PRAISE FOR
HELEN HARDT

"These two are downright lovable! You are rooting for them to get together from the get go. The chemistry between them is smoking HOT, and...once they get in bed you will need a fan."
~Guilty Pleasures Book Reviews

"Helen writes these books with such grace and finesse that you feel as though you've been transported back in time and are walking among the characters. You feel every bit of passion, anguish, and love emanating from the pages. It envelops you and leaves you grasping at the hopes that these two wonderfully in love couples get to have the HEA they both deserve."
~Bare Naked Words

"Flawlessly written, and in my opinion a work of art..."
~Girly Girl Book Reviews

Craving

STEEL BROTHERS SAGA
BOOK ONE

Craving

STEEL BROTHERS SAGA
BOOK ONE

WATERHOUSE
PRESS

DEDICATION

For my mother

WARNING

This book contains adult language and scenes, including flashbacks of child physical and sexual abuse, which may cause trigger reactions. This story is meant only for adults as defined by the laws of the country where you made your purchase. Store your books and e-books carefully where they cannot be accessed by younger readers.

CHAPTER ONE

Jade

Talon was the brother I'd never met.

When Marjorie and I were in college, her older brothers, Jonah and Ryan, often visited. They were tall, muscular ranchers from Colorado, complete with cowboy boots and Stetsons. All the Steel siblings, Marj included, had dark hair that was nearly black. I admit I swooned a little when I first saw her brothers. Who wouldn't want to meet a couple of ruggedly handsome cowboys who were also billionaires from their ranch and wine business? They were too old for me, of course, and neither gave me a second look. And that was okay, because I was in love with Colin.

Still, my heart always beat just a little bit faster every time Jonah and Ryan Steel came around. Marj laughed at me. They were her brothers, after all, and she had spent most of her youth the target of their merciless teasing. But even she admitted they were nice to look at. Of course they were. Marj looked just like a female version of the two of them. The Steels had definitely been gifted in the area of physical beauty.

I felt like the ugly stepsister around Marj. Though I'd always liked my thick brown hair, it seemed juvenile next to Marj's nearly ebony tresses. My eyes were more gray than blue, without the depth of Marj's dark-brown ones that seemed to look straight into a person's soul. Like her brothers, Marj was tall, a few inches taller than I, and I was no slouch at five-feet-seven-and-a half. Even her body was perfect. She was long and lean like her brothers, while I was busty to the point that I had given up button-down shirts.

I smiled. Marj used to envy my boobs—even after I'd educated her on the evils of boob sweat and never being able to find a sports bra that fit. I would've gladly traded my boobs for her perfect-sized body.

The plane landed with a jolt.

"Ladies and gentlemen, please remain seated as we taxi to our gate. Thank you for flying with us today, and we welcome you to Grand Junction, Colorado."

I reached in my purse for my cell phone and clicked it on. A text from Marj.

Welcome! Can't wait to see you. Unfortunately something came up, and I won't be able to pick you up. Talon will be there. I've shown him your picture, and he'll be waiting at baggage claim.

I let out a sigh.

The brother I'd never met.

Talon had been deployed in Iraq during the years Marj and I were in college together. That was why he had never come to visit. He was the middle brother, between Jonah, the oldest, and Ryan, the youngest. Marjorie was the baby of the family.

Marj never talked much about Talon. He was a mystery to me, though if he was as good-looking as his brothers, I wouldn't have any trouble looking at him for the hour ride from the airport to the Steel ranch.

The plane finally halted, and people began to rise, pulling their luggage out of the overhead compartments. I was trapped in a window seat, and the elderly couple sitting with me didn't seem in any hurry to get moving.

So I waited.

And I sighed again.

My life had certainly taken a detour. Colin and I were supposed to be on our honeymoon right now, but him leaving me at the altar had changed those plans. Oddly, I wasn't as upset as I should've been. In truth, I'd known for some time that Colin and I had grown apart. I just hadn't wanted to admit it myself. When I finally realized that the agony coursing through me was actually laced with relief, I needed a change. Marj, who had been in Denver for my wedding as my maid of honor, convinced me to come to the western slope of Colorado and live at her ranch. I could find a job as an attorney in the small town of Snow Creek, and if not there, I could commute to Grand Junction.

So what the hell? I had left Denver, the only home I'd ever known, and here I was, having just landed in Grand Junction.

The elderly couple finally moved, though at tortoise speed, and I stood and stretched my legs. I grabbed my carry-on out of the overhead bin and walked off the plane and into my new life.

I followed the signs to baggage claim and strode toward carousel number five.

I knew him before he even turned around.

So tall. Taller than either of his brothers, with that signature Steel black hair curling over his collar. The white shirt stretched over broad shoulders and then tapered down to a trim waistline and a gorgeous ass in dark jeans.

I gulped.

Well, what had I expected? For him to be waving a sign that said Jade Roberts on it? Why hadn't I gone to the bathroom to check myself out? I no doubt looked like I had been run over by a truck.

I walked up behind him and cleared my throat.

He turned, and two nearly black eyes scorched into me. His skin was nicely tanned and his nose almost perfectly formed except for a barely noticeable crook. He must have broken it once. His strong jawline was covered in black stubble—about a day's worth, maybe more. His lips were full and dark pink. And that corded neck... What might that bronze skin feel like against my fingertips? The first two buttons of his stark-white shirt were open, and a few black chest hairs peeked out. My nipples poked against my bra, and my skin tightened, as if I'd been shrink-wrapped.

"You Jade?" he said in a husky voice.

I nodded, unable to speak. Talon Steel was a god come to life. My heart hammered. How could I be so attracted to a man when, in a parallel world, I was supposed to be married to another right now? Colin and I might not have been in love anymore, but we still had feelings for each other. But being left at the altar... It screwed with a girl's head.

"Just point out your bag to me, and I'll grab it for you."

I nodded again and walked to the carousel. No worries. My bag was always the last one off. I was usually left standing with only one or two other people, convinced my bag was on its way to Timbuktu. Right now, I relished the wait. I could stand here and enjoy the hypnotizing effect of the revolving bags as I got myself together.

No way. My bag inched down a little ramp and onto the carousel. So much for my time-out. I grabbed the purple suitcase and lugged it off the carousel when a warm hand brushed against mine.

"I said I'd get it for you." Talon seized the bag from me. "Come on. I'm parked on this level."

I followed him. What else could I do? Clearly, he wasn't much of a conversationalist, and truth be told, neither was I. I hated small talk, but I'd be trapped with him in a car for an hour. Without talking, that hour would be damned long.

The man even walked sexily. He had to be six-three at least, maybe six-four. I had to power walk to keep up with his long strides and was huffing and puffing before long. Of course, the view of his ass wasn't torture. His black cowboy boots clomped heavily along the tile floor. Once we reached the door, it opened automatically, and he went through first.

Not much of a gentleman, but what did I care? I just wished he'd walk a little slower. I needed a little more time before the dreaded car ride.

I followed him to a shiny burgundy Mercedes. The Steels had money. A lot of it. While I went home from college during the summers and did secretarial work for my father's construction company, Marj took whirlwind tours to Europe and cruises to the Greek Isles. One time, during spring break of her junior year, she invited me on a Caribbean cruise with her, all-expenses-paid. I'd had the time of my life despite being separated from Colin.

Talon deposited my suitcase in the trunk and then eyed my carry-on. "You want to put that in?"

I nodded and handed it to him. Then I walked to the passenger door and let myself in.

Talon opened his door and took the driver's seat. He turned to me. "You don't talk much, do you?"

I couldn't help letting out a laugh. I hadn't said a word yet, had I? He must've thought I was some kind of mute. "Thanks for picking me up. I got a text from Marj saying she couldn't make it."

"Yeah, she had to go on a job interview."

"Really? I thought she was going to be working on the ranch."

"We thought so too. But then it turned out that the local paper in Snow Creek just lost its star reporter, and Marjorie is gunning for the job."

"Good for her."

Marj enjoyed journalism. She'd minored in it at school. Her major had been agriculture, as she figured she was destined for ranch work. Her real love, though, was cooking. I'd tried to talk her into culinary school scads of times, but something kept her from taking that leap.

"So Marjorie tells me you're a lawyer?"

"Yeah. I actually won't get my bar results for a few weeks yet, but I'm optimistic."

Talon nodded, keeping his eyes on the road as he pulled out of the airport parking lot.

A few minutes passed with no talking. I looked at my fingernails, picked at a piece of dry cuticle. I eyed my purse on the floor of the car and grabbed it, pulling out my cell phone. Normally I hated when people hid behind their cell phones, but right now, I needed something to occupy myself. The awkwardness in this car was so thick I could've cut it with scissors.

Say something, Jade. Anything. This silence is deafening.

But to say something, I had to actually *have* something to say. For some reason, Talon Steel paralyzed me. He was perfectly cordial but not friendly. Impenetrable. Like a suit of invisible armor covered him from head to toe. He had been in the Marines. Most likely he had seen some pretty nasty shit there, stuff I couldn't even begin to comprehend. He'd been back now for several years. Marj said he had been honorably discharged the summer after we graduated college.

Still, who knew what he had experienced?

I cleared my throat. "Are there any positions open for attorneys in your little town?"

Talon shook his head. "I sure wouldn't know."

"Marj said there might be."

He let out a chuckle. "I sure don't know how she would know either."

Okay. That line of questioning hadn't led to anything. "How is Marj doing? I've really missed her."

"I think you'd know how she's doing better than I would. Didn't you just see her last week at your...wedding?"

Yes, yes. I did just see her at my wedding that didn't happen. Thank you so much for bringing that up. So much for trying to make conversation. "I didn't actually get married."

"I know the whole story. And even if I didn't, you're coming out here without a husband and without a wedding ring, so I could figure it out."

Had he actually looked closely enough at me to notice I wasn't wearing a wedding ring? Didn't seem possible. All the Steel brothers would know of my humiliation by now. I fidgeted with my phone a little more, but the battery was about to die. I checked the clock on the dashboard. Damn, we had only been driving for about five minutes. How was I going to get through this?

"Are you hungry? I can take you through a drive-through or something."

Had he just spoken? Come to think of it, I was little hungry. I'd refused to pay for the crappy overpriced airplane food. Eating would give me something to do with my mouth so I didn't have to talk. "Yeah, if you don't mind. Anything's fine. A burger, whatever."

He pulled into a Wendy's and, without asking me, ordered two number one combos with Cokes. I nudged his arm a little.

Without looking at me, he said into the speaker, "Sorry, make one a Diet Coke."

A little presumptuous. Truth was, I didn't drink soda. Never had. The carbonation bothered me. I nudged him again. "Iced tea for me, please."

He let out a huff. "Sorry, nix the Diet. Make it an iced tea." He turned to me. "Does that satisfy you?"

I shook my head. Was this guy for real? "As a matter of fact, no, it doesn't satisfy me. You ordered me a burger, not asking me what I wanted on it or anything. I could be a vegetarian for all you know."

A partial smile curved the left side of his lips upward. "You just said anything was fine. 'A burger, whatever,' I believe were your exact words."

My cheeks heated. Yeah, I had said that. Now I looked like a moron. Great. I played with my fingers until the employee handed Talon the bag of food and the two drinks through the window. He handed the drinks to me, and I checked to see which one was the iced tea. I set his in the cupholder next to the driver's seat and inserted the straw into mine.

He tossed the bag on my lap. "Unwrap mine for me so I

can eat it while I'm driving."

No "please." No "would you mind?" Just an order. Well, he *had* been in the military. Maybe he was used to giving commands. Or maybe he was just rude as hell. I didn't know Marj's other brothers that well, but when I'd met them, they had been perfectly friendly. So what was up with this guy?

Since I was still embarrassed about my burger blunder, I did as he asked—or rather told—me to do. The burgers were identical, so I didn't need to worry about which one was his. I unwrapped it, folded the paper over, and wrapped it back up so half of it was out and he could eat it easily while he drove. I handed it to him.

He grunted.

Apparently, that was what passed for "thank you" in the vocabulary of Talon Steel.

I opened my burger and took a bite. Christ, mayonnaise. Not that I had anything against mayonnaise, but I tried to avoid excess fat when I could. No point in voicing this. What was done was done. The burger tasted so good—or maybe I was just *that* hungry. Now if only I could make it last for another forty-five minutes. I took small bites and chewed them until I had masticated the food into a pulp.

Still, the clock showed thirty minutes to go when I had finished the burger and the accompanying fries.

I stared straight ahead, ignoring the magnetic pull to turn and look at him. The man was obviously an asshole, so why was my libido so interested? My nipples were still tightening against my bra, aching for lips.

His lips.

Damn, this was going to be a long half hour.

CHAPTER TWO

Talon

Everything about the woman was sexy.

Marjorie had told me she was pretty, and I'd seen photographs, but they didn't do Jade Roberts justice. Even the way she ate was sexy—how she licked her lips after every bite and then daintily touched them with her napkin. Still, a lone crumb from her hamburger bun stuck to the left edge of her lower lip. Damn, to be that crumb. I wanted to lick it off and then trace the rest of her lips with my tongue before plunging it inside her sweet mouth and kissing her hard.

The paper from her burger crinkled as she wadded it up and put it in the bag. When she reached to grab mine out of my lap and her fingers grazed the inside of my thigh, my dick stiffened. Yeah, just what I didn't need—a boner in the fucking car. She wadded up my paper and tossed it in the bag as well.

Should I say something? I had no idea. She was Marjorie's friend, not mine. If only Ryan or Jonah had been able to pick her up. Twenty more minutes...

"I'm really excited to see Marj," she said.

Clearly, she was making small talk. Had she forgotten that she just saw Marj last week at her aborted wedding? It was the second time she'd made that goof. I couldn't help a small chuckle, but I managed to keep it silent. She was cute.

"Yeah, she's really excited about you coming out here to live."

"I really appreciate you guys letting me stay with you on the ranch until I get settled."

"Not a problem. If there's one thing we've got, it's room."

"Oh, yeah, I know. I visited Marj at the ranch sophomore year during spring break. You weren't...uh..."

"I was in Iraq." For the life of me, I couldn't figure out why people were so loath to say the word "Iraq." I was there. I saw a bunch of shit no human should ever have to see. But it was a fact, so why beat around the bush about it? It sure wasn't the first time I'd seen nasty-ass shit.

She cleared her throat. "Yeah."

Silence for a few beats. Then—

"I think it's really heroic what you did over there. I really respect our military."

"I didn't do it to be a hero."

"Oh, I didn't mean to imply—"

"I'm no hero, blue eyes." Had I just called her blue eyes? "In fact, I'm about as far from a hero as you'd get."

I didn't know what I expected her to say to that, but I sure as hell didn't expect what she said.

"It really doesn't matter what you think, does it? I think anyone who serves our country is a hero. That's my personal definition, and I'm sticking with it."

I shook my head. Such naïveté. Had I ever been that naïve in my life? Not since my first decade on this earth, and even then I don't think I was quite as innocent she was now.

She'd learn eventually. I hoped it would be a while. I wouldn't mind seeing the innocence in those soft blue eyes a little longer.

"I don't know what to say to that."

"You could say 'thank you.' Isn't that customary when someone gives you a compliment?"

"You didn't give me a compliment."

"Sure I did. I said you were hero. It's a great compliment. I wish someone would call me a hero. I'm no one's hero, and I never will be."

"And I told you, I'm no hero."

"I suppose heroism, like beauty, is in the eye of the beholder, then."

I looked straight ahead, resisting the urge to turn toward her. I was driving, after all. The road into Snow Creek was never busy. We had to drive through the small town to get to Steel Acres.

"So where can I get a good deal on a used car? I need something to get around in."

"You'd be better off going into Grand Junction for something like that. But there's no hurry. We have about five cars on the ranch that aren't being used right now. You're welcome to use one of them."

"Oh, no. I can't impose."

"You're already imposing, staying with us." I regretted the words as soon as they left my mouth. She didn't deserve to be treated this way. I just wasn't used to mincing words.

"I...I'm sorry. You just said...you had plenty of room." Her voice cracked a little.

Shit, now I had upset her. Truth was, I didn't know how to deal with people. Five years in Iraq didn't teach me that, and God knew my life before then hadn't taught me jack shit.

But something about her raised my hackles. I couldn't quite put my finger on it. All I knew was that I had to keep her at arm's length. Couldn't let her in. Couldn't let anyone in. Only problem was, up until now, I had never wanted to let anybody in. After less than an hour with this woman, my whole philosophy seemed to be shattering.

Those damned blue eyes...

"All I meant was that we have extra cars, and you're welcome to use one."

"That's not what you said."

I let out a heavy sigh and slowed the car down, stopping on the shoulder. I turned and looked into those amazing eyes, the color of tanzanite. My heart skipped. "Look, you're Marjorie's best friend in the world, and you are very welcome at our home. I didn't mean to allude otherwise. I'm..." Why did I have such a hard time saying that one damned word? I breathed in and let the air out slowly. "Sorry."

Her smile lit up face. Those cherry-red full lips, looking so kissable, gave way to big dimples on each side of her cheeks. Her blue-gray eyes sparkled. "There, was that so hard?"

Brown hair fell across her shoulders in waves. I itched to touch the hair, the silkiness of her cheek, the moist scarlet of her lips.

Damn it. I wanted her.

And I had never wanted anything before in my life.

★ ★ ★ ★

"Jade!" My sister came running as soon as we got in the door.

My mutt, Roger, panted at her heals.

"Hey, boy." I scratched him behind the ears.

Jade fell to her knees. "How cute! Hi there, baby."

Roger took to her immediately, licking her face.

Marjorie laughed. "I forgot how much you love dogs." She turned to me. "Jade goes crazy whenever she sees a dog." Back to Jade. "I'm so sorry I couldn't come to the airport. Did Talon take care of you?"

For a moment, my stomach dropped. Would she tell Marjorie how rude I had been?

But Jade just smiled. "Oh, of course, everything went fine. Did you get the job?"

Marjorie shook her head. "Nope. Somebody else beat me to it. So I'm back to learning the ropes here. I guess three years of travel while you went to law school was enough." She laughed.

I loved my sister, but she was a little spoiled. Okay, a lot spoiled. But she didn't shy away from hard work. I'd give her that.

"So how was the drive from the city?" Marjorie continued.

"Just fine. Talon even treated me to a burger on the way home. I was starving."

"I'm so glad to hear that. Tal can come off a little abrupt sometimes. But he means well, don't you, Tal?"

Mean well? I'd do anything in the world for my baby sister, or either one of my brothers, for that matter. But did I ever mean well? That was a damned good question—one I'd probably never find the answer to.

So I sidestepped it. Just like I'd been sidestepping for twenty-five years. "I assume she's going to take the empty bedroom next to yours, right, Marj? I'll take her stuff up."

"Oh, you don't have to—" Jade began.

"Oh, let him," Marjorie said. "Might as well put all that good muscle to use."

Jade's cheeks pinked. Goddamnit, did she get red over

the rest of her body too? On her chest? On those amazing voluptuous breasts that I could see even under the shapeless top she wore? The girl was stacked. No doubt about it—a goddamned brick house.

"So next to your room, Marj?"

"Of course. It's a great room, Jade. It has a private bathroom and everything."

"You guys really don't have to go to all this trouble."

Marjorie laughed. "Trouble? The room is empty, for God's sake. As are three others. Jonah lives on his own ranch house down the way, and Ryan lives in the guest house out back. Tal and I are the only ones who live here anymore."

Like I had a choice. When I got back from overseas, Jonah had already built himself a house, and Ryan had taken over the guest house. I was stuck in the main ranch house. I had the master suite, but still I felt closed in. And now, with Jade living here... I'd better get to drawing up some plans for my own house...far away from this one.

I grabbed Jade's suitcase and her carry-on and walked down the hallway toward Marjorie's room. I deposited the luggage in the extra bedroom. My suite was on the other side of the house, thank God.

I needed to stay as far away from Jade Roberts as possible.

I just wasn't sure any amount of distance would ease my craving.

CHAPTER THREE

Jade

I punched my pillow for what seemed like the hundredth time. The bed was comfortable enough, and so was the pillow, for that matter. It was just strange, and until I got used to a new bed, I often couldn't sleep. Whenever I stayed at a hotel, I never slept the first night.

Maybe a cup of tea would help. Caffeine or not, tea always relaxed me. And I'm talking tea, not an herbal infusion that people like to call "herb tea" when there's not a speck of real tea in it. I got up and quietly stole out of my room, down the hallway, to the mammoth kitchen in this amazing ranch house. I turned on the light...and gasped.

Talon sat at the kitchen table, a glass of water in front of him, Roger at his feet, tail wagging. Talon's magnificent chest was bare, his dark nipples surrounded by black chest hair— just enough to make him deliciously masculine but not too hairy. His right arm sat on the table, his forearm beautifully corded, and his upper arm... Oh, God... The muscles bulged even while he was sitting in a relaxed position.

Why hadn't I bothered with a robe? My boobs were plainly visible beneath the tight white tank top I wore. A pair of Colin's old boxers covered my lower half. I'd thrown out most of his stuff, but these were just so comfy. I crossed my arms over my chest quickly, hiding my hard nipples.

"I...I'm sorry," I stammered.

He didn't respond.

"Why are you sitting here in the dark?" I asked.

"Couldn't sleep."

That didn't really answer my question, but I decided not to push it. "Neither can I. I'm sorry to disturb you. I just thought I'd see if you guys had any tea. It relaxes me."

"The small canister on the counter." He pointed.

I wanted to go back and get a robe, but that would just make me look even more conspicuous, like I was trying to cover myself up. Which of course I was. I fumbled with the tea bag and started looking through cupboards for a mug.

"Cupboard to the right of the oven," Talon said, not turning his head.

I opened the cupboard door, and indeed, coffee cups and mugs appeared. I grabbed one, filled it with water, and placed it in the microwave for a few minutes. As usual, the two minutes were the longest two minutes ever. Talon still sat, facing away from me, not drinking his water.

When the microwave dinged, I grabbed my cup, added the tea bag, and set it on the counter. Should I sit down at the table and join him? That same wall encased him, and right now, it seemed to encompass the entire table. Only Roger's wagging tail breached it. He stayed at Talon's feet, and as much as I wanted to squat down and pet his soft head, I held back.

I did not feel welcome.

"Come on and sit down if you want," he said.

I grabbed my tea and sat down across from him. Sitting next to him didn't seem right, but sitting across from him turned out to be a big mistake. He was right in my line of vision. I couldn't *not* look at him.

His hair was tousled and sexy, and he raked his fingers through it, mussing it further. His gorgeous brown eyes were sunken and rimmed with dark circles.

"I...I'm sorry you can't sleep," I said.

He cleared his throat. "Don't be. I never sleep."

That couldn't be possible. All humans had to sleep. But again, I wasn't going to push it. "I don't normally have any trouble," I said, "but the first night in a new bed is always troublesome for me. I'm sure I'll be fine tomorrow night."

"Yeah, you'll be fine. The demons in this house can't get to you." Talon pursed his full dusky lips.

Demons? What the hell was he talking about? He probably had nightmares from his time in the Marines. Perhaps he even had post-traumatic stress disorder. Was he getting any therapy? Certainly wasn't my place to ask.

"I don't really have any demons. Except, of course, my ex-fiancé, who totally humiliated me a little over a week ago."

Talon raised his eyebrows. Had I actually piqued his interest?

"I'm sure that was rough."

His tone unnerved me. While it seemed to hold sincerity, something bit through it. A touch of sarcasm? I wasn't sure what he meant by the comment, so I decided to take it at face value.

"Honestly, I'm more embarrassed than anything else. I really don't think we were in love anymore. We were together all four years of college in Denver, and then I stayed and went to law school and he headed to New York to intern for his father's company. Somehow we held it together, but long-distance relationships are hard. In retrospect, we shouldn't have stayed together."

Talon stood. "I'm sure you'll be just fine. Believe me, things could be a lot worse."

My skin warmed. How dare he belittle this? I wasn't sitting in here asking for his pity. I had told him point-blank that the relationship had been a mistake and we should have called it off years ago. Of course things could have been a lot worse. Things could *always* be worse.

I stood as well and looked him straight in his blazing black eyes. "You're right. I will be fine. Did I ever say I wouldn't be? I know there are a lot worse things in the world than being left at the altar. However, that doesn't take away the fact that I was completely humiliated."

Talon shook his head, chuckling. "I get it. You're fine."

His words crept under my skin, and my hackles rose. Why did everything he said cut through me like an ice pick?

"You know, you hardly know me. Why are you being so judgmental?"

"I know you more than you think, blue eyes. I know you've had a life so full of privilege that the worst thing in the world that has ever happened to you is you got humiliated on your wedding day."

"For your information, my life has not been full of privilege. I had a modest upbringing"—I did a one-eighty around his gourmet kitchen, Viking stove and all—"which clearly you did not."

He chuckled again, and goddamnit, my dander rose.

"Blue eyes, there are some things money can't buy. Modest upbringing or not, you had a college education. You had a law school education. Once you pass the bar, you'll be able to get a job that pays decent money. And with your looks and that luscious body of yours, you'll have no problem attracting another guy in no time. So don't tell me you don't have privilege."

I had to think to understand his last words. I was stuck on the "looks and luscious body" part. Was he attracted to me? This western god? Attracted to me?

I opened my mouth to speak, but before any words came out, he grabbed my arm, pulled me toward him, and crushed his mouth to mine.

The kiss was raw. He forced his tongue between my lips and took, just took.

My legs quivered. Oh, God...

Seven years of kissing Colin...and it had never been like this.

He devoured me, and I melted into him. He grabbed the back of my hair and yanked on it as he continued to plunder my mouth. Electric jolts arrowed straight to my pussy. No man had ever yanked on my hair before, and oh my God... I returned his kiss with greed. Such a soothing salve for my shattered ego. This man...found me attractive... Was kissing me—

He ripped his mouth from mine and sucked on my neck, trailing tiny kisses up to my earlobe.

"God, blue eyes..."

My legs nearly gave way, but he steadied me.

"That guy you almost married," he whispered into my ear. "Did he ever kiss you like this, blue eyes?"

I opened my mouth, but all that came out was a sigh.

Talon thrust his tongue into my ear canal. I nearly melted into a puddle right there. *Take me to your bed*, I said in my mind. *Take me to your bed and fuck me silly.*

"Tell me," he demanded again. "Did he ever kiss you like this?"

"No."

And he clamped his mouth to mine once more. Again our tongues swirled together, and again my legs threatened to give way. I slid my hands up his hard arms, relishing the muscle covered by smooth bronze skin. I gripped his shoulders and then wrapped my arms around his neck, trying to close whatever distance remained between us.

Closer... Wanted to be closer—

But he broke the kiss with a loud smack, releasing my hair so I nearly tumbled backward. I caught myself by grabbing the back of the chair. I whimpered at the loss of his lips, his arms, his need.

He stood, staring at me. No...*glaring* at me, those black eyes burning two holes in my skin.

Was he going to say anything? What was I supposed to do now? Should I apologize? But I hadn't kissed him. He had kissed me. Would *he* apologize?

No. No apology. He walked past me, out of the kitchen, and down the hallway toward his room, the blond mutt loping on his heels.

I plunked down in the chair and wrapped my hands around my warm cup of tea.

His full glass of water still sat, untouched.

★ ★ ★ ★

Rita's Café was a cute little mom-and-pop diner on the main drag of Snow Creek, Colorado. I sat across the table from Marj. She had insisted on taking me out to breakfast my first full day in Snow Creek, treating me to what she called "the best coffee in the universe." I was skeptical. I liked really strong coffee—*really* strong, as in it plops when it's poured. Most restaurant coffee was hot brown water. I raised my cup to my lips and took a sip.

Yup. Brown water. But I didn't have the heart to say so to Marj.

I drew in a deep breath, gathering my courage. I was going to ask Marj about her brother. I wouldn't tell her about the stolen kiss last night, at least not yet. But something was up with Talon Steel, and Marj probably knew what it was.

"After we're done here," Marjorie said, "I'll show you around Snow Creek. It's the most adorable little town. There's one law firm in town where you might be able to find work. And there's always the city attorney's office too."

"I haven't passed the bar yet," I reminded her.

"For a genius like you, that's just a formality. You know you'll pass, Jade."

I had felt pretty confident coming out of the test, but I'd also known people who felt just as confident or more so and hadn't passed. "I hope so. Otherwise, I'll have to wait another six months try again. But no worries. I can always get a job waiting tables or something while I study. I'm not going to be a burden on you guys."

"Who says you're a burden?"

Ah, good. The opening I was waiting for her. "Well, your brother, for one."

"Talon? Why would he say such a thing?"

"He didn't say those exact words. But while we were driving home yesterday, he mentioned that I was imposing." Okay, so I fudged a little. He'd actually said I could drive one of their cars. I was the one who'd used the word imposing, and then he'd repeated it.

"I'm sure he was just kidding, Jade. Tal is... Well, that's just the way he is."

My curiosity was piqued. "What do you mean 'just the way he is?'"

"You know he was overseas with the Marines. He doesn't talk about that. The truth is he's always been the kind of guy who keeps to himself. I'm much closer to Joe and Ryan than I am to Tal. He's definitely a loner."

"Yeah, I can kind of see that. I got up last night in the middle of the night to get a cup of tea, and he was sitting alone in the dark in the kitchen."

"He has trouble sleeping. He gets up at night a lot."

"But why does he sit in the dark? What doesn't he turn on the TV or read a book or something?"

Marjorie bit her lip and fidgeted with her hands. "Talon has always been a little bit...off. But he's a good man, Jade. He just has...issues. I mean, he was in Iraq. I have no idea what he saw over there, and he never talks about it, at least not to me. But it had to have some kind of an effect on him."

"Do you think he has post-traumatic stress disorder?" I asked.

Marj shook her head. "I've considered— Oh!" Her eyes widened as the door to the coffee shop clicked open.

I turned around, and my heart nearly stopped. Talon Steel strode in, his ass looking delectable as ever in snug jeans, the sleeves of his black western shirt rolled up, his gorgeous bronze forearms visible.

"Hey, Tal, over here." Marj gestured for him to join us.

My skin prickled. All I could think about was that kiss

last night, his tongue devouring me as if I were his last meal. I hadn't seen him since then. I wasn't sure how to react.

"I'm just getting a coffee to go, but thanks." He walked to the counter.

"Please, join us." Now why in hell had those words come out of my mouth?

Marjorie looked at me like I had two heads, her brow furrowing. "Yeah, come on over, Talon. You have a few minutes to hang out with your little sister and her friend, don't you?"

Talon turned away from the counter, his dark eyes a mixture of fire and...was it sadness? "Yeah, sure. I guess I have a few minutes."

"My brothers don't deny me anything," Marj said, smiling. "Of course, they're also overprotective as all get out. The price I pay for being the youngest and the only girl."

Yes, Marj was the youngest. I had never even thought to ask the ages of her brothers. "How old are all your brothers?"

"Jonah is thirty-eight, Talon is thirty-five, and Ryan is thirty-two."

Wow. Talon was ten years older than I was. Of course, I knew he was older. I just hadn't considered how much older. Marj was twenty-five, the same as me. Sounded like she was an afterthought. "I guess I didn't realize they were that much older than we are."

"Oh, yeah, I used to chase after them when I was a kid and drive them crazy."

"You must have had a fun childhood."

"Well, I never knew my mother..."

I let out a breath. God, I was such an idiot. Her mother had killed herself when Marj was only two. "I'm so sorry. I don't know why I said that."

Marjorie attempted a smile. "It's okay. I mean, I did grow up on a gorgeous ranch with everything that money could buy and three older brothers who adored me."

"Adore you?" Talon sat down and set his coffee and the scone on the table. "Why do you think we would adore you, squirt?"

I let out a chuckle. The nickname squirt did not fit Marj. She was model tall.

"So what are you doing in town today, Tal?" Marjorie asked.

"Just had an appetite for one of Rita's scones." Talon took a bite of the confection, crumbs falling to the table. "What are you all doing here?"

"I'm just showing Jade around town. Had to introduce her to Rita's coffee."

"Yep," Talon agreed. "Best coffee this side of the Rockies."

They were delusional, but I smiled anyway. If that was what passed for good strong coffee around these parts, I needed to stop at a store and pick up a coffee maker, grinder, and some decent beans.

"The city attorney's office isn't far from here," Marjorie said. "I know the city attorney. His name is Larry Wade. We could stop by, and you could introduce yourself if you'd like."

I looked down at my Daisy Duke shorts and scarlet tank top. I was hardly dressed to meet a potential employer. "Not today. I mean, look at me."

Talon turned toward me and met my gaze, his dark eyes burning. The few clothes I had on were being melted off by his piercing stare. My nipples hardened under my bra and soon were visible—two pencil erasers encased in red. As well endowed as I was, I made a point never to wear padded bras. I didn't need any extra. Of course, the price was whenever I was cold—or incredibly aroused—my headlights flashed.

Talon's lips trembled just a bit. Was he holding back a smile? He didn't smile a lot. He had noticed my nipples—I was sure. At least the warmth of my skin and my skittering heartbeat were sure. I crossed my arms over my chest...which made it pretty difficult to drink coffee. But the coffee sucked anyway.

Talon finished up the scone and wiped the crumbs from the table into his hand. "I've got a few errands to run, ladies. See you back home for dinner."

Yes, dinner. The Steels had a housekeeper and cook who came every day—Felicia. I wasn't sure when I would get used to being cooked for and cleaned up after. This was so far from how I had lived for so many years. My dad was in construction and made a decent living, but that was light years away from how the Steels lived. We never even had a cleaning lady, let alone a housekeeper and cook who came daily.

I couldn't help watching Talon as he walked out the door. He was one fine-looking man. With one fine-looking ass. My palms sweated, and I rubbed them on the denim of my shorts.

My breath caught.

I would never forget our kiss.

CHAPTER FOUR

Talon

The boy huddled in the darkness, his worn T-shirt and the ragged gray blanket his only warmth, and they did little. His eyes had long ago adjusted to the darkness of the dank cellar where he was kept. Nighttime was the hardest, even though he was left alone then.

Aloneness came with its own demons.

Isolation. Fear. Vulnerability.

Frigid air pricked at the boy's skin. Haunting squeaks drifted toward him. Cancerous blurs emerged against the walls, dancing eerily to a discordant violin. Black claws descended, and the cold concrete walls inched forward slowly.

The boy's breath grew rapid, and he scooted backward, the concrete floor chafing his bare skin. Couldn't breathe... The ceiling descended, blackness engulfing him.

And the walls continued forward. Always the walls. Cold and hard and impenetrable. They laughed maniacally, their voices low and terrorizing, as they enclosed the boy.

Breath. Need a breath... Air...air...

"You are nothing," the walls taunted, their distorted faces appearing as they creaked closer. "You will die here. Used and abused and worth nothing more than the ragged blanket you sleep on. No one cares. No one is coming for you. No one but us.

We will take you into hell..."

★ ★ ★ ★

I sat at the kitchen table again, a glass of water in front of me that I never touched. Why did I always get a glass of water when I came to the kitchen at night? Seemed like the thing to do. When a person got up in the middle of the night, he got a drink of water. I wasn't thirsty. As usual, I hadn't turned on the light. I always sat in the dark. I was more comfortable that way.

Didn't make sense. All the worst times in my life had taken place in the dark. Still, darkness gave me a cloak of comfort that I didn't understand. I had stopped trying to understand myself a long time ago.

I blinked my eyes when the light came on. Jade again. Did that woman never sleep?

She wore a robe this time. Too bad. Her body was a goddamned work of art. The most luscious rack I'd ever seen, and I'd had plenty of women. Women had been throwing themselves at me since I was fifteen. I took what they offered. Why not? I enjoyed myself, and so did they. I never really wanted any of them. They fulfilled a physical need, nothing more.

"Sorry. I didn't think you'd be here tonight again." Jade shuffled over to the canisters and pulled out a tea bag.

"I didn't think you'd be here again either." I turned back around and stared at my glass of water.

Her nipples weren't visible tonight, though the robe she wore was skimpy, showing her long shapely legs, her well-formed ass. My cock stirred. What the hell was wrong with me? I'd been around plenty of beautiful women. I'd had tons of women more beautiful than Jade Roberts.

Okay, maybe only a few who were actually *more* beautiful than she was. She was a goddess. Still, I'd had beautiful women, so what was it about her?

The microwave dinged, and Jade walked back over to the table with her mug of steaming tea. "I don't want to disturb you. I'll just take this to my bedroom." She turned to leave the kitchen.

"Don't go."

Had those words come from my mouth? What did I want with her? I was only sure of one thing. I did not want her to leave the kitchen.

She turned and faced me. "Honestly, I didn't mean to disturb you."

"Why can't you sleep?" I asked. "Is something wrong with your bed?"

Jade shook her head. She knelt down to give Roger a pet—"How are you doing, boy?"—and sat down at the table. "No. My bed is perfectly comfortable. I don't know why I've been having trouble sleeping. Maybe I'm not as over the whole wedding thing as I thought I was. Maybe I'm anxious about my bar results. Maybe I'm worried about getting a job and imposing on you guys for too long. Probably all of the above."

"You don't have to worry about the last one. We have plenty of room. You're welcome to stay here as long as you need to. Marjorie wouldn't have it any other way."

"That's kind of you. I appreciate it more than you know. But I'm just not the kind of person who can sponge off of others. Freaks me out."

"Freaks you out? What do you mean?"

Jade let out a sigh. "My dad was always really adamant about making his own way in the world, and he transferred those values to me. We had a modest life, but we were always fed and clothed. And I knew he loved me."

"So you're close to your dad?"

She nodded. "I miss him."

"What about your mom?"

"I haven't seen my mom since I was a kid. She left us for her career."

"Her career? What kind of career would she leave her kid for?"

Jade shook her head and let out a sarcastic chuckle. "You ever hear of Brooke Bailey?"

"Yeah. She was a supermodel a couple decades ago, right?"

Jade nodded. "She was. She's also my mother."

I arched my eyebrows. Brooke Bailey had been the hottest thing walking when I was a teen. Jonah had nursed a major hard-on for her while we were growing up. The signature poster of her in the royal-blue bathing suit had hung on the wall right by his bed. She was taller than Jade and thinner—leaner and not as buxom. Her hair was a dark blond compared to Jade's soft brown. She must've gotten her father's hair.

But Brooke's eyes—they watched you from the wall. Every guy fantasized that Brooke was looking at him, smiling for him, her nipples hardening and poking through that blue spandex for him. The camera loved Brooke Bailey. She must have made a mint on that poster. So why had Jade had such a modest childhood?

I gazed at her.

And then I saw it.

Jade had Brooke's eyes—that steely blue-gray that seemed to penetrate through every layer of a person.

That's what had first drawn me to Jade—those eyes. I felt naked, like she could see right through me, into the very recesses of my broken soul. It scared the hell out of me.

So why did I want her so much? I hadn't been able to get that kiss out of my mind. Her lips were so full, so red, and she tasted like champagne and strawberries. I had never tasted anything when I kissed a woman. Something about the kiss with Jade had been different, but I couldn't quite put my finger on it. All I knew was that I desired her.

In my bed.

She was my sister's best friend. I couldn't just bed her and forget her like I did with the others. Even more scary? I didn't want to.

Those eyes... I could never let her get close to me. She would see right through all of the walls that I had built up around me, all the secrets I'd buried deep inside. I could never tell her the truth about why I didn't sleep, about the demons that haunted me in my dreams. I could never tell anyone.

"Really?" I finally replied to her revelation.

She looked down to her teacup. "I know it's hard to believe. I don't look anything like her."

"You have her eyes." I couldn't help myself. It just popped out.

"You think so?"

I nodded. "Joe was obsessed with Brooke Bailey when he was younger. He had that blue swimsuit poster that she made. You know, the one where you could swear she was looking right at you and smiling?"

Jade rolled her eyes. "That poster embarrassed the hell

out of me while I was growing up. Most people didn't know Brooke was my mother, and I kept as quiet as I could."

"Why would you be embarrassed? That poster was a hit. Your mom is beautiful."

"Yeah, more beautiful than I'll ever be, but that's not why it was embarrassing."

I didn't agree that Jade wasn't as beautiful as Brooke. Brooke was model beautiful, but Jade... Jade was stunning, warm, inviting.

"Then why?"

"Well...it's kind of hard to say..." Her cheeks flushed an adorable pink.

"Come on," I urged. "Tell me."

"Well...because pretty much every teenage boy I knew had masturbated to my mom's hard nipples poking through that blue suit, that's why."

I let out a chuckle. Poor girl did have a point. "I'm sure the poster made a lot of money for you."

"I never saw any of it. Her second husband took most of it and gambled it away. After she divorced him, she came back, wanting to work things out with my father and me. I was around fifteen at the time, and I was having none of it. Neither was my father."

The pain of loss washed over me. I knew what it felt like to lose a mother. My mother had been great up until... I shook my head to erase the images that tried to sneak in. I was twelve when my mother killed herself. Marjorie didn't even remember her.

"I see. So it was the classic 'choosing the career over the family' kind of thing."

Jade nodded. "That about sums it up. She was more interested in being Brooke Bailey than she was in being my mom, until she lost everything."

"What's she up to now?"

"I haven't the foggiest, other than she's broke and botoxed." Jade took a sip of her tea. "And I don't care."

I nodded. What could I say to that? She had every right to feel the way she did.

"I guess I should get back to bed." She stood.

But I didn't want her to leave. I enjoyed talking to her. I really didn't talk to much of anyone other than Marjorie and my brothers. I found myself wanting to talk to Jade, and that had to stop. The more I talked, the more cracks got into my wall. I could not risk my wall coming down. I would die.

So I had to let her go. I couldn't let her in, as much as I wanted to.

But I stood anyway, went after her, grabbed her, and turned her to face me.

"What is it?" Her eyes were wide.

"This," I said and slammed my mouth onto hers.

God, the same strawberry-champagne flavor... She returned my kiss, twirling her tongue against mine. My cock stiffened under my lounge pants. I wasn't wearing a shirt, and I desperately wanted to feel her breasts against me. Still kissing her, I untied her robe and slipped it over her shoulders until it ended up in a silky puddle on the kitchen floor.

Her beautifully full breasts were bound in a white tank top. Such beauty shouldn't be bound. It should be free. I broke the kiss and looked down. Her dark areolas were visible through the white cotton, her nipples puckered and hard. I cupped one breast in my left hand and kissed her again.

She groaned into my mouth. I felt the vibration more than heard it. My cock was full-on hard now. I desperately wanted to push her down to her knees, force her mouth onto my erection, and make her suck me into oblivion.

Instead, I kept kissing her, thumbing her erect nipple. When she sighed into my mouth, I gave the nipple a little pinch.

She jerked against me but did not stop me. She continued to kiss me, letting her soft sweet tongue wander into my mouth. I drank from her, quenching a thirst that I hadn't realized I had. She was so beautiful, so giving, so...everything that I was not. Soft where I was hard.

Whole where I was...broken.

Could she heal me? Could anyone heal all the holes in my soul?

As we kissed, I almost believed that she could.

But I knew better.

I broke the kiss with a loud smack.

No one could heal me. I would forever be broken.

She looked up at me with those steely eyes, her lips puffy and swollen, her nipples still hard through the white tank top. How I ached to hold her close to me, kiss the top of her silky hair, whisper into her ear that everything was all right and would always be all right.

But that would be a lie.

Nothing would ever be all right again.

I walked around her, my cock still hard and aching, left the kitchen, and went back to my bedroom. Roger trailed at my heals, panting. Damn dog was always happy.

Once in bed, I eased my desire with my own hand. Still, Jade's beautiful face, those eyes that penetrated through all my layers, haunted me well into the night.

I didn't sleep.

I never slept.

CHAPTER FIVE

Jade

He did it. He really just left me standing in the kitchen after giving me a kiss even more amazing than the last one. I didn't know what to make of it. Should I talk to Marj about it? Would she even want to know? Would she be comfortable with her brother kissing her best friend?

I let out a heavy sigh and took a few more sips of my tea, which had grown lukewarm. I would have to stop these little midnight visits to the kitchen.

I picked up my robe and put it back on, a shiver overtaking me. My nipples were still hard against the fabric of my tank. God...when he touched them, pinched them...I'd nearly shattered right then and there. Two kisses from Talon Steel had affected me more and been more exciting than seven years of kisses with Colin Morse.

Thank God he had left me at the altar, or I'd be married to one man without ever knowing what it felt like to love another.

I shook my head rapidly to clear it. I was not in love with Talon Steel. I'd known him for two days. He was such an enigma. He didn't sleep, ended up in his kitchen every night, and now he had kissed me twice for no apparent reason. He'd never said anything about it. Not like there was a lot to say, but shouldn't he at least mention it to me in passing? Apologize if he didn't mean to do it? And I sincerely hoped he meant to do it.

My legs trembled, and I sat back down at the table. Damn. Colin had never made my legs tremble, at least not like this. Talon Steel was fucking amazing. Flawless looks, the best kissing in the world... But he still wore that armor.

My talk with Marj hadn't revealed anything. Clearly, she didn't know her brother any better than I did. Maybe the people I should be talking to were Jonah and Ryan, but I had only seen them in passing since they both lived outside of the main house.

In the morning, I'd go out on the ranch and talk to one of them. Or I could drive over to the vineyards. That was where Ryan would be. He was the winemaker.

Finally, I stood. Time to get back to bed. But I wouldn't sleep.

If only I had brought a vibrator with me...

★ ★ ★ ★

In the morning after breakfast, I told Marj I would do some exploring on my own. I hopped in the Ford Mustang they had allowed me to use, set my GPS, and drove over to the Steel vineyards. I didn't want to bother Ryan, but it couldn't hurt to see if he had a few minutes to talk to me.

The scenery was lush and green—acres and acres of pastureland for their beef cattle, and little houses dotted the area as well, where their hired people lived. When I passed all of the pastureland, I came to the orchard. The apple and peach trees were in bloom, and the sweet smell of their blossoms wafted into the car. I inhaled deeply. Marj raved about Western slope peaches. She also said that Ryan, as well as making traditional wine from grapes, made an apple wine and a peach wine in a dry style. Most fruit wines I'd tasted in the past were so sweet. I was excited to try Ryan's offerings.

When I finally drove to the end of orchard, I came to the vineyards. They were also in bloom. I'd have to ask Ryan what kind of grapes he grew here. The Steels made a Merlot, a Cab, a Rhône blend, a traditional table red blend, and several others. Could he possibly grow all of those grapes here? Or did he bring some in from California? All good questions, and I was actually interested. That would give me a good segue into talking about Talon. I could start with Ryan by telling him I had an interest in the wine business. That wasn't even a lie. I loved a quality glass of wine. Enology had always interested me.

On that job issue... Maybe Ryan could use me at the winery. At least until I got my bar results. I'd been working since I was sixteen years old. Didn't feel right to me not to be earning something. All through college and law school, I worked twenty to thirty hours a week, waiting tables during college and then as a law clerk during law school.

Perfect... Of course, I was putting the cart before the horse. Maybe Ryan didn't need any help at the winery right now. After all, he wouldn't actually be making wine until harvest time. But it didn't hurt to ask.

I drove up the gravel driveway to the winery office and tasting room. I'd been here once before when I visited Marj on the ranch during college. We'd thought it great fun to get to taste all the wines even though neither of us was twenty-one yet.

I parked and walked in. A woman sat behind a small desk,

typing on a computer.

"Hi," I said. "Is...Ryan around today?"

"Yeah, he's over in the warehouse, tasting wine from some of the barrels. Is he expecting you?"

"No, not really. I'm Jade Roberts, Marjorie's friend. I'm staying at the ranch for a while until I get settled here. I was wondering if you guys needed any help here around the vineyards. I'm looking for work."

"You'd have to ask Ryan about that. I don't really know."

"Can I just go over and...ask him?"

The woman nodded. "I'm Marion, by the way. Tell him I said to go on over. You can see the warehouse from here."

"Thanks so much."

I left the office and walked toward the big warehouse where the barrels were housed. Steel Vineyards was a state-of-the-art establishment, but still I imagined Lucy Ricardo stomping grapes. I let out a giggle. I'd loved Lucy since I discovered the black-and-white reruns when I was a kid. What would grapes feel like between my toes?

I hesitantly opened the door to the warehouse. I had been here before, but I'd forgotten how huge the stainless steel barrels were. The place was spick-and-span spotless. I'd been surprised when I first saw the place several years ago. I had been expecting old wooden barrels. Nope, not for Steel vineyards. Everything up to date and state of the art. Several employees milled about, none of them paying me any mind. I looked around until I saw Ryan over in the corner with a wineglass, taking a sample from one of the barrels.

I gathered my courage and strode over.

"Hi, Ryan."

He looked up. Same dark eyes as Talon, but not as

brooding. "Oh, Jade. Hey, great to see you. Sorry I haven't been up to the house."

"No worries. I've only been here a few days. I wanted to come by and say hi."

"Great. I'm glad you did. Here, you want to taste this with me?"

"Sure." I nodded. "What is it?"

"It's my version of a dry rosé made with Grenache, Syrah, and Cinsault. Kind of like a French rosé." He handed me a glass of the pink liquid.

I took a sip. "Wow, it's really good." Here was my chance to impress him. "It's very fruit forward, raspberries on the nose. But I like the acidity. Makes it feel dry even with the fruitiness."

Ryan smiled. "Pretty good for an amateur. I'm getting all that plus a little bit of plum, tiny bit of sweet pepper."

Sweet pepper? Like red bell pepper? I definitely didn't get that, but I wasn't about to tell him. "Oh, yeah, now that you mention it..."

"This will be ready for bottling come fall." Ryan looked around. "So what have you been up to since you've been here?"

"Not a lot. Marj showed me around the city. But until I get my bar results, which won't happen for a few weeks or so, I can't get a job practicing law."

"Just relax, then. We've got all kinds of stuff to do around here. You won't be bored."

"It's not being bored I'm worried about. I like to be earning something, and...I was wondering if maybe you could use some help around here. I love wine, and I'd love to learn more about it."

"Well, we get the busiest around harvest time and bottling

time. Both of those happen around the same time in the fall. Bottling goes into the winter sometimes. So there's not a lot to do around here right now, but I suppose you could always help Marion in the office if you don't mind busy work."

"I don't mind busy work at all. I've been doing clerical stuff for my dad for years. I'd love it, but if you don't need the help..."

His eyes brightened. "Actually, I think Marion would appreciate it very much. And also"—he stroked his chin—"I think I could use you in the tasting room. If you're truly interested in wine, I could give you a little guidance, and you could run tastings."

My mouth dropped open. "Really? I would love that."

"The pay's not much. Not for someone who's waiting for a job as a lawyer. Fifteen bucks an hour. But I could probably get you twenty to thirty hours a week between helping Marion and helping in the tasting room."

"Hey, the pay is great. I've been working since I was sixteen, and I just hate not to be earning something. I really appreciate the fact that you guys are letting me stay here, but I don't want to be a total sponge."

"Are you kidding me? Marjorie has been so excited to have you. And we have room and plenty of everything to go around. But I understand how you feel, and I actually really could use your help."

"This is so awesome, Ryan. Thank you so much."

He grinned. He resembled Talon quite a bit, except his nose was still perfect. Obviously, it hadn't been broken. Is this what Talon would look like when he smiled? I had never seen Talon smile. Not really. What would it take to get a true smile out of him?

"Let's go back to the office. We'll fill out some paperwork, and I'll introduce you to Marion."

"We've already met. I asked her where to find you."

"Great. Let's take a walk."

As we walked, I itched to bring up Talon. How exactly did one bring him up in conversation? *Hey, what's going on with your brother?*

When we got back to the office, Ryan filled Marion in, and she set about rooting out the tax forms I had to sign.

Once everything was in order, Ryan said, "The tasting room is just behind the office. Let me show you. People visit the winery a lot during the summer, and we offer free tastings of our current releases."

The tasting room was basically just a conference table with a buffet on one end that held lots of wineglasses. A bar sat along the far wall.

"The wines are back here." Ryan pointed to a refrigerated wine cabinet. "You just open four or five bottles of our current releases and pour. Simple enough. Answer questions about the wine if the people have any. I'll have you sit in on a few that I do and that Mike does. He's my second-in-command around here, although he's off for a week on vacation right now."

"This is awesome, Ryan. I'm so excited."

"You'll find it's not as glamorous as you think. But I enjoy it."

"Are you kidding? You're an artist."

"Well, I've won a few awards in my day." He grinned again.

I sucked in a deep breath and let it out slowly. Now or never. "Ryan, could I ask you question?"

"Sure. Go ahead."

I bit my lip. "I was wondering about your brother. Talon. He seems... I don't know."

"Have you had a run-in with him?"

Well, yeah. He kissed me twice in the middle of the night. "No, no, nothing like that. He's the one who picked me up at the airport a few days ago. He was just so..."

"A little off?"

I nodded. "Yes, that's it exactly."

Ryan blew out a breath. "You know he was in Iraq for a while."

"Yeah, I know. I figured that's what it was."

"Well...there were things before then, even. But it's Talon's story to tell, not mine. If he's bothering you, just ignore him."

"No, that's not what I meant. He's not bothering me. I just would like to know more about him."

"He's pretty much a closed book."

"I figured as much." That armor I had sensed the first time I met him—so apparent, although invisible. I could feel it, as if it were a living, breathing entity enclosing him.

"Don't let him get to you," Ryan said. "He's been through a lot. Just hang out with Marjorie, and starting tomorrow, you can hang out here with Marion and me and the rest of us. When did you say you get your bar results?"

"It could be as soon as a few weeks to a month. Or it could be longer. I frantically check the website every day to see if it's been updated."

Ryan laughed. "I imagine that's pretty nerve-racking."

"No kidding. Those were the most challenging two days of my life. And I'd better pass, because I am certainly never taking the damn thing again."

"Well, if you don't pass and you don't want to take it again, maybe you can become a winemaker." He smiled.

Gorgeous smile. Funny, though. It didn't affect me at all. I didn't feel any pull. It was Talon, who never smiled, who drew me like a magnet.

"I'll have to think about that." I laughed. "What time do you want me here tomorrow?"

"Let's say nine for now. When things get busier, we start at eight, and sometimes even seven."

"Not a problem. I can do that." It would give me something to focus on. And I'd better start sleeping if I had to get up early, which meant no more midnight rendezvous with Talon.

All for the best.

I thanked Ryan again, stopped at the office and said goodbye to Marion, and drove back to the main house.

I walked in the front door. "Marj?" I called.

No response. I checked my watch. Noon. No wonder I was hungry. I walked into the kitchen, this time in broad daylight, and there was Talon sitting at the table, that adorable dog at his feet.

He was staring at a full glass of water.

CHAPTER SIX

Talon

"So is this your MO at noon as well as midnight?"

I looked up. Jade. Well, what had I expected? She lived here now.

"Don't mind me," she said. "I'm just going to make myself a sandwich."

"Felicia can make you something."

Jade turned her head. "Where is she?"

"She ran to the market."

"If she's not here, how can she make me anything?" Jade walked to the refrigerator and opened it.

"She'll be back."

Jade laughed. "I'm perfectly capable of fixing my lunch. Can I get you anything?"

"No. I'll wait for Felicia to get back."

"Suit yourself."

Jade rumbled about in the kitchen, and within a few minutes, sizzling sounds and the robust scent of cheddar cheese drifted over to me.

"What are you making?"

"Grilled cheddar and tomato sandwich, one of my favorites."

My mouth began water. Damn, that sounded good. But I

couldn't ask her to...

"Sure I can't make one for you?"

"Well...I don't know how long Felicia is going to be. I am kind of hungry..."

She clomped over to me and stood at the other end of the table, glaring at me with her steely eyes. "I am more than happy to make you a sandwich. It is not a problem. It is not a bother. But you have to tell me that you want it."

God, when she looked at me, I became defenseless. She could see right through those walls. I knew it. And somehow, I could tell that she knew it too.

I couldn't let her in. I'd already kissed her twice. If I let her make me a sandwich... Oh, fuck. It was a goddamn sandwich. "I want it," I said.

She pursed her pretty red lips. "A 'please' might've been nice, but I'll take it." She walked back to the counter and brought over a sandwich on a plate. "You can have this one. I'll make myself another."

"I didn't mean to take your sandwich."

"It's no bother," she said through gritted teeth. "You're letting me live in your house, Talon. And you know what? Even if I weren't a guest in your home, I would still offer to make you a sandwich. Do you know why?"

Was I supposed to answer? Or was it a rhetorical question? I arched my eyebrows.

"Because I'm a nice person. Because it's a nice thing to do."

She walked back to the cooktop. I turned around and watched her create another sandwich for herself. She was at ease in the kitchen. I didn't have a lot of memories of my own mother, but of the few I had, none of them included her standing in the kitchen making a meal for me. For any of us, for that matter. We always had a cook and housekeeper. One of the benefits of being born a Steel, I guess. There didn't seem to be many more benefits, at least not in my case.

I turned back around and took a bit of bite of my sandwich— "Shit!"

"Sorry. The cheese is going to be really hot. You might want to wait a few minutes before eating it."

If only she had given me that warning ten seconds earlier. The skin on the roof of my mouth was bubbling. Once it cooled down though, and I took another bite, the sandwich was really good. Delicious, even. Had Felicia been home, she would've whipped up some enchiladas or tamales for me. She was an amazing cook, and not just her native food either. But damn... Even as I sat thinking of Felicia's prime rib, a rack of lamb with rosemary and mint, her roast pheasant with cherry and walnut chutney...I swear to God, nothing tasted as good as that damned grilled cheddar and tomato sandwich that Jade had made for me.

A minute or two later, Jade sat back down at the table with her own sandwich. She pulled one of the pieces of bread up, and steam flew out from the melted cheese. "This helps cool it off," she said.

I took another bite of mine and swallowed. "It's really good."

"Simple grilled cheese and tomato. Even better with a homemade tomato bisque."

"Where did you learn how to cook?" I asked.

"I'd hardly call this cooking. I'm not Marj. But I do know how to make things other than grilled cheese. I told you that my mom left my dad and me when I was quite young. He's not a bad cook, but he worked so much that I had to learn to do the cooking once I was old enough. I learned most of it from my grandmother, my dad's mom, but she passed away by the time I was ten. I still had her old and worn-out *Better Homes & Gardens* cookbook. It's not gourmet, but it's good and edible."

"Well, this is a really good sandwich. I never would've thought of putting tomato on it."

"I actually came up with that one myself, although years later I found out that a lot of people like grilled cheese and tomato, which is why grilled cheese and tomato soup are so popular together."

"It's delicious." *Thank you.* The words sat on the tip of my tongue. Why couldn't I utter them? Jade had done something nice for me, and the sandwich truly was delicious. It had been so long since I'd said those words to anyone and meant them. Rather, I changed the subject. "What have you been doing today?"

"I drove over to the winery to talk to Ryan."

A sharp pain stabbed me in my gut. Why the hell was she talking to Ryan? Ryan was known as the most jovial and best-looking Steel brother. The guy always had a smile on his face. No baggage for that one. Of course not. I had saved him that day.

"He's going to give me some work over at the winery until I get my bar results."

Thank God. So that's all it was. Jade was interested in wine.

"What kind of work?"

"Nothing too exciting. Mostly helping Marion around the office with busy work. He did say he would train me to do tastings. I'm really excited about that opportunity."

"Yeah, he opens up the winery for tastings all day on Friday and Saturdays. We get quite a good crowd there. He doesn't charge for the tastings, but that doesn't matter, because most people end up buying a case or two of wine."

"Do you like wine?"

"I'm more of a bourbon or whiskey man myself. Peach Street is my favorite."

"I've never heard of that."

"It's made here in Colorado. It's some smooth stuff, let me tell you. Colorado makes some amazing whiskeys. Breckenridge and Stranahan's are two other great ones."

"I'll have to try them sometime. I'm not much into hard liquor, or beer, for that matter. My preference is wine when I drink at all. Which isn't a lot."

No longer scalding hot, the rest of my sandwich was amazing. The sharpness of the cheddar and sweet acidity of the tomato combined with the whole-wheat bread into a succulent delicacy. I opened my mouth to say again how delicious it was but decided against it. No sense beating a dead horse.

Jade finished her sandwich just as I took the last bite of mine. She stood, grabbed her plate and then mine, walked over to the sink, and ran water over them.

For an instant, I imagined we were husband and wife. She had made my lunch for me and picked up my plate. No one other than Felicia, or whoever the cook/housekeeper of the day was, had ever picked up after me. Not my mother, not my father, and certainly not my brothers or sister. Was I supposed to say thank you for that as well?

Why was it so hard? Usually I said thank you to Felicia. That was impersonal. It was a trained response. I took Felicia for granted. I knew I did. I pretty much took everything for granted.

Jade tussled around the kitchen, putting something in the microwave. "I'm making a cup of tea," she said. "You want anything?"

There she went again. For the life of me, I couldn't figure out why this was so amazing to me. "No thanks." Although a cup of tea did sound good.

I rose, walked to the cupboard, pulled out a mug, and filled it with water. When the microwave dinged, and she took her cup out, I put mine in.

"What in the hell are you doing?" she asked me, her eyebrows arched.

"I'm making some tea."

She shook her head. "What? The tea I offered wasn't good enough for you?"

My cheeks warmed. "No, I...I just didn't want to be a bother."

She shook her head again, letting out a heavy sigh. "I really don't get you, Talon. I was over here making a cup of tea. It would not have been any trouble to make another cup of tea. In fact, I could have put both cups in the microwave at the same time, and they'd be done by now."

Great. Now I felt like a piece of shit. Of course, since I always felt like a piece of shit, this was really nothing new. "Now you don't have to bother."

"Oh, for the love of God!" She pounded her fist on the counter. "Damn it, that hurt!"

"These counters are solid granite."

"Yes, yes. And I'm used to cheap Formica. Well, you got that right. Enjoy your tea." She took hers and turned, walking toward the table.

But she passed the table and headed for the hallway.

Something stirred within me. I wasn't ready to let her go yet. I wanted to spend more time with her. But how? If I asked her to stay and drink tea with me, she probably would. *So ask her, Talon. Just fucking ask her.*

But my lips stayed clamped shut. If I let her anymore near me, the walls that were already beginning to crumble in her presence would come crashing down.

What was it about her? Why did I want her so much?

I had to stay away from her. Ryan probably didn't have room for me in the guest house, but Jonah might have some room in his house. I'd go over and see him this afternoon and find out. And then I'd go into town and start the process for a permit to build my own structure here on the ranch. I needed to get far away from Jade Roberts. For her own good as well as mine.

★ ★ ★ ★

Jonah was in his office, decked out in full cowboy regalia, ready to go out in the field and check on some steers. He looked up when I entered.

"Hey, Talon, what are you doing out here?"

"It is one quarter my ranch. Shouldn't I know what's going on from time to time?"

"Sure. But you never come out here. I take care of the beef, Ry takes care of the vineyards, and you take care of the orchard. We don't bug each other."

"I didn't come out here to bug you, Joe. Actually came out ask you favor."

"Anything for you if I can. What you need?"

"It's time for me to build my own house here on the land. I've got a spot in mind, and I wanted to go over it with you, make sure you didn't need it for pasture or anything. Then I plan to go into town and file the papers for the permit. I'll drive into Grand Junction and hire an architect later this week."

"Are you sure that's a good idea? That will leave Marjorie in the big house all by herself."

"She's a big girl. And she's got her friend with her now."

"I suppose. One of us is going to have to take over the big house eventually, though, and I figured it would always be you, Tal. I mean, I've got my own place already, and Ryan's comfortable in the guest house. Marjorie will probably eventually meet someone and move off the ranch."

"Is it a goddamned crime for me to want my own house?"

"No, of course not. Calm yourself down, for God's sake."

"I just can't stay there anymore, Joe."

"Why? What the fuck is wrong with that house? It's beautiful. Felicia comes in every day and takes care of everything. You don't have to do a damn thing."

"You don't understand. I have to get away from..."

"From what? Not Marjorie?"

"Of course not Marjorie. She's my sister. I love her."

"Then—oh my God." Jonah raked his fingers through his dark hair that was beginning to gray at the temples. "It's that friend of hers, isn't it?"

I looked down at my feet. "I don't know what you're talking about."

"I knew there'd come a day. She's trying to knock down your walls, isn't she, Tal?"

"No. At least...I don't think so. I mean, she's not *trying* to."

"Getting under your skin, is she?"

I sat down in the chair across from Jonah's desk. I didn't say anything. There was nothing left to say. I was an open book to my older brother. I had been since I'd come back.

"Are you ready to get some help, Tal?"

Help. Poor Joe didn't know this, but no help existed for me. I was a product of so many different hells, and no one could help me. I had to live alone. Nothing else would work for me. "We've had this conversation before," I said. "You couldn't help me. Dad couldn't help me. There's no way some stranger can."

"There are strangers who have the right training to help someone like you. In fact— Oh, fuck, never mind. If you want to build a house, build a fucking house. Maybe Marj will want the ranch house. Maybe she'll never marry, or maybe she'll marry some poor pauper who wants to live big in the main house. Who knows?"

I unrolled the land plats I had brought with me. "I'm looking at this place." I pointed to the beautiful area I had chosen to build my home on. "It's right on the lake, and you don't currently use it for grazing land."

Joe grabbed the plat and took a look. "I don't see why you can't have it. But you know it's open grazing out here, so the animals could make their way to you."

"I have no problem with that." I liked animals. They understood me. They didn't press. They didn't judge. They didn't ask questions I couldn't answer. That silly mutt Roger had come around about a year ago, begging for food. I'd fed him, and I'd made a friend for life. The little guy doted on me, followed me everywhere, and I loved it. I loved him, as much as I was capable. Animals were easy to love. All Roger asked was a meal every day, a warm bed at my feet, and a scratch behind the ear now and then, and he gave me his loyalty unconditionally.

"It's pretty far removed from the rest of us."

"And?"

Jonah shook his head. "And nothing. I guess that's how you want it, Tal. One more wall you can lock around yourself."

"When you've walked a mile in my shoes, brother, you can judge me." I stood.

Jonah stood as well. "Talon, I would have gladly walked in your shoes to spare you the pain."

"You can't say that. You don't know..."

"You're right. I don't know. I don't pretend to know everything you've been through. But that doesn't mean I wouldn't have done anything to protect you. You're my younger brother." He let out a heavy sigh. "It should've been me."

"We've been through this time and time again. There was nothing you could have done."

"I should've been there to protect you. You were there to protect Ryan, and I should've been there for you."

"And what would that have accomplished? You would've gone through the hell instead of me? Or maybe we both would have? Is that truly what you wanted?"

"Of course not. What I would've wanted was for neither of us to go through it. But if it had to be one of us, I would've preferred it to be me."

My skin prickled. The thought of either of my brothers enduring what I had nauseated me. "That's the dumbest thing I've ever heard, Joe. Look at me. I'm alive. What more can I want?"

"You're not alive, man. You're a goddamned corpse

walking around—no feelings, all those walls. That's not living, bro."

"I'm doing the best I can. This is all the living I know right now."

"Talon, that's a fucking lie and you know it. You know what? I changed my mind. I *do* need that little plot of land for pasturing. I don't want you building a house there, or anywhere, for that matter. If Jade is getting inside your skin, I'm all for it. You won't let any of the rest of us in. If she can get in, maybe she can help you."

"Fuck you," I said through gritted teeth. "I'm going to go start the process for the permit. That land belongs to me too, damn it."

My older brother sat down and threaded his fingers through his tousled hair once more. "Fine."

I turned and walked out the door.

Right into Jade Roberts.

CHAPTER SEVEN

Jade

The Great Wall of Talon Steel stopped me in my tracks. Damn. "Sorry."

"What are you doing here?" He didn't smile.

Of course, he never smiled.

"I came to see Jonah. Why is that any of your business anyway?"

"Joe's getting ready to head out to pasture and check on some steers. And everything that happens on this ranch is my business, blue eyes."

I doubted that, but why argue? Besides, my tummy was fluttering from the "blue eyes." I had a feeling he could call me just about anything and I'd react. "I haven't seen him since I've been here, and I want to say hi and thank him for letting me stay."

"I see. Well, don't let me get in your way." He turned and walked away.

I knocked on the door and then opened it. "Is anyone here?"

"Yeah, come on in." Jonah was in the corner, checking the spurs on his boots. "Hey, Jade."

"Hi. Sorry if I've come along at a bad time."

"Not at all. I have a few minutes. What's on your mind?"

Talon. But I couldn't say that. "Not a whole lot. I just wanted to come by and thank you for letting me stay at the main house with Marj."

"Oh, that's no problem at all. As you've seen, we've got the room. We're happy to have you."

"I'm glad. I really appreciate all you guys are doing for me."

"Any friend of Marjorie's is a friend of ours."

"Yeah... Well, I'll see you around. I'll let you get back to your work." I turned.

"Jade, wait a minute."

I turned back. "Yeah?"

Jonah walked toward me, his spurs clacking on the floor. "There's something I want to ask you, if you don't mind."

"Not at all."

"I understand you're helping Ryan over at the winery."

"Yeah. I'm really excited about it." Was that what he wanted to know about?

"So..." He hedged a bit. "What do you think of my brother?"

Ryan? That was who we were just talking about, right? "He's great."

"Great. Hmm."

"Yeah. I mean, he didn't have to give me a job at the winery."

Jonah shook his head. "Oh, no, I'm not talking about Ryan. I'm talking about Talon."

Talon... What could I say about Talon? *Oh, he's the best kisser in the world, but other than that he hardly speaks to me, and when he does, he's usually rude.* "Well... He... I don't really know what to say. Talon keeps to himself."

"Have you and he..."

What in the hell was he talking about? And then it dawned on me. Talon might have told Jonah about our kisses. Did brothers talk about things like that? I had no idea.

"Have he and I what?"

"Never mind."

But suddenly I wanted to know exactly what he meant. Talon was such an enigma. "I'd really like to know what you're going to ask. In fact, I'd really like to know more about Talon."

"Why is that?"

"Well, he's so...closed up, you know?"

Jonah nodded. "He's been through a lot."

"Yeah, I know. Overseas. The Marines."

"Yeah...overseas..." Jonah's dark eyes held a faraway look. A hint of sadness.

"I asked Marj about him, and she said that's just the way he is. Ryan didn't say much more, except that it wasn't his story to tell. What story is he talking about, Jonah?"

Jonah looked above me, his gaze seemingly fixed on a spot on the wall. "Whatever story he's talking about, it's not mine to tell either."

That was no help. Why was I not surprised?

"But could you do me a favor?" Jonah asked.

"Sure. What do you need?"

"Don't give up on Talon. There's something about you... He's responding to you in a way I've never seen him respond to anyone."

"How could you think that? You've never seen us interact."

He smiled, handsome as anything, just like Ryan, but lacking the heat I felt when Talon looked at me.

"Call it a hunch."

Hunch? I was supposed to "not give up" because of Jonah's hunch? "I'm afraid I don't understand what you're asking."

"Try to spend some time with him. Get him talking."

"He barely says two words to me, Jonah."

Jonah let out a laugh. "That's probably two more words than he says to anyone else."

I couldn't help it. I laughed too. "Does he ever smile?"

Jonah sighed. "Not a lot, I'm afraid. But that's part of my hunch. I have a sneaking suspicion that you might be able to get some smiles out of him."

"Did he tell you about—" I clamped my hand over my mouth. What was I saying? I hadn't even told Marj about the kisses. I certainly wasn't going to tell Jonah.

"Tell me what?"

"Never mind." I turned around and ran out the door.

God, sometimes I was such a complete moron.

But I had made up my mind about one thing. I was going to learn more about Talon Steel. One way or another, I would find out what made him tick.

Those walls were coming down.

★ ★ ★ ★

I'd been sleeping better, but I purposely set my phone to buzz at one in the morning. Maybe I could learn more about Talon during one of his midnight kitchen raids. I walked out to the kitchen, but he wasn't there.

The next night, even though I was exhausted from my first day working with Ryan at the winery, I did the same thing.

My phone buzzed for me at one in the morning. I rose,

took a quick bathroom break, combed my hair, and pinched my cheeks. I purposely didn't put on my robe. I was wearing my trademark cotton/spandex white tank and old boxers.

I crept out into the kitchen. When I turned on the light, there sat Talon, at the same place at the table, staring at a full glass of water, his dog at his feet.

"Where were you last night?" He looked up.

"I actually do try to sleep most nights." Which was a lie, of course. He hadn't been there last night, at least not at the same time. Was he messing with me?

I gave Roger a quick pet and then walked to the counter to begin my ritual. "Do you want some tea?" I asked over my shoulder.

"No," he said without looking up.

Okay. Evidently, things were going to continue as usual. What was I doing? I had work in the morning, and here I was setting my damned alarm to go off in the night. This was ridiculous.

When my tea was ready, I walked to the table and sat down in my usual spot next to Talon.

"So do you ever actually drink that water you pour for yourself?"

He pursed his lips and then brought the glass to his mouth and took a drink. "Satisfied?"

Satisfied? Seriously? "Do you really think I care if you drink your water?"

"Well, you appear to, since you asked."

"Unbelievable." I rolled my eyes and dipped my tea bag in and out of my water.

"What's unbelievable?"

"How you can be so rude about something so

insignificant."

"Rude? Me? You're the one who asked me about my water."

Touché. He was right. While the content of my question was innocuous, my tone had been a little snide. "Okay. I'll admit I might've used a slightly rude tone when I asked. But I truly am interested. You're here nearly every night, you pour yourself a glass of water, and then you sit and stare at it. What is that about?"

"You wouldn't understand."

I looked straight into his burning dark eyes. "Try me."

He picked up the glass, walked to the sink, and poured it out. He came back to the table and pounded it with a loud bang. "There. I took care of it."

"And that is supposed to be significant?"

"Trust me. It is."

I turned my attention back to my teacup. "If you say so."

He stood and took the water glass to the sink. He stayed for a moment, his back to me, his ass looking delectable in his sleeping pants. His skin was tan, and the strong muscles of his back seemed tense. How I longed to massage all the tension out of him. Would I ever get that chance?

I'd have to break down a lot of walls to be able to do anything for his tension. Was I ready for that? Having just come away from a broken engagement?

I let out a soft chuckle. Whether I was ready mattered little. Talon was not ready and probably never would be.

He turned around and gazed at me. "What's so funny?"

Shit. Had he heard my laugh? "Nothing."

He walked toward me, aggression in his demeanor. "Are you fucking laughing at me?"

"No, I—"

He pulled me up and out of my chair so I was facing him, our chests nearly touching.

"You think it's funny that I can't sleep? That I sit here with a glass of water? Is that why you get up every night, to laugh at me?"

I trembled before him—from fear or arousal, I wasn't sure. He gripped my upper arms, his knuckles whitening with the pressure he was exerting.

I should stop him. I should stop him now before this goes one minute further.

But I didn't want to stop him. Yes, he was gripping me hard, harder than he should. But his touch on my skin, his hands on my flesh... It all felt right, somehow.

"Answer me, goddamnit."

I shook my head. "Of course I wasn't laughing at you. I wouldn't do such a thing."

He sneered at me. "Yes, because you're such a nice person, right?"

"Yes." My lips trembled.

"Are you, Jade? Are you really a nice person?"

"Of course I am."

He still gripped me firmly. "Then you should probably stay the hell away from me." He released me quickly.

I stumbled backward, catching myself by grabbing the back of the chair.

This man was dangerous. Brooding and dangerous. And sexy as hell. His dark-walnut hair framed his face in soft tousled waves. His onyx eyes gleamed, boring holes in my center as he stared at me. His muscles were tense, his whole chest clenched. He needed something. Anything, to release the tension.

"I...I guess I'll get back to bed." I turned to leave.

But he grabbed me again, this time pulling me right up to his chest, only the thin cotton of my tank separating us.

"I'm going to tell you this once, and I expect you to listen," he said, his eyes burning.

Was I supposed to nod? I simply arched my eyebrows.

"Do not come to the kitchen in the middle of the night anymore."

"Why not? If I can't sleep, the tea helps me relax—"

His lips slammed down on mine.

Oh, God...

He forced my mouth open with his tongue and plunged inside. His kiss was...feral—more feral and animalistic even then the previous ones. Oh, yes, he needed to release tension... and I would willingly help. He gripped my shoulders, bringing us closer and closer together, as if he wanted to disappear inside my skin.

I returned his kiss, not only because I wanted to, but because he seemed to need it so much.

We kissed for several minutes until finally he eased up, and the kiss became softer. He unclenched his fingers from my shoulders and trailed one hand up my neck to cup my cheek.

And I was lost. I could never resist a face toucher. I loved the feeling of being so treasured by someone. I wasn't laboring under any delusions that Talon Steel treasured me, but oh, the touch of his calloused fingers on my bare cheek... I was in heaven, floating on a magical cloud.

The kiss was still deep, and I still returned it passionately, but it was soft now, almost...loving. He unclenched his other hand from my shoulder and slid it down my arm, my skin prickling in its wake. My nipples were so hard I felt sure they were poking him. I longed for him to slide his hand up my side and cup one of my breasts, but we were too close together for that. I ached for his touch.

My sex throbbed. I knew I must be dripping, and all I had on were these loose boxers. God, I wanted his fingers on me, in me, stroking me to completion while he continued to kiss me.

Bravely, summoning all the courage in my arsenal, I clasped the hand that was holding on to my wrist and drew it toward my mound.

He broke the kiss abruptly, forcing me backward, his dark gaze burning into mine. "You don't know what you're asking for, blue eyes."

My courage still coursing through me, I regarded him. "I do, actually."

"I will hurt you." Sadness laced his voice.

Why would he think he would hurt me? Was he even talking about emotional hurt? Did he actually think he would physically hurt me?

"I'm a big girl, Talon. I can make my own choices. If I get hurt, it will be my own doing."

"You don't know what you're dealing with. You have no idea how much I ache for your pussy right now. I want to stuff you so full of my cock that you can't see straight. I've wanted you since the first time I laid eyes on you, Jade. I don't know why, but you have a hold on me."

My skin warmed, my pussy pulsing. Was this truly happening? "Then take me to bed. I'm going willingly."

"I'll never love you."

Bam! A brick settled on top of me. At least he was honest. I could give him that. I responded the only way I knew how.

"I'm not asking for your love."

He let out a chuckle. "Sooner or later, all you women want love."

I chuckled back at him. "Seriously? Look where so-called love got me. Left at the damned altar. Humiliated in front of my family and friends. Why in hell would I want to repeat that?"

"Maybe you don't want love today, and maybe not tomorrow. But you will someday."

"And who's to say you and I are going to be together someday?"

Another chuckle. "I can guarantee you we won't be together someday. I don't love, blue eyes. I take. I take what others are willing to give to me, but I can't give anything in return. It's not in me."

"I think you're probably selling yourself short, Talon, but what does it matter? Tonight doesn't have to make a future, does it? Tonight can simply be about what it is—two people enjoying each other's bodies and releasing some tension." I touched his shoulders, gently massaging them. "And damn, you've got a lot of tension built up."

"I don't want to fuck you to release tension, blue eyes."

"Then why do you want it?"

"Not because I love you."

Yes, yes, hit me over the head with it. "You've made that clear. What you haven't made clear is why you want me."

"Because I crave you. I crave your lips, your tongue, your body pressed against mine. I crave your sweet little pussy, your lips around my cock. I want to take you, own you, possess you for a night. I want to fuck you and fuck you and fuck you until neither one of us can take it anymore." His eyes glowed, his dark nipples hardened, and his erection was apparent underneath his pajama pants. "I'm so hard for you right now, like granite. And maybe, Jade, maybe if I fuck you and take you, I'll get this goddamned craving out of my system."

My knees buckled beneath me. My skin was blazing and my pussy throbbing. He wasn't offering me love. He wasn't even offering friendship. What he was offering was a good old-fashioned fuck with his body that had been carved by artists in heaven.

I didn't think about the consequences, about having to live under the same roof with him and what that would mean. I didn't think about how it would feel to see him every day and not be able to touch him. I didn't think about what the night might ultimately mean to me and the sadness I might feel at never being able to have it again.

I should have thought of all those things.

But I didn't.

Instead, I met his dark gaze.

"You want to fuck me so bad? Then do it, Talon."

CHAPTER EIGHT

Talon

I grabbed her arm and jerked her toward me. God, those breasts, against my chest...her hard nipples poking me... I was so fucking hard, so fucking ready to stick my cock inside her. In her mouth, in her pussy, in her ass. Wherever she let me. And she would let me go wherever I wanted. I could see it in her eyes, those steely blue orbs that haunted me. She'd let me have whatever I wanted tonight.

Why was I hesitating? I was Talon Steel. I took what was offered. I never felt the least amount of guilt.

I looked down at her red lips, swollen from the kiss I had given her. Fuck, that kiss... I'd been like an animal marking his prey. God help me, I couldn't get enough of her lips, enough of her luscious tits pressed against me, enough of her blue gaze that crashed right into my soul.

I would be her undoing. I knew that without question.

But I didn't care. I had to get my cock inside her. And if she was willing? Who was I to refuse?

I swept her into my arms and carried her down the hallway into my suite. I wasn't going to be gentle. I was never gentle. And even though with her, I almost wanted to be, I was so fucking turned on now that I couldn't be.

I set her down next to my bed. She turned to face me, her

gaze never leaving mine as she slowly pulled the white tank top over her head. Her ample breasts fell gently against her chest, her brownish-pink nipples taut and hard. She cupped them for a moment, as if holding them out in offering, but then slid her hands down her sides and over her hips, taking her boxers with her. When they were a plaid puddle on the floor, she stepped out of them.

Fuck me. She was shaved bare, her ruby pussy lips on full display. I nearly creamed myself right there. I had to squeeze the base of my dick to calm myself down. Jesus, I was like a teenager around her.

She took a step toward me, placed her silky hands on my hips, and brushed my lounge pants down over my legs and onto the floor.

Her eyes widened when she saw my cock. I couldn't help a small smile. Seconds later, though, she met my gaze, slid her hands up my abdomen and neck to cup my cheeks.

"Take me, Talon," she said. "Take what you need."

I could have thrown her on the bed and fucked her silly right then and there. She was ready. The lips of her beautiful pussy were already glistening.

But no. I wanted to go slowly, to savor her. I had to make this night count, make it everything it could be. I had to, because I needed to make damn sure this need went away after tonight.

"Get on the bed," I said.

She smiled—oh my God, she was fucking beautiful—and complied.

"How do you want me?" she asked.

"I'm going to suck on your nipples, blue eyes. I'm going to suck them until they're raw and aching. Tell me you want that, baby. Tell me you want my lips all over your nipples, all over your breasts."

"Yes," she breathed, her eyes fluttered closed. "I want that. I want you to suck my nipples."

I flicked my tongue over one hard bud. "I want to suck and suck on them, baby, until your pussy is so wet and dripping for me, until you're begging for my cock."

"If it's begging you want, I'm ready now."

I shook my head. "No way. I'm going to make you really want it, really ache for it. By the time I'm done with you, blue eyes, you are going to be rode hard and put away wet."

I took one of her dark-pink nipples between my lips and sucked.

She writhed beneath me, moaning. "God, that feels so good."

I continued sucking and tugging, while I found the other with my hand, giving a light pinch.

She jerked beneath me.

God, her pussy. I could smell her... Her arousal. That scent that made me crazy. I sucked harder on her nipple, pinched harder on the other. Her hips began moving, wafting more of her scent toward me.

She had a musky odor that reminded me of a ripe peach. Goddamnit, I loved peaches. I wanted to slide down her luscious body and lick her sweet cream. But I wasn't done with her nipples yet. I wanted her so tight, so on edge that she was begging for me.

She writhed underneath me, moaning, groaning. Each time I gave her nipple another light pinch, she jolted.

"Oh my God, Talon. God..."

I let her nipple drop from between my lips with a soft pop,

and I looked into her steely eyes. "You like that, baby?"

"Oh, God, yes."

I continued working her nipples while I trailed my hand down her soft skin to that oasis between her legs. I found her clit easily and pushed on it. She jerked with a loud sigh.

She began moving in rhythm with my finger as I teased her clit.

She was so fucking wet—wet with that fragrant nectar of hers. I resisted the urge to dip into her channel with my fingers. No, I was going to go slow. I would make her want me so badly she couldn't take it anymore.

She threaded her fingers through my hair as I started sucking on her nipple again, all the while teasing her clit.

"Please, please..." she begged.

Again I let the nipple drop from my mouth. "Please what?"

"Please... Your finger... Your cock... I need you inside me."

"All in good time." I returned to her nipple, sucking it, kissing it. I worked my tongue around her areola and then up over the full globe of her breast. Her skin was like silk under my lips, and she was so responsive. So warm.

A few seconds more, and I dropped her nipple again and removed my hand from her clit. I quickly turned her around and pushed her on the bed so she was lying on her tummy. Her beautiful ass, creamy and milky, drew my attention. I gave her a soft slap and then shifted her knees forward so her ass was the air. Her beautiful red pussy was on display, ripe for me to take it. And her puckered little hole... Goddamn...the woman was killing me.

I couldn't wait anymore to taste her. I shoved my face between her butt cheeks and inhaled her musky odor. I swiped my tongue along her slit and nearly unraveled. God, she tasted so fucking good. Better than any pussy I had ever tasted, and I'd had more than my share. Even her little asshole tasted sweet.

I slid my tongue through her folds again. She moved her hips backward, moaning.

"Your pussy tastes so good, blue eyes." I dived back in again, sliding her labia along my teeth, nipping, biting, sucking. Couldn't get enough of her sweet pussy.

When I finally took a break and kissed the sweet curves of her ass, I inserted two fingers into her cunt. Immediately she clenched around me, jerking backward.

God, she was coming. And it was the most exciting thing ever. Her moans and clenches fueled my desire. She was going to come and come and come all fucking night. She responded to my touch like no other had.

"Talon, what are you doing to me? Damn, it's good." She kept driving into my fingers, her spasms increasing.

And I was beyond thrilled.

"Yeah, baby, come all around my fingers." I hoped to God she wasn't a one-orgasm woman, because I was far from done.

I nursed her through the end of her spasms, and she collapsed on her belly.

I turned her over. I could've slid my cock into her heat in that moment, and damn, I was tempted, but I had to savor her. This would be the only time I had her, and I had to get enough to ease my desire. Make it go away forever.

"Sit up," I commanded. "I want you to suck my cock."

Her eyes fluttered open. Her lush body was flushed pink. She was clearly still reeling from her orgasm, yet she obeyed me, sitting up and wrapping her slender, warm fingers around my erection.

"How do you like it, Talon? Licking? Kissing? Sucking deep?"

"All of the above." I closed my eyes. "Just get those lips around my cock."

She bent forward and obeyed, kissing my tip. I damn near exploded. Then she tongued my tiny slit, swirling her tongue around the head. God, I was sensitive. I clenched my teeth, forcing myself to stay in check. This had to last if I was going to get her out of my system.

She slid her tongue down the underside of my cock to the base and up again. Then she swirled around the head again and clamped her lips over it, taking me to the back of her throat. She held it there for a few seconds, and I had to force myself not to release down her throat.

"Damn."

She continued sucking me, making me crazy, until I couldn't hold off any longer. I grabbed on to her head, forcing her down upon my cock and then up and back down, up and back down. I ached to come down her throat, to watch my semen wet her mouth, watch her lick my saltiness from her lips.

No way. I was coming in that hot little pussy of hers.

I had planned to take her from behind, doggy-style. That way I wouldn't have to look at her face, but suddenly I wanted more than anything to see those eyes when I came inside her and as she shattered again around my hardness. I grabbed her hair and forced her off of my cock, and laying her down on her back, I spread her legs. Her red pussy lay beckoning, already swollen from her first orgasm. How easy it would be slide right in, find my solace within her sweet body.

But I wasn't looking for solace. Solace didn't exist for me. What I needed now was release, pure and simple—an end to my aching need.

So instead of sliding into her, I thrust into her harshly, taking her. Taking what she was giving me, what she had told me to take.

And my God, she fit me like a fucking glove. The suction around me, every little ridge inside her cunt, the edge of her cervix—all of it had been created as a perfect mold to my cock. She was milking me, and I hadn't even pulled out and thrust in again yet.

I was so on edge. I could spill at any moment. How would this help my need if I couldn't make it last?

"Please, Talon. Please fuck me. I need it. Now."

Her words were my undoing. I pulled out and thrust back into her, finding in her body the release I needed. Only one more thrust and—

The convulsions started at the base of my cock and in my balls, traveling at light speed through my arousal as I filled her with my come.

What was I, a fucking teenager? Two thrusts and I'm coming? A thirty-five-year-old guy who couldn't hold his spunk?

She didn't get to come again.

What a fucking failure I was.

I pulled out, my cock already going limp. And I had forgotten to look into her eyes. That filled me with the most sadness of all.

She gently cleared her throat. "Are you...done?"

Embarrassment flooded through me. But what the hell did I care what she thought? This was just a fuck, after all. If it hadn't been to her liking, oh well. She had come at least once. It wasn't a complete loss.

"I'm..." was all that came out. I rolled over so I was lying on my back, next to her.

"You're what? Sorry? Why? It was wonderful."

"Don't lie to me."

"Who's lying? No one's ever gone down on me like that before. And my nipples are still quivering from the treatment you gave them." She leaned up on one arm and pressed her lips across mine.

Tenderness. She was giving me tenderness. And I didn't deserve tenderness.

I didn't want tenderness.

I'd done what I wanted to do. I'd fucked her. Yeah, I'd wanted it to last longer, but it hadn't.

It was over.

It wouldn't happen again.

CHAPTER NINE

Jade

He didn't respond to my kiss.

My skin tingled all over, and my pussy was still throbbing. His cock hadn't been inside me for long, but God...for the few seconds he had penetrated me, I'd felt complete in a way I hadn't ever.

Or maybe I was just horny.

I was wildly attracted to Talon Steel. No denying that. But on the other hand, how much of this was the rebound thing? I *had* just been left at the altar.

And now I had to live here in the same house with him. Had this been a complete mistake?

But as I looked at him lying on his back, his arm over his forehead and his eyes closed, I couldn't think it had been a mistake. Perhaps it would be awkward between us from now on, but I would never regret this.

I couldn't help a smile. He had come very quickly. That meant he had wanted me, or at least that he found me wickedly attractive. I'd take either at this point.

Now what? It was the middle of the night. Should I get up and go back to my own room? Did he want me to stay?

I wanted to stay. Talon Steel was so... I couldn't quite put my finger on it. All I knew was I had an overwhelming need and desire to offer him comfort. I had no idea what might be comforting for him, but something in me knew he needed it.

Slowly I trailed my hand over his forearm. He jerked at first.

"Shhh," I said softly. "Let me."

He relaxed slightly. Though still tense, at least he didn't make me stop. I feathered my fingers up his forearm, his upper arm, to his shoulders. Then down over his abdomen, tracing gentle circles around each of his nipples. I glided my hand down his chest over his abs, down to his dark thick patch of pubic hair. I entwined my fingers in it, purposely avoiding his cock. This wasn't about sex. This wasn't about turning him on. This was about giving him comfort.

I sat up a little so I could move my hand down his thick muscular thigh, his calf, all the way down to his ankle and his foot, I gently trailed my fingers over his instep and then moved to the other foot, the ankle, the calf, the thigh back up to his pelvis, his beautiful torso, to his shoulder and then his other arm, all the way down to his hand. I squeezed each finger gently and then went back up his arm across the shoulder and back down his other arm to the hand near me.

I pulled the blankets over our bodies, entwined my fingers with his, and lay back down next to him on my back.

I would stay until he told me to leave.

★ ★ ★ ★

I was sitting in a plush seat of the Boettcher Concert Hall in Denver, my fingers weaved around Talon's. I massaged his thumb with mine. He looked at me and smiled. Smiled! A symphony orchestra was playing Vivaldi's The Four Seasons.

The music drifted toward me, the beauty and gentility of spring... lovely. And then summer. The birds singing through the fields, the sweet summer breezes, and then the violent lightning storm of cellos.

I opened my eyes.

Oh! I was still in bed next to Talon. The music was coming from his phone. He must have set the alarm. Still he lay, not moving, his arms haphazardly strewn over his forehead. Our fingers were still intertwined. Roger lay sleeping at his feet.

Now what? Should I wake him? Should I get my clothes on and leave?

That would be the easiest course of action. Put on my clothes quietly and sneak out before he woke.

But if I did that, he might never acknowledge that last night had taken place. So I gathered my courage, gulped, and gently nudged him.

He shot up in bed. "What?"

"Calm down. It's just me."

He turned to me, his eyes full of smoke. "What are you doing in here?"

"Don't you remember? We fell asleep together after we..."

He raked his fingers through his disheveled hair. "Oh, shit."

Not exactly what I'd wanted to hear. "You sweet-talker, you," I said.

Talon grabbed the covers, tented them, and looked underneath. "Fuck." He swung his legs over to the side of the bed, got up—God, his ass was great—found his pajama bottoms, and quickly put them on. "Listen. Last night never happened. You got that?"

Was he fucking kidding me? "I hate to tell you this, Talon, but last night most definitely did happen. And quite frankly, it was pretty awesome."

He ambled across his bedroom, darting his gaze from here to there. Most likely he was purposely avoiding mine.

"Last night meant nothing. It was a mistake. I... You mean nothing to me. Nothing, you got that?"

His words cut through me like a dull butcher knife. He had wanted me. I had seen it in his eyes, felt it in his touch. Heck, he had said the words. It might've been a fuck, but it wasn't just any fuck. Maybe it hadn't crossed the line over to lovemaking, but it was more than just a quickie. Something had happened between us last night, and goddamnit, he was not going to get away with this.

"I don't believe you," I said.

"Well, start believing. Last night meant nothing to me."

I sniffed back some tears that threatened, rose, and stalked toward him, still naked. "You wanted me as much as I wanted you."

He still refused to meet my gaze. "Wanting has nothing to do with anything."

"Perhaps not, and maybe I don't mean anything to you. If that's the truth, I will accept it. But you have to convince me with something other than your harsh words, because your body sang an entirely different tune last night."

He huffed, saying nothing. He continued stomping around his room, looking for God knew what.

I figured that was my exit cue, but damn it—no. If he wanted me to leave, he was going to tell me so. I walked back over to the bed, sat down, and then—crap. I had to work this morning. Ryan was expecting me over the winery. What the hell time was it anyway?

"What time is it?" I asked Talon.

"Six a.m."

"Six a.m.? Are you crazy?" I didn't have to be at work until nine. "What are you doing up so early?"

He turned, finally looking me in the eye. "In case you've failed to notice, I have a ranch to run. We start early around here. All this finery didn't just appear. We've all worked really hard for it."

Bam! He sure as hell knew how to make me feel insignificant. Again, tears threatened, and I tried hard to will them back.

To no avail. One trickled down my cheek. I got up and lowered my head to hide my tears from him. I grabbed my boxers and tank top, got them on as quickly as I could, nearly stumbling as I did so, and left the room without saying anything. I couldn't say anything. I was too choked up. I walked briskly down the hallway, past the kitchen, and down the other hallway to my own bedroom, where I shut the door, threw myself on the bed, and cried into my pillow.

CHAPTER TEN

Talon

What had I done? Why couldn't I control my desire? What was it about her that got to me? I wasn't used to wanting something. I never had to want women. They always just appeared, throwing themselves at me. I wasn't stupid. I took them up on it most of the time. Why not? As long as I used a condom, I was safe.

Fuck!

I hadn't used a condom with Jade.

Damn, how irresponsible was she? She didn't know me from Adam. I could be carrying around all sorts of crap. I wasn't, of course. If anyone practiced safe sex, it was me. After what I'd been through, I didn't take any chances. I was damn lucky I hadn't been infected a long time ago.

Now I'd have to talk to her. She was a smart girl. Definitely not stupid, that one, which didn't make sense. Why hadn't she insisted on a condom? She was probably on the pill or something—otherwise she would be worried about pregnancy. But what about disease? What had she been thinking? Did she have indiscriminant sex often? Should I be worried?

Goddamnit.

I pulled a T-shirt on and left the suite, walking quietly to the other side of the house to her room. I knocked. No response.

"Jade?" I knocked a little louder.

"Go away," she said, her voice muffled.

"We need to talk," I said.

A minute later, the door opened and she appeared, her eyes streaked with tears.

A brick hit me in the gut. What had I done? I flew into a rage, wanting to beat the shit out of anyone who made her cry.

And then it dawned on me.

I had made her cry.

"What do you want?" she asked.

"Can I come in? I need to talk to you."

"Sure. Yeah, I agree. We should talk." She opened the door wider, turned, walked back to her bed, and sat down.

I thought about sitting next to her on the bed, but I couldn't be that close to her. I didn't trust myself. So I grabbed an armchair from the corner and scooted it toward the bed.

"So what did you want to talk about?" She grabbed a tissue from her nightstand and blew her nose.

"Well...about last night..."

She nodded. "Yeah?"

"I want to apologize for..."

She arched her eyebrows.

"For not using a condom."

Her eyes popped open into circles. "*That's* what you want to apologize for?"

"Yeah. It was really irresponsible. And I want to make sure—"

"Let me guess," she cut in. "You want to make sure I'm not harboring some disgusting disease that I might've infected you with."

"Well, yeah..."

"Jesus Christ." She shook her head.

"What did you think I wanted to talk about?"

"Oh, I don't know. The fact that we just had sex, perhaps? The fact that you basically told me it meant nothing? The fact that I know that's bullshit?"

"So you're saying that safe sex isn't important?"

"Oh, for God's sake, Talon. Of course safe sex is important. You have nothing to fear from me. I have been monogamous the last seven years, and I've been on the pill for the last ten. You know I just ended a long relationship. I'm the one who should be concerned about you."

"You certainly weren't concerned last night, because you didn't insist that I use a condom."

She let out a huff. "Absolutely right. I got lost in the moment. It was stupid, and it was irresponsible. But I promise you, I do not have HIV. I do not have herpes. I do not have gonorrhea or syphilis or chlamydia. I do not have any other disgusting little mite growing down there."

"All right."

She was telling the truth. I knew it. Her face had turned pink, and more tears flooded her eyes.

I was a jerk.

"But since you're so concerned," she continued, "why don't give me a rundown on your sexual history? I would bet it's way more exciting than mine."

My sexual history... She had no idea. But I was clean. I always used condoms, and I got tested for everything every six months, whether I'd been active or not. Maybe it was a little OCD, but I couldn't help it. "I was last tested two months ago. I can show you the results if you'd like."

"The results don't mean jack shit if you had sex with someone other than me in the last two months."

I had. A cocktail waitress had thrown herself at me in a bar in Grand Junction about a month ago. But I'd used a condom that night, as well as the next night when I saw her again. Other than that, I hadn't had any encounters since my last test. A little slow for me, but it wasn't like I ever went out looking for it. They usually came to me, and as long as the woman didn't look dirty, I allowed it. A man had needs, after all. I took what was offered.

I didn't want to tell Jade about the indiscretion, but I had just fucked her. She had a right to know she was safe.

"Only a couple of times in the last two months, and all with the same woman. I used a condom every time."

A look of distress cast a shadow over her pretty face, but only for a split second. "Then why didn't you use a condom with me? Surely you keep a good supply on hand."

I did. She was right about that. What could I say to answer question? That I'd wanted her so badly I'd lost my mind? That I'd been so crazy with desire I had forgotten to be safe? That had never happened before, even in Iraq, where everyone was so needy and was looking for comfort wherever he could find it. If I didn't have a condom on me, I didn't do it, no matter how beautiful or desirable the woman was, no matter how much my cock wanted release. I never had intercourse without a condom. Ever.

Until last night.

"I guess I just...forgot."

She nodded. "I see. And I understand."

"No, you don't understand. You think I just wanted you so much that I forgot. That's not the case at all."

"It's not? I readily admit that's absolutely the case with me. I knew I was safe from pregnancy, and I knew I was disease-free, yet I knew nothing about you. But I will admit to you, Talon, that I wanted you so much, I was so star-crossed with desire for you, that I forgot to be careful. I don't condone it. I'm embarrassed to say it. But that is the goddamned truth."

My cock stirred. She had worked up quite a head of steam, and her body flushed all over a shade of pink so perfect... I wanted her again.

How was this happening to me?

I knew. I had come so quickly that I hadn't had enough of her to ease my ache yet. I would have to fuck her again.

Now seemed like an opportune time.

I stood and stalked toward her.

"What are you doing?"

"What we both want right now." I bent down and kissed her lips.

She turned away from me, my lips sliding across her cheek.

"How dare you? You just said I meant nothing to you. That last night meant nothing. You came running into my room, worried that I have given you some horrible, disgusting, blistering disease. And now you want to fuck me again?"

"Yeah. I do." What else was there to say?

"Get the hell out of my room."

"I think this is actually *my* room, since you're living in my house." Had I really just said that? Christ, how petty.

"You're going to play that card, huh?" She rose. "That's fine. I feel like I'm imposing on you guys anyway. I'm making a little working for Ryan, and as soon as my bar results come in, I'll find a job as an attorney. If not here, in Grand Junction.

I think maybe I'll go into town this morning and find my own place to live."

Now what had I done? The thought of her leaving tore me in half. "Look, Marjorie wants you here."

"But clearly you don't."

"The ranch is one quarter mine, but it's also one quarter Marjorie's. So if she wants you here..."

"If she wants me here, what? You'll put up with it? How noble of you."

"I want you here," I whispered under my breath.

She kept moving about the room, so I knew she hadn't heard. Thank God.

She walked into her adjoining bathroom and said over her shoulder, "I need to get ready for work. Please let yourself out."

The whoosh of the shower sailed into the bedroom. She was naked now, rivulets of water meandering over her perfect body. My cock was granite. God, I wanted her.

I was going to take her.

I quickly strode to her bedroom door and locked it. Then I took off my T-shirt and pajama pants and walked into the bathroom. God bless my father for installing clear glass shower doors. None of that frosted glass in his house. I could see her clearly, her mahogany hair wet and slick, pasted over her shoulders and breasts. So beautiful.

I had to have her. I opened the shower door.

She gasped, nearly losing her footing. I grabbed her forearm and steadied her.

"Get out of here! What do you think you're doing?"

"Joining you." I stepped into the shower.

"I'll scream, Talon. I'll wake up the whole household."

"Felicia's not here yet, and Marjorie could sleep through World War III, as you probably know."

"Still, I'll—"

I crushed my lips to hers. She opened for me almost immediately. Yes, she wanted this as much as I did. A quickie in the shower and then maybe a nice long romp on her bed. After that, I would be sated. I could go on with my life, and she hers.

I thrust my hard cock against her soft belly, wanting so much to be inside her. But not quite yet. I needed her soft lips on me.

I brushed my fingers up her arms to her shoulders, softly gripping them. "Get on your knees. Suck me."

"You're kidding right? After you just—"

I stopped her with a finger to her lips. "Please," I whispered.

Her eyes softened, and she obeyed, dropping and taking the head of my bobbing cock between her beautiful red lips. I closed my eyes and leaned back, letting the water pelt my face as she kissed and licked my cock, her lips like heaven. She fisted me at the base, pulling my skin taut as she moved her mouth up and down over my erection.

I was ready to blow. But I had to get inside her. Inside that sweet, wet pussy. On the other hand, I could shoot my load down her throat, and by the time we had dried off and gotten to the bed, I would be ready for her again. In my soul, I knew this.

I feared I would never get enough of her.

I abruptly stopped that line of thought, concentrating on her dazzling lips sucking my cock. This would be it. This had to be it. This quickie in the shower and then a long and amazing fuck on her bed. We had time. She didn't have to be at work until nine, and I had hired help who would cover for me in the fields. Not a problem.

"God, that feels so good," I rasped. "Yeah, baby, suck my cock. Take all of me."

I grabbed the back of her head, entwining my fingers in her soft, wet hair. Gently, I began moving her head back and forth to my rhythm. She didn't resist me.

What a gift. She wilted to my will. Let me take what I needed.

Take what you need from me. The words she had said to me last night.

"Baby, baby, I need to fuck you now. Come here." I drew her to her feet and then lifted her, setting her down on my cock. "Ahhh..." The sigh left my lips in a groan. "So good. You fit me like a glove. A perfectly fitted glove."

She sighed into my neck, giving me little nibbles. I trembled, my legs threatening to give way, but I stood firm. Had to. Had to have her... Now... In the shower... So good... I lifted her and brought her back down upon my cock—up, down, up, down—oh, God, what a good little fuck she was.

"Talon," she said into my neck. "Take me, Talon."

"Yeah, baby, I'm taking you. I'm taking you into the goddamn stars."

"I feel so good. You feel so good inside me."

"That's right, baby. Let me fuck that sweet pussy of yours. So good."

I lasted longer this time. But damn, not by much. When my balls tightened, I knew I was about to explode. No condom again, but who the fuck cared? We were both clean, no chance of pregnancy—

"God!" I cried out as I filled her with my semen.

She sighed against my neck. "Yes, Talon, Inside me. Inside me."

When I finally regained my senses, she was weeping against my neck. Had she even had an orgasm? How selfish was I?

She released her legs from around me, and I set her gently on the shower floor.

"Why are you crying?" I asked.

"Because... Because..."

I wasn't going to push it. "I'm sorry, Jade. I should've let you come first."

She shook her head. "I don't care about that."

"You don't care if you come?"

"Well, I care." She bit her lip. "It's just that...this wasn't about me, Talon. This was about you."

CHAPTER ELEVEN

Jade

He looked down at me, those brown eyes blazing. The shower still pelted us with droplets of water. I blinked the wetness out of my eyes.

Was he going to get weird again now that he was done? What was he thinking? I could ask, but I wouldn't get a direct answer.

Since I didn't know what else to do, I grabbed my shampoo off of the bath shelf. I hadn't washed my hair or my body yet. I was still warming up when he'd walked in on me. I squeezed a good amount into my palm, rubbed it between my hands, and smoothed it over my wet hair.

"Let me do that for you." Talon threaded his strong fingers through my hair and massaged the shampoo into my scalp.

I trembled, nearly losing my footing. Such a tender thing from someone who didn't seem to have much tenderness to give. Or maybe he had a lot of tenderness to give but just didn't know how to give it. Seven years with Colin, and he had never washed my hair. We'd taken our share of showers together over the years, but that was only to fuck. We washed ourselves.

I closed my eyes and let his magic fingers take me to another world. He continued massaging, slowly but firmly, and kept at it long after my hair was clean. The suds dripped over my forehead and into my eyes. Now I couldn't open my eyes without rinsing off my face first. But I had no desire to open my eyes as long as he was massaging me.

Finally, he turned me around so I was facing the pelting water, pushed my head slightly down, and rinsed my hair. A few moments later, he turned me back around and toweled off my eyes with the edge of a soft bath linen.

More tenderness. Next, he squirted some conditioner into his hand, rubbed his hands together, and smoothed it over my hair, making sure to get it all over the ends.

I couldn't help a small smile. I picked up the shampoo and squirted some more into my hand. "Now you."

"That's okay."

"Please. I want to. Let me."

He was so tall that I had to stand on tiptoe to give him as good a massage as he had given me. As if reading my mind, he bent his knees slightly, and I was able to thoroughly wash his hair. So thick, such a rich dark brown, almost black. His eyebrows were thick and black also, but perfectly shaped, no unibrow in sight. Did he have them waxed? The image of rugged Talon with little wax strips on his brows made me smile. Clearly he didn't manscape. His chest was perfect—just enough dark hair that he looked like a man. I looked down to the thick black bush surrounding his cock. Nope, no manscaping needed. He was perfect just as he was.

When he bent over, I rinsed his hair and then dried his eyes as he had mine. Next, we each took some body wash and rubbed it all over each other, scrubbing ourselves clean together.

"Done?" I asked.

He nodded. I turned off the water, tossed him a towel,

and grabbed one for myself. I wrapped it around my body as I always do and then took another one, making a turban out of it to dry off my hair. He simply toweled his hair dry, and it fell in wet waves against his neck.

He was so beautiful. Those dark eyes—I could look into them forever and never tire of them.

I shook my head. "Well, I have to get ready for work."

"Not quite yet."

I arched my eyebrows. "What do you mean?"

"I mean, I'm not done with you yet. And you're not going anywhere until I am."

"Ryan expects me there at nine."

"It's seven. It takes you a half hour to drive over to the winery. You're already washed."

"I have to dry my hair and—"

His mouth came down on mine. I sighed into him. Again... Had he just said we were over? Had he just said... Oh, hell, I didn't care. I would take what I could of him. This would clearly never be a real relationship. He was wrestling too many demons, or so it certainly seemed. I could at least enjoy the present. I had never been so attracted to a man. This— whatever it was between us—made my entire relationship with Colin seem like a middle school crush.

Talon was still naked, and he wrested the towel from around me. It dropped to the floor in a plush red puddle. My turban still bound my hair, but he made short work of that also, pulling it off. My wet tresses clung to my shoulders and back.

The kiss became more urgent. He nibbled at my tongue, my lips, my nipples hardening into sharp knobs pressed into his gorgeous chest. My pussy was throbbing, I wanted him so badly. Our mouths still melded, he began walking forward, forcing me backward into the bedroom, until the back of my knees hit my mattress. He pushed me down, still kissing me, his body on top of mine. He braced himself on his elbows so his weight wouldn't crush me.

And still we kissed, a drugging kiss, a kiss that left nothing unsaid. A kiss of want, of ache, of desire and passion. He took from me with that kiss, and I opened my mouth to him and took from him as well.

When he broke the kiss and inhaled, he clamped his lips onto my neck, sucking on me, kissing me.

"Mine," he growled.

Did he even know what he'd just said? I wasn't sure, but I didn't rightly care at the moment. He continued kissing down the front of me until he reached one of my turgid nipples. He sucked it into his mouth hard, and I squealed. The pain lasted only for a moment, and then unbridled pleasure coursed through me, landing right in my pussy. God, I must be soaking wet. This was so crazy, but what was happening seemed so right.

Just go with it, Jade. Enjoy.

As he sucked on one nipple, he pinched the other between his thumb and forefinger. The pleasure shot straight between my legs. I fluttered my eyes closed. I needed this so much. Needed him so much...

I opened my eyes quickly. *No, you don't need him. Just enjoy. Savor this moment. It probably won't happen again.*

I closed my eyes again and let the feelings take me. He released my nipple and rained hard kisses down my belly to my vulva.

"So hot, baby. I love how you shave down here. So fucking

hot." He flicked his tongue over my clit.

I nearly shattered.

He plunged two fingers into my heat. "I want to fill you up, baby. I want my cock everywhere, in your mouth, in your pussy, in your ass. I want to take you everywhere. Want to mark you. Mine."

And I exploded against his fingers.

"Yeah, baby, come for me." He jammed his fingers against my G-spot, rubbing, rubbing, rubbing...

My whole body clenched, every cell sizzling, illuminating, pushing outward. Nirvana. I was flying, soaring to the stars.

"God, so hot."

High, higher still. His fingers still abrading the anterior of my pussy, my walls still spasming, my body still floating, electricity still surging through my cells...until...

"Talon! I...can't...take..."

"Oh, yes, you can, baby. You can take it all." He continued finger-fucking me, hitting that spot again, again, again, again...

The orgasms kept coming, ripping through me like lightning. This orgasm was rapturous.

"Please... Please... Enough..."

"I owe you. You didn't come in the shower."

That was what this was about? "Talon, please... Inside me... Now."

Finally, he released me, pulling out his fingers. He crawled up over me and stuffed his cock into me.

"Ah," he groaned. "Yeah, baby, it's so good." He kissed my lips, my cheeks, and then trailed over to my ear. "Did you like that, blue eyes? All those orgasms? Do you even know how hot you are?"

Oh...my...God. All I could think of was his perfect huge

cock burning me and fucking me and plunging in and out. Never had I felt so full, so complete. This man's cock was pure heaven. If only this could last forever...

But it wouldn't.

Stop it, Jade. Just enjoy the moment for as long as it lasts.

I whimpered when he withdrew his cock.

He lay down on his back. "Get on top of me. I want to watch you ride me."

I obeyed, sinking down onto his hardness. God, it felt so good. I wanted to sit for a few moments, just savoring the fullness, but the urge to thrust soon overwhelmed me. I rose and went down, rose again. Soon his hips followed my movements, thrusting, plunging, pushing, fucking. So, so good.

"You're beautiful, Jade." He cupped my breasts, pinching my nipples lightly. "Your breasts—I've never seen any so perfect."

He sat up, our chests meeting, and plunged up into me. After a few moments of that, he lifted me off of him.

"Get on your hands and knees."

No sooner had I complied than he plunged into me from behind. Doggy-style. Wow, a different angle made all the difference. A sharp slap on my ass brought me almost to the edge again. He fucked me hard, driving into me, his cock completing me. And when those tingles crept across my skin—

I jerked when a soft caress drifted over my anus.

"Easy, baby. Has anyone taken you here? Anyone taken this gorgeous ass?"

"N-No."

He continued fucking me. "It will be mine. Only mine."

No one would ever fuck me there. But I didn't need to say

that right now.

"Yeah, baby. Feels so good. I love fucking you."

He continued pounding me, pounding me, pounding me until—God, did I have anything left?—I exploded into another climax, this one radiating from my nerves inward to my pussy, convulsing, throbbing, resonating throughout my entire core. I screamed and buried my face in the covers, hoping to muffle myself.

"That's it, baby. You scream. Show me you like it."

He kept thrusting, thrusting, thrusting... He had just come in the shower, so he probably still had a long way to go.

As much good as it was, my body was tired, sated, I was ready to be—

"Fuck!" He pounded into me one last time, hard, and released, keeping his cock lodged in me. With every convulsion, every spurt of his seed, my pussy became more his.

Only his.

When he finally withdrew, I straightened my legs and collapsed on my belly. God. I needed to go to sleep, but I had to get to work.

And what was Talon going to do? Was he now going to become distant as usual?

I didn't know, and I was too relaxed and sated to care. If only I didn't have to go to work today, I would lie there and bask in the beauty of what had just occurred.

The weight on the bed shifted, and I looked up. Talon had risen and was putting on his pajama pants. He looked down at me.

"That should do it," he said.

"That should do what?"

He didn't respond. He simply pulled his T-shirt over his head and left my bedroom.

CHAPTER TWELVE

Talon

I walked back to my own bedroom.

And already I wanted her again.

What would it take to get rid of this need? This all-consuming ache for another person? I didn't even know her very well yet.

I had taken her this morning, just as I'd taken every other woman who came to my bed. She hadn't offered herself to me like they had, but I had taken her anyway. She hadn't resisted, but still I felt a twinge of guilt. For some reason, I didn't want to just take her. I wanted it to be mutual. I wanted her to want me as much as I wanted her—which was really odd, since most women wanted me way more than I wanted them. I was simply taking care of the physical need. But with Jade...

Damn. A flaw in my reasoning emerged. I kept thinking that if I could have her once, and then once more, I would get rid of this all-consuming need. The problem was, the more I had her, the more I seemed to want her.

I was screwed. Completely screwed.

She wouldn't allow me to fuck her forever. She would eventually either tell me to stop, or she would want more—a relationship. And that was the one thing I couldn't give her. I had no business being in a relationship with anyone. Not when

I was so messed up.

Shit. I had to get out to the orchards. Check on everything. But I needed some alone time first. I quickly texted my foreman and told him I'd be an hour or so late coming down. Then I opened the door to my room, shut and locked it, and lay down on my bed, closing my eyes. Roger jumped up and snuggled at my feet.

Maybe just another hour of sleep—if I could be so lucky.

★ ★ ★ ★

"Hey, handsome." Julie grabbed my arm and pulled me into her apartment. "Long time no see. Whatcha been up to?"

The little cocktail waitress was still hot as hell. Small in stature but nice and curvy, she wore a tight T-shirt and athletic shorts.

I didn't answer her. I wasn't in the mood to talk. I was in the mood to fuck—to fuck the memory of Jade Roberts right out of my head. After a hard day in the orchard, I'd driven to Grand Junction for a quick bite to eat and hopefully a quicker romp in the sack.

Julie was a fun little fuck. She smiled as I grabbed her and pulled her tight little body into mine. I leaned down and kissed her, forcing my tongue into her warm little mouth. She was so much shorter than Jade. My neck was ready to break.

No. No thoughts of Jade.

I deepened the kiss, searching, wanting, waiting for... that champagne and strawberry flavor that intoxicated me. Instead I got fresh mint. Not bad. I could make that work. I pulled her up against my pelvis and ground into her.

Nothing.

No erection.

I wasn't even breathing hard.

I broke the kiss.

"What's wrong, handsome?"

I didn't answer.

Julie took my hand and squeezed it. "Wanna go into the bedroom?"

I let out a sigh and shook my head. No use. Another woman wasn't going to help.

Damn, nothing would help. Nothing except Jade. I wanted to lose myself in her.

"I have to go," I said to Julie.

"Come on, handsome. Let me help you take the edge off."

If only she could. "Not tonight. I'll see you later."

"Okay, maybe another time..."

I walked out of her apartment and didn't look back.

★ ★ ★ ★

"Can't reach it, boy?" Tattoo chuckled.

The boy didn't know their names, but the one with the tattoo—some kind of colorful bird wrapped in flames and rising from what looked like ashes—always took the lead.

The glass of water sat less than an inch from the boy's reach. Full, with ice, and the boy was dying of thirst, his mouth parched. His lips were so dry the bottom one had cracked in the middle, and he tasted the tang of blood on his tongue.

"Look at him reach." The one with the low voice laughed.

This was a game they liked to play. And even though logically the boy knew he would never be able to reach the glass of water, still he tried, stretching his arm as far as he could, thinking maybe, just maybe, today was the day his arm had grown a little bit, or that he could stretch his muscles those few more millimeters necessary...

It didn't happen.

The three men laughed at him, taunting him. "Thirsty, boy? You want that water, boy?" Their devilish laughter echoed in his ears.

If only he could reach just a little farther...

He imagined the cool crisp water flowing down his throat, soothing the dryness, easing the ache of hunger that was always present, hydrating his dry lips, healing them.

Always that glass sat there, always slightly beyond his reach.

Always...

★ ★ ★ ★

A new memory—how could I have forgotten? That fucking glass of water still tormented me. Again, I sat in the kitchen, staring at it. Never drinking it. Only that tiny sip that had barely wet my tongue the other night when Jade bothered me about it. The sip had felt wrong, like I deserved punishment for taking it. I didn't know why. I drank plenty of water. I didn't get dehydrated at all, but that midnight glass of water—the one that I poured myself, added ice to, and sat on the table before me—that was the one I couldn't touch.

I hadn't seen Jade since this morning—yesterday morning, since it was after midnight—when I left her bedroom. I assumed she went to work and then came home. I hadn't gotten home from Grand Junction until nearly eleven.

Julie's words rang in my mind. *Okay, maybe another*

time...

But I knew then and I knew now. There would be no other time with her or with anyone.

Until I got Jade Roberts out of my system, I wouldn't be with other women.

Fatigue gripped me. God, I was so fucking tired. Always tired. If only I could get one whole night of sleep...

I looked over at the full glass of water, condensation forming on the outside of the glass. And again the maniacal laughter... I could still hear all three of them in my ears, laughing at me, taunting me with that glass of water.

I stood. "Damn it!" I said aloud. I picked up that fucking glass of water and hurled it onto the floor where it shattered into hundreds of little pieces.

Then I sat back down in the chair, letting the darkness take me, my head in my hands. Melancholy enveloped me. Sadness overtook me.

But I didn't cry.

★ ★ ★ ★

"You want that water, boy?"

The boy nodded. It would do no good, but he nodded anyway as he always did. Maybe this would be the one time when they felt sorry enough for him to give him the water.

"I'll give you the water if you cry, boy," Tattoo said, his eyes glowing beneath his black mask. "Go ahead. Cry for it. Cry like the little pansy you are."

The boy was all cried out. There probably wasn't enough water in his body to make tears.

But that water—that tall, clear glass of water—pulsed like a heartbeat. It was laughing too, ridiculing him, jabbing at him.

"You can't have me. They'll never let you have me..."

The boy closed his eyes, squeezing them together, desperately trying to conjure just one tear, even knowing that he still wouldn't get the water if he cried. He bore down, clenched all his muscles, trying, trying...

"Come on, boy. Just cry for me. Cry one tear, and I'll let you have the water."

The boy didn't cry.

★ ★ ★ ★

The next morning, I rose early and walked into the kitchen to clean up the mess I'd left. I didn't want anyone slipping and getting hurt. Leaving the shattered glass and water on the floor had been self-indulgent. Two others lived in this house, and I had no right to put them in danger.

To my surprise, the kitchen floor was spotless. Felicia hadn't come in yet, so either Jade or Marjorie had cleaned it up. My sister wasn't known as an early riser, but she was used to my outbursts every now and then. I hoped it had been her. Otherwise Jade would come to me, asking a bunch of questions I didn't want to answer. That I *couldn't* answer.

It was a quarter to six, and I wanted to head out to the orchards early since I'd spent all yesterday morning shirking my duties. I had been pretty lax about the orchard lately, and I figured Jonah was due to stop by anytime to give me one of his big brother lectures on pulling my weight. I sure as hell wasn't in the mood to listen to him, especially since he would be right.

I was rinsing out the coffee carafe when Marjorie loped up behind me.

"I cleaned up your mess earlier."

Thank God. I didn't turn around. I measured coffee out of the grinder.

"You might've left a note or something. I could've cut the hell out of my foot, you know."

I couldn't argue. She was right. I shouldn't have left that mass. What if she—or Jade?—had slipped and fallen on the broken glass? It could've been pretty nasty.

I turned. "You're right. I'm really"—I hacked the dreaded word from my lips as it kicked and screamed to stay put—"sorry."

"I'm just glad I found it this morning instead of Jade. It would have freaked her out. She should be up pretty soon. I think she meets Ryan over at the winery at nine."

I poured water into the coffee maker and pressed start. "Today's Saturday."

"True. I don't know if she's working over there on Saturdays."

"What are you doing up, Sis? You're not usually an early riser, especially not on the weekend."

"Hey, there's a first time for everything. I thought I'd head over to the orchards with you. I guess it's about time I started earning my keep around here."

I let out a chuckle. "Suit yourself. It's pretty boring right now. Lots of busy work."

"I don't mind busy work."

"Good thing."

I wanted to ask her about Jade. Had she confided in Marjorie about what had happened between us? My guess was no, or Marj would've come to me by now. "Marj?"

"What?"

"Your friend... Jade..."

"What about her?"

"I...was wondering about her ex-boyfriend." I wasn't, but it was a good way to find stuff out about Jade without asking more personal questions.

"Colin? He's an ass."

"Well, yeah, sure. He left her at the altar. But what kind of relationship did they have?"

"They were together all the time during college. He's a trust fund kid. His dad's a financial guy in New York, but they come from old money. Not that they have Steel money." She smiled. "Anyway, after graduation she stayed in Denver and went to law school, and he went to New York to intern at his dad's office, so it was long-distance. But they kept it going, determined to make the wedding date they had actually set three years before at college graduation. Obviously, it didn't quite work out that way."

"Do you think this Colin messed with her head?"

"Maybe a little. I mean, she was totally humiliated. But she seems okay. I think the relationship just ran out of steam, and neither of them wanted to admit it. I think, in the long run, she's just as happy that they didn't get married. She was just really embarrassed that day. I felt so bad for her. I was standing next to her as the maid of honor, waiting to walk down the aisle, and we were waiting...waiting...waiting... The best man, the groomsmen, and the ushers were all there, but no one seemed to know where Colin was. We tried to keep it from Jade for as long as possible, but finally we couldn't put it off any longer. She was a trouper. She went up and told the congregation that there wouldn't be a wedding. That Colin hadn't shown up."

My heart nearly broke for her right there in the kitchen. If I ever saw that Colin...

"Like you said, she seems okay now." I poured two cups of coffee and handed one to Marjorie.

"I think she is. She's a little tense right now, waiting for her bar results. They should be here pretty soon. Of course, she's brilliant, so I know she passed. But it will be a load off her mind when she knows for sure."

"Yeah..." I wanted to know so much more about Jade, but I didn't know how to ask Marjorie. "You think she's happy out here?"

"She's only been here for a couple weeks, Tal. But she likes working with Ryan at the winery. And I know she'll be happy once those bar results arrive. She'll be able to find a job here or in Grand Junction."

I nodded. "She told me about her mom. That she's that supermodel."

"Brooke Bailey? Yeah. What a shallow bitch."

I nodded. That was for sure. People who didn't want to stay and raise their kids shouldn't have kids. Which was exactly why I would never have kids. I'd be a terrible father.

"All in all, she seems pretty well-adjusted."

Marjorie nodded. "Jade's the best. Best friend a girl could have. She has certainly helped me through some hard times. Like any BFF would."

I took a few more sips of my coffee. "I'm going to shower. Meet me in about half an hour, and we'll drive over to the orchards."

Marj smiled. She looked so much like my mama—a woman she didn't even remember. She had the same nearly black hair and dark-brown eyes of all the Steels, but her face was shaped a little differently from ours. She had the soft lines and tiny little bow mouth that Mama'd had.

I missed my mother sometimes. But things had never been the same between us after...

Things were never the same, period.

CHAPTER THIRTEEN

Jade

I slept late. It was Saturday, and I didn't have to go to work. I wanted to make sure I got up well after Talon had risen and headed out. At ten a.m., I finally rose. I knocked on Marjorie's door, but she wasn't there. Maybe she was in the kitchen or in the family room watching TV, maybe outside. Nope. After taking a walk around the entire house and the patio, I could not find her. Just as well. I needed some alone time to think.

The coffee in the coffee maker was cold. I started a fresh pot—a *strong* fresh pot—and then headed back to my room to shower while it brewed. The doorbell waylaid me.

Who could be coming at this hour on a Saturday? Then I laughed to myself. This hour? It was ten, not six a.m. It could be anyone. Of course, if they were looking for either Talon or Marj, they'd be out of luck.

Still in my boxers and tank top that I'd slept in, I walked to the door and looked out the peephole.

I rolled my eyes. Who should be on the other side of the door but my ex-fiancé, Colin Morse.

I hadn't seen him since the rehearsal dinner the night before the wedding. He had never bothered to show up later on the wedding day to apologize or anything. I had no idea where he had gone, and at this point, I didn't rightly care.

Curiosity more than anything forced me to open the door.

He looked the same—handsome in a refined and priggish way—why had I never noticed that before?—with blondish hair, greenish eyes, boringish khaki trousers and white cotton dress shirt. His gaze zeroed in on my breasts. I crossed my arms.

"What are you doing here, Colin?"

"Can I come in?"

"No."

"Come on, Jade."

"Fine." I stepped backward.

He strode into the foyer. "I took the red-eye to Grand Junction. I've been here since six this morning. It took me a while to find this place. It's not exactly on a map."

"The Steel property is pretty big."

"I'll say."

"So what are you doing here?"

"I...I want to tell you how sorry I am."

"You know, Colin, if you'd had the balls to tell me this before the wedding, or at least at the rehearsal dinner, we could've saved a little bit of money by canceling. Not a lot, mind you, but a little."

"I didn't really think this was about the money."

Unbelievable. Colin had grown up with a silver spoon shoved so far up his ass he didn't know reality. "You didn't? You know my dad lives a modest life. You know I do too. He spent twenty grand of his hard-earned savings to give me the day of my dreams, and we weren't able to get any of that back. Not a freaking penny."

"I intend to pay your father back, Jade."

"Great. I'm sure he'll appreciate it." I tapped my bare foot.

"Did you really come all this way just to tell me that?"

His cheeks reddened. "No. I...I came to tell you that...I think I made the biggest mistake of my life."

He could not be serious. "Yeah? And what might that be?"

"Letting you go."

I shook my head, laughing. "This is rich."

"I'm serious, Jade. I still love you. I never stopped loving you."

"Then why in the hell didn't you want to marry me?"

"I got scared."

"Scared. Okay. And you think I wasn't scared? Binding yourself to another person is a pretty scary thing, Colin. But we had seven years under our belts."

"Yeah, I know. You were my first and only serious girlfriend. I just started wondering if..."

"If what? If something better was out there?"

He bit his lip.

That fucking bastard.

"Well, here's news, Colin. We are over. You blew it."

"Come on, Jade. We should be back from our honeymoon by now, settling in together. Both of us starting our careers at Dad's Denver satellite."

"Yeah, we should. But you know what? I'm here, hanging out with Marj and her brothers, and I'm having a great time. I'm really glad to be here. My bar results are due any day now, and in the meantime, I'm working for one of Marj's brothers at the winery. I'm learning lots of stuff that I'm becoming passionate about. All in all, I'm glad we didn't get married. I think it really would've been a mistake. So I should thank you."

His lips trembled. "Please don't say that."

"Why not? You embarrassed and humiliated me in front of all of our family and friends, Colin. At the time, I didn't think I could ever forgive you for that. But I can now, because I think it was the right thing in the long run."

"Jade—"

"I don't want to hear it. Now, if you'll excuse me, I have lots to do today." I took his arm and started walking him out the door.

He turned and grabbed me, pulled me into him, and pressed his lips to mine.

I gasped, and he slid his tongue into my mouth. Everything about this kiss felt wrong. I tried pushing him away, but his strength defeated mine.

"What the fuck is going on here?"

The voice came out of nowhere. Heavy footfalls. Toward us. Powerful arms wrenched me away from Colin's grasp.

Talon stood, glaring, his eyes afire. "Who the hell are you?"

Colin stumbled backward. "It's okay. I'm her fiancé."

"Her *what?*" Talon said through clenched teeth.

"Talon, it's all right," I said, wiping Colin's taste from my lips. "He was just leaving."

"You *never* touch her again."

Colin stood his ground. He wasn't as tall as Talon, but he was buff, a great athlete. "Or what?"

In an instant, Talon jammed his fist into Colin's cheek. Caught off guard, Colin fell against the wall. Talon grabbed him by the neck and punched him again, this one landing square on Colin's nose. Blood oozed from his nostrils, while Talon gripped his shoulders and threw him to the floor, kicking his stomach. Colin groaned, covering his nose.

"Talon," I yelled. "Talon, stop! Please!"

He kept kicking Colin, who lay on the floor doubled over.

I grabbed Talon around the waist, my heart thundering. "Please! You're really going to hurt him."

No change.

"Please! For me!"

Talon froze mid-kick. His facial features went blank, and he backed away.

I bent to Colin. "Are you okay?"

He nodded. "I'll be fine, I think," he choked out. "I've taken worse on the football field."

"I'll show you worse."

I looked up. Talon's dark eyes were glazed, ferocious.

"Oh, no, you don't, Talon. Don't just stand there. Go get him an ice pack for his nose."

Talon hesitated for a minute but then walked to the kitchen. A few seconds later, he came back with a plastic bag filled with ice. I held it to Colin's nose.

"Does he need an ambulance?" Talon asked.

Colin coughed. "Of course I don't need a damned ambulance, you Neanderthal. I can take as much as you can dish out."

"Oh, yeah?" Talon's eyes lit with fire again.

"You two stop this right now." I stood and faced Talon, my hands on my hips. "You owe Colin an apology."

"The hell I do."

"I don't need a goddamned apology from him." Colin stood, holding the ice bag to his nose. "I'm staying at the Hotel Coronado in Grand Junction. I want to take you to dinner tonight."

"Over my dead body," Talon said.

"Talon, I will decide who I have dinner with, got it?" I helped Colin up and over to a chair in the living room. "You sure you don't want me to call someone?"

He shook his head. "Just give me a few minutes to collect myself. I'll be fine. I've been in worse shape than this."

Back in the foyer, Talon seethed. I looked away from him. What I had just witnessed disgusted me...and unnerved me. I did not want to see him right now.

After about fifteen minutes, I walked with Colin to his car. "Text me when you get to Grand Junction safely."

He nodded. "I still hope you'll meet me for dinner tonight."

I shook my head. "No, Colin. That's not going to happen. I'm sorry."

He drove away.

I walked back into the house. Talon was in the kitchen, sitting at the table with that goddamned glass of water again. He looked up at me when I walked in.

"What the hell was that all about?" I said.

"He was kissing you."

"Why is it any of your business who I kiss?"

"Well...he walked out on your wedding, so he shouldn't be—"

I clenched my hands into fists. "For God's sake, Talon, do you have feelings for me or not? How did it make you feel to see him kissing me?"

"I don't know..."

"You don't know? You nearly beat him to death. I can't believe you got so violent."

"I...don't know why either."

"Were you jealous?"

"Of course not."

"Just as well"—anger boiled within me—"because whatever this little thing was between us, it's over. I mean really over. I don't want anything to do with you. I'm going to talk to Marj about moving out."

"Marj is out at the orchard. And she wants you here."

"Either I'm leaving or you are, and I don't think you are."

"But what about...?"

"What about what? We shared a few kisses, a few romps in bed. It was beyond great. But you are so screwed up that I can't get through to you. I just witnessed you nearly beat the life out of a man. Frankly, Talon, you scare me."

I walked back to my bedroom. Leaving was my only alternative. There was no getting around it. Something lived inside Talon, something poisonous, something I might never understand, and as long as he kept himself closed off from me and everyone else, I couldn't risk being around him.

I refused to lose my heart to someone who was incapable of giving me his.

CHAPTER FOURTEEN

Talon

I wanted to go after her. I wanted to with everything in my body and soul. I wanted to grab her, kiss her, make her forget how angry she was.

God... When I saw that man with his hands on her, something in me snapped. Green rage boiled through me. I had to get him off of her, off of my woman.

But she would never be my woman. I had nothing to offer. Nothing but a few midnight kisses and romps, as she called them.

I would still be beating the guy if she hadn't stopped me. I'd been crazy, unable to stop. I wasn't even thinking, and my hands and feet were acting of their own accord. A primordial need to pummel him into soup had consumed me, and all logic had fled.

I could've done serious damage to him. He deserved it, for humiliating Jade the way he had, but I knew better. Knowing better hadn't stopped me though. It never did.

Icy chills gripped the back of my neck.

This couldn't go on.

I wasn't ready to give up. I wanted to *live*.

I stood abruptly, grabbed the keys to my truck, went out the back way, and drove over to the ranch office where Jonah would be. I stormed into the office, past the office manager to Joe's office.

"Talon"—my older brother looked up from some documents he was reading—"what are you doing out here?"

"I'm ready, Joe. I'm ready to get some help."

★ ★ ★ ★

Joe had handed me a business card of a psychologist in Grand Junction, Dr. Melanie Carmichael. He didn't know much about her other than she was supposed to be tops in her field and that she'd had a lot of success treating patients with histories similar to mine. He had even offered to go with me and to get Ryan and have him go as well. But no, this was something I had to do alone.

I called the number right away, and even though it was a Saturday, Dr. Carmichael agreed to meet me in her office.

I pulled up into the Heritage Medical Group offices and parked my car. She said she'd leave word with the security guard to let me in, since the doors were locked on weekends.

I stood at the door, my palms leaving sweat marks on the glass. Had this been a huge mistake? A security guard sat at his desk inside. I knocked on the door. The man looked up and came to the door.

"Mr. Steel?"

I nodded.

He opened the door and let me in. "Dr. C's up on five, Suite 524. I'll have to key in the elevator for you. They're locked on weekends."

I nodded again and followed him to the elevator. He keyed in a code.

"Good luck," he said.

Good luck? I warmed all over. Of course, he knew what field Dr. Carmichael was in. This shouldn't be a surprise to me. But I wanted to disappear.

As the elevator moved up five floors, I kept thinking of an excuse not to go and see Dr. Carmichael. I could go home and tell Jonah I'd gone. I could make up some kind of psychobabble jargon. He wouldn't know the difference.

But this woman had been kind enough to come and open her office for me on a Saturday. Standing her up would be rude as hell. If I was truly going to try to change, this was the first step.

When the elevator dinged at the fifth floor, my feet became leaden. I felt like I was walking through sludge as I trudged to room 524. I walked in, but of course, there was no receptionist. It was Saturday. Where was the doctor? As I was looking around, thumbing through the magazines on the coffee table, a tall woman with strikingly light-blond hair and green eyes walked out from an adjacent room.

"You must be Mr. Steel," she said.

I cleared my throat, my cheeks warming. "Yes, I'm Talon Steel."

She smiled and held out her hand. "Dr. Melanie Carmichael. So nice to meet you. Would you like to come on back?"

I swallowed. In for a dozen... I followed her into her office. Her desk was in a corner, and the requisite couch sat against one wall. I was so not lying on the couch. A couple of recliners in forest-green leather sat around a marble coffee table. She sat down in one of them and motioned for me to take the other. Moving slowly, I did.

"So what can I help you with today, Mr. Steel?" She crossed her legs and smiled.

I sighed. Where did I begin? I didn't have enough hours left in my lifetime to explain what had brought me in here, and most therapy sessions only lasted an hour. So I figured I'd start with what had prompted me to call.

"I beat the shit out of a guy today."

She nodded. "I see. Why do you think you did that?"

Wasn't she supposed to tell *me* why? "He was kissing my sister's friend."

"All right. And that kiss bothered you?"

I nodded.

"Why did it bother you so much? Is your sister's friend your girlfriend?"

I shook my head. "No. I don't have girlfriends."

"You don't? Handsome man like you? Why not?"

"I'm just not wired that way, Doctor."

"Wired that way? Do you mean you're gay?"

I shook my head. "No. I'm not gay." The whole gay line of questioning gave me a chill. I had never been attracted to men, yet...my history... I couldn't go there. Not yet.

"Then why don't you have girlfriends?"

"I just...don't."

"Okay. What types of relationships do you have with women, then?"

"Well, the only woman in my life right now is my sister, who lives with me. Other than that, the only kind of relationships I have with women are sexual."

"So you're a love 'em and leave 'em kind of guy, huh?"

"Yeah, I guess so. At least the leave 'em part."

"You use women, then. Is that what you're telling me?"

"Oh, for God's sake. No, I don't use them. They offer something to me, and I take it. What the hell is wrong with that? They're getting what they want, and I'm getting what I want."

"I'm not here to judge you, Mr. Steel."

"Mr. Steel sounds ridiculous to me. Call me Talon."

"All right, if you prefer. Talon. As I said, I'm not here to judge you. I'm here to help you. So let's go back to why you beat up the man today. That appears to be the catalyst for bringing you in here, am I right?"

I nodded.

"Have you seen a therapist before?"

I shook my head. God knew Ryan and Jonah had been after me for a decade to see one. Instead, I went off to Iraq, hoping to get my brains blown out. No such luck.

"Do you have a history of violence, Talon?"

I shook my head again. "Not really. I was in the Marines, stationed in Iraq for several years. I saw a lot of shit go down there, and I did things I would prefer not to think about, but it was all in the line of duty."

"Did you kill a man there?"

More things I didn't like to think about.

Before I could answer, Dr. Carmichael spoke again.

"Let's not go there quite yet," she said.

Thank God.

"Let's go back to today. Who was this girl that the guy was kissing? Your sister's friend. Tell me about her."

How could I tell her? How could I make her understand the ache inside me? I could talk for hours about Jade. I could talk for thirty minutes on those steely blue eyes of hers alone. They gripped me, tore at me, drew me to her. Emotions were rising to my surface—emotions I thought I was incapable of having.

"She's my sister's best friend, and she moved out here to our ranch after she got left at the altar on her wedding day."

"Oh my gosh," Dr. Carmichael said. "That's terrible."

"She seems to be handling it okay. The guy kissing her was her ex. He showed up this morning."

"Are they reconciling?"

"Doesn't look that way. I mean, he totally humiliated her."

"But they probably still have some feelings there."

I tensed up in my chair, gripping the arm, my knuckles whitening.

"So you have feelings for this Jade."

"What makes you say that?"

"Well, first, the fact that you beat up her ex. Second, because you've got the arm of that chair in the devil's clinch."

I let out a breath and consciously relaxed my hand. Yeah, she was good.

"Tell me what you were feeling while you were beating him."

"It was like I wasn't myself. Almost like my arms and legs were acting on their own. The rage was so real. It took me over so that I wasn't even there—just the rage was."

"Why did you stop beating him?"

"Jade asked me to."

"So Jade got through to you, through the fog."

She had. Through the fog... The words Dr. Carmichael used resonated with me. It had been like a fog. A thick hazy fog. A red sickness that simmered within me.

"So is the man okay?"

"Yeah. I was pretty hard on him, broke his nose. He'll

have held a few bruises, but he'll live."

Dr. Carmichael nodded. For the first time, I noticed that no notepad sat on her lap. No pen. I was one patient of many.

"Why aren't you taking any notes?" I asked.

She smiled. "I like to focus on the patient during the session. I'll make notes afterward."

"What if you forget something?"

She laughed. "I've been using this system for the ten years I've been in practice. Trust me, it works for me and for my patients."

I nodded.

"So how are you and Jade now?"

"She's pretty pissed." Pissed enough to leave the ranch. A dagger jabbed me in the stomach.

"I can understand that."

"After what he did to her, I don't know why she didn't want me to beat him to a pulp."

"Part of her probably did. But she was being rational, Talon."

Rational. The word hung in the air, ridiculing me. In other words, I had *not* been rational. Couldn't really argue there.

"So how did you leave things with Jade?"

And again, the dagger. "She doesn't want to have anything to do with me. She says she's moving out of the ranch house."

"And how does that make you feel?"

How could I answer that? I hardly knew Jade Roberts, but I had been more intimate with her in these last weeks that I had ever been with anyone in my life. I had a constant need for her, a constant ache...

A craving.

"Talon"—she leaned forward, her eyes serious—"this is

only going to work if you open up and are honest with me."

I nodded. She was right. Rationally, I knew she spoke the truth. I cleared my throat and looked down at my lap.

"Do you think you might be more comfortable with a male therapist? I have several colleagues who are excellent."

"Honestly, I don't know. I'm not sure I'd be comfortable with any therapist. But my brother Jonah says you come highly recommended."

"That's kind of him."

I nodded. I was nodding a lot.

Her gaze turned serious again. "Talon, I know you didn't drive all the way here into Grand Junction on a Saturday to *not* talk to me. Obviously, Jade and your feelings for her are what caused the issue this morning. Are you in love with her?"

My whole body tensed, and I stood and walked over to the desk and back. "How could I be in love with her? I've only known her a couple of weeks."

"Then how do you feel about her leaving? Will you miss her?"

Miss her? Those words didn't even begin to encompass how I would feel if she left. Not having Jade around would be like a Colorado summer without the sun, a meadow without columbine, the Rocky Mountains without Ponderosa Pines and Aspens.

"I will miss her."

Dr. Carmichael nodded. "Why do you think it was so hard for you to voice that?"

"I don't know. Isn't that your job? To figure me out?"

"Talon, correct me if I'm wrong, but I think things inside you run a heck of a lot deeper than you're letting on. These feelings for Jade that are troubling you—there's a reason why you can't admit them. Tell me, were you close to your mother?"

Christ, my mother. Time for a Freudian analysis. "My mother died when I was twelve."

"I'm very sorry to hear that. Were you close to her before then?"

"When I was really little, yeah. But then she changed."

"How did she change?"

"She got very depressed. My sister was born prematurely when I was ten, and she almost died. Maybe my mother had postpartum depression. I don't know."

"That's quite possible. Are you saying she took her own life?"

I nodded. She might very well have had postpartum depression, but that wasn't why she took her own life.

"How about your father? Were you and he close?"

I was surprised she didn't ask me anything further about my mother's suicide. Wasn't that a shrink's wet dream? "No, not really. He was closest to my older brother, Jonah. Come to think of it, he was pretty close to my younger brother, too, and of course to Marjorie, the only girl. She was Daddy's little girl if there ever was one."

"I see. Tell me about your family dynamic. You say you have an older and younger brother."

"Yeah. Jonah is thirty-eight, I'm thirty-five, and Ryan is thirty-two. Marjorie didn't come along until a lot later. She's twenty-five."

"So she doesn't even remember her mother."

"That's right."

"So back to your father. How old is he now?"

"He died seven years ago, right after Marjorie left for college. Heart attack."

"I'm very sorry about that."

I bit the inside of my cheek. "Well, like I said, we weren't all that close."

"Let's talk a little bit about your childhood, then. Were you and your brothers close growing up?"

"Yeah, when we were little."

"What do you mean by that—when we were little?"

"I guess I mean up until about the time I was ten."

"So what happened when you were ten?"

I stood up, my heart pounding out of my chest. The walls—dank concrete walls—surrounded me. Closed in on me...

I drew in a deep breath. "I have to leave now."

"We still have a lot of time. I'm happy to stay and help you as much as I can today."

"No. Don't worry. I'll see that you're paid for your time. Double for coming in on the weekend."

"Talon, that's not nec—"

I walked out the door quickly, beads of perspiration emerging on my forehead, my heart beating a rapid staccato.

Before I had gotten to the door, my legs turned to gelatin and gave out from under me, and I fell.

Dr. Carmichael came running out of her office. "What happened? Are you all right?"

Purple haze...and then the concrete walls again... Closing in...

I tried to breathe...

Air...needed air...

Then flames...

Morphing into wings of purple and gold.

A phoenix rising...

And then blackness.

CHAPTER FIFTEEN

Jade

"Jade, you can't leave." Marjorie unfolded my clothes as quickly as I was folding them. "You just got here. Between you working for Ryan at the winery and me working around the ranch, we've hardly spent any time together."

I swallowed. My heart was breaking, and not just because I would be leaving Marj. "I'm so sorry. I'll find a place in town. We'll still be able to hang out."

"But it won't be the same." Marj grabbed my pair of black patent leather pumps and threw them back in my closet.

"Look"—I walked to the closet and retrieved the pumps—"I don't belong here. I just can't..."

"Can't what?"

"I can't stay around your brother. He nearly beat Colin into a pulp this morning."

"That's not like Talon," Marj said. "He's actually a peaceful kind of guy."

"An ex-Marine? Doesn't really reek of peaceful."

Marj flung a pair of jeans out of my suitcase and onto the floor. "At least Colin wasn't hurt."

I picked up the jeans. "Wasn't hurt? Okay, so there isn't any lasting damage, but his face is pretty beaten up, his nose is most likely broken, and he's damned lucky he doesn't have any broken ribs from all the kicking. If he wasn't an athlete and didn't know how to protect himself..." I couldn't finish.

Marjorie finally stopped going through my suitcase and sat down on the bed, her brows arched. "Why do you suppose it bothered Talon so much to see him kissing you?"

Marj had always slept like a baby. Four years of rooming with her in college had taught me that. As Talon had said, she would sleep through World War III. So it was no surprise that she had no idea what had gone on between Talon and me. Just as well. How exactly was I supposed to bring the subject up? *Oh, by the way, I've been having a little midnight fuck fest with your brother.* Really didn't think that would go over too well.

"Talon's been a little off lately," Marj continued.

Off? The man was way beyond simply *off.*

"This morning I woke up early. Came to the kitchen and found a broken glass. Water and shattered glass all over the floor. I cleaned it up. Thankfully I'd put my slippers on this morning."

Shattered glass of water... "Do you know what happened?"

She didn't need to answer. Talon had been sitting at the table with his glass of water, as usual, and for some reason, he decided to break it. Or maybe it was an accident. But why would he have left it there for anyone to walk into?

"I'm pretty sure Talon threw the glass." Marj bit her lip. "It wouldn't be the first time."

What did Marj know? "So you know that he goes out to the kitchen most nights and sits with a full glass of water?"

Marj nodded. "I rarely get up during the night. I sleep the sleep of death, as you know. But every once in a while I get up and walk around. Talon is usually in the kitchen, sitting with a glass of water. Sometimes I sit down with him and we chat for a few minutes. This morning was the second time I've woken up to a broken glass of water in the kitchen. It's possible that it's happened other times and either Felicia or Talon himself have cleaned it up."

I frowned. "Is this something new since he got back from overseas?"

"As far as I know. At least breaking the glasses. He's always gotten up at night, ever since I can remember. He's just a really light sleeper. He's had insomnia most of his life."

"Has he seen a doctor?"

"Honestly, I don't know. I was just a kid for most of the time, and then I went off to college and then travels. But now that I'm an adult, I've noticed more things about my brother."

I sat down next to her. Time for brutal honesty. "Marj, I think Talon needs help."

Marj nodded and bit her lip. "Remember when you asked me whether he had post-traumatic stress disorder? I think he does, from being in the military."

"Yeah, that would make a lot of sense. Have you talked to him about it?"

She shook her head. "No, but Joe and Ryan have. Talon refuses to see anyone."

Talon... He'd already shown me so much, and even though I had to leave, part of me wanted to stay. Part of me wanted to help him, be with him, show him that everything would be okay. But I had no training in psychology. Lawyers were trained to analyze and argue, not delve into someone's emotions and psyche.

"Look, Jade, you don't have to leave because of Talon. He's harmless."

"Harmless? Anyone could have slipped and fallen on that

mess you cleaned up this morning. And you didn't witness his attack on Colin."

"In Talon's defense, Jade, Colin is an ass."

I couldn't help a slight chuckle. She had the right of it. "Well, I'm afraid I still can't—"

A fist pounded on the door. "Marjorie, you in there?"

"She's here," I said. "Come in."

The door burst open, and Jonah rushed in. "Marj, thank God I found you. We need to leave. Talon's in the hospital."

★ ★ ★ ★

Marj and I sat in the waiting area while Jonah spoke to the nurse in charge at the emergency room in Grand Junction. I strained to hear but could only make out mumbling. My heart beat rapidly, and fear pounded through my veins. He had to be okay. He just had to be. He'd come to mean so much to me in so little—

But no. We could not be together. That poison inside of him... That unknown...

And he didn't want me anyway. Said he could never love me.

But, God, please let him be okay. I can't lose him. I'm falling in—

Stop! Don't go there, Jade. You're not in love with this man. You are not.

After what seemed like an hour, Jonah came back to us.

"What happened, Joe?" Marj asked.

"Apparently he fainted at the doctor's office."

"Doctor?" I said. "What doctor? Is he sick?"

Jonah raked his fingers through his mop of dark wavy

hair. He looked so much like Talon, except his hair was starting to gray at the temples. "Jade, I'm not sure I should—"

"Joe, Jade's family," Marj said.

"It's okay." I patted Marjorie's thigh. "I understand. There's something your brother doesn't want me to know."

Joe shook his head. "No, I think it's all right to tell you. Marj would probably tell you anyway. Today Talon went to see a psychologist."

My heart thundered. He was getting help. Thank God. But why had he fainted?

"The therapist, Dr. Carmichael, isn't exactly sure what happened. He had already left her office and was in the waiting room when he fainted."

"Is he okay?" Marj asked.

Jonah nodded. "Yeah, he'll be fine. It was nothing serious, and luckily he didn't hit his head very hard when he fell. No concussion or anything. We'll be taking him home with us in a little while."

My heart thundered again a mile a minute. Taking him home with us... I shouldn't be here. I would only make things worse for Talon, and I couldn't bear that.

"Marj?"

She looked to me, her eyes sad. "Yeah?"

"I...think I'll go ahead home now."

"Just how do you think you're going to get home? We all came together."

What a moron. I hadn't thought that far ahead. I just knew I had to get the hell out of there before Talon came out—

Too late. He walked toward us, two women flanking him. One was clearly a doctor by her white coat. The other was blond and dressed in black slacks and a red satin blouse.

The doctor held out her hand to Jonah. "Mr. Steel, I'm Dr. Morgan, your brother's neurologist. And this is Dr. Melanie Carmichael." Dr. Morgan gestured to the other woman.

Dr. Carmichael held out her hand. "Mr. Steel, nice to meet you. I'm so sorry about what happened at my office."

"Oh, come on, Doc. It's not your fault. I'm fine," Talon said.

"Your brother is fine," Dr. Morgan agreed. "We did some neurological testing. He hasn't suffered a concussion or any other significant injuries. This was just a simple fainting spell."

Talon's cheeks blazed a rosy red when he looked at me. I couldn't help a small smile. He was embarrassed that I was seeing him like this.

"Jesus, Joe, you didn't have to bring the cavalry."

"Tal, the phone call we got said you were in the emergency room. That was all I knew. So of course Marj and Jade came along." Jonah gestured to the doctors. "I'm sorry. This is my sister, Marjorie, and her friend Jade."

We all shook hands while Talon stood, his hands in the pockets of his jeans, looking as handsome and yummy as ever except for the pure exhaustion weighing down his features.

Talon was tired.

Of course he was. He never slept. His beautiful eyes were always just a little bit sunken, and dark circles shadowed them. He was so damned good-looking I hadn't noticed before, but they were there.

They always had been.

Dr. Morgan turned to Talon. "Mr. Steel, get some sleep." She handed him a slip of paper. "I've written you a prescription for Ambien. It's a common sleeping pill, and it's not habit-forming. Use it. Life is a lot easier when you're well rested."

Talon took the prescription and shoved it in his pocket.

"Here's my card also." She handed it to him. "I want to see you again in a week."

"That's ridiculous. I don't need to see a neurologist."

"Have you fainted before, Mr. Steel?"

Talon shook his head. "Of course not."

"All right. But if this happens again, I want to see you. In the meantime, I suggest you continue seeing Dr. Carmichael."

If possible, Talon's cheeks reddened even further. "I don't need therapy."

Dr. Morgan sighed. "Well, you can lead a horse to water... It's been very nice meeting you, Mr. Steel. Please, take the Ambien. Get some rest. Physically, you're fine. All of your test results were great. Your blood counts are normal. Everything looks good. It was nice meeting all of you." Dr. Morgan turned and headed back down the corridor.

"Talon," Dr. Carmichael said, "I'm so glad you're feeling better. You have my number if you need anything. It was nice meeting all of you." She left as well.

"I don't see what all the fuss is about," Talon said.

"You fainted," Jonah said. "That's what all the fuss is about."

"I'm not sure I even fainted. Probably just stumbled."

"Talon—"

"Do we have to discuss this right now, Joe?" Talon darted his gaze toward me.

Jonah let out a heavy sigh. "Let's just get you home. You need a good meal. And then you need a good night's sleep. You've obviously been working too hard."

"That's right," Talon said. "I've been working too hard. That's all."

Good save. But Talon wasn't telling us everything. As much as I wanted to know what it was, and as much as I longed to help him get through whatever was torturing him, I could not.

I would be leaving—this evening if possible.

CHAPTER SIXTEEN

Talon

"The last thing you need to do is leave, Tal. You have to work through this. We all do."

I shook my head at Jonah. He and Ryan had joined me in the den at the main house the day after I fainted. I didn't know where the girls were. I was just glad Jade wasn't anywhere near. She hadn't left yet, and now she wouldn't have to.

I was leaving.

"I've thought about this a lot. You need to get on with your lives, both of you. So does Marjorie. And so does her friend. All I do is disrupt everything."

"Where you think you're going to go?"

"Does it matter? Maybe I'll reenlist."

"Please," Ryan said. "Don't do that. We need you here. Nothing was the same when you were gone last time."

"No one needs me. I destroy everything I touch. I can't stay here and do what I've done to the two of you to our little sister. Or to Jade."

God, no, not to Jade. Jade was sunshine, rainbows, the fresh air of the Colorado Rockies. She was everything that was good in the world, and if I stayed, I would destroy her.

I could not live with that. As much as I wanted her, I had to let her go.

"You haven't done anything to us," Jonah said.

I shook my head. "Do you think I can't see it? What happened to me lives in the two of you. Maybe not in the same way, but you're just as affected by it as I am."

"Talon—" Jonah began.

"Don't start, Joe. You blame yourself for the whole ordeal. I know you do. I've heard you say it time and time again. It should've been you. You should've been there to protect me. Well, you weren't there. I've never blamed you for that, so you need to stop blaming yourself."

He turned to Ryan. "And Ryan, you got away. That was a good thing."

"I only got away because of you," Ryan said, casting his gaze downward.

"So what? The fact is, you got away. I wanted you to get away. I would do it again tomorrow if I had to."

"You were stronger, bigger. You could've run, Tal. Why didn't you run? Why did you sacrifice yourself to save me?"

I shook my head. I was thankful my little brother had been spared. And my older brother as well.

"Why can't the two of you just be happy? Be happy this didn't happen to you. I sure as hell am."

Jonah sighed. "Talon, it's not that we…"

"It's not that you what? Why are you afraid to say it? Just say it, goddamnit! 'I'm glad it didn't happen to me.' You *should* be fucking glad. You should be down on your knees thanking whatever deity you believe in that it didn't happen to you. It's okay to say that. It's okay to be happy that you didn't go through the horror I went through."

"Talon," Ryan said.

"Say it. Both of you. I want you to fucking say it. Say 'I'm fucking glad none of that shit happened to me.'"

My brothers both remained silent.

Not that I expected anything else. I sure as hell was glad that it hadn't happened to them. It was understandable why I was having a hard time letting the whole damn thing go. Them? I really couldn't understand anymore.

Maybe I didn't want to understand. Maybe I was just waiting for the day when all of this would go away in a puff of smoke. But I knew better. That day would never come. This was my burden to bear.

I would never be free of it.

"I didn't think you could say it. And that's okay. But I do need to leave. Try to understand." I walked toward the door and then through it, leaving my brothers behind.

I headed toward my suite, and then, on a whim, turned around and headed back the other way, to Jade's bedroom. It was Sunday. She might be sleeping in. I hadn't seen her or Marjorie yet that morning.

I knocked gently.

No response.

I knocked harder.

A few seconds later, Jade opened the door. Her hair was tangled and sexy in a messy disarray around her shoulders. She wore her signature white tank and boxers, white cotton socks on her feet.

Her nipples poked through the white fabric, red-brown and luscious. My groin tightened.

"Did I wake you?"

She yawned. "Not really. I was kind of in that alpha mode, you know? Hovering between asleep and awake?"

No, I didn't know what she meant. "Can we talk for a

minute?" I asked.

"I suppose so. Although I don't think we really have anything to talk about."

I walk through the door and shut it behind me. "Just a few minutes."

"Sure, come on in," she said sarcastically.

Her duffel bag sat at the end of her bed, packed. A suitcase lay open on the floor, filled with clothes and shoes. She really was leaving.

Now she didn't have to.

"I just wanted to tell you that I'm leaving the ranch," I said.

"You? Why are you leaving? It's your ranch."

How to put this... "My being here... It's affecting my brothers. And I don't want it to affect you and Marjorie."

"You don't have to worry about me." She gestured to her duffel bag and suitcase. "As you can see, I'll be leaving later today."

"But now you don't have to. You can stay here with Marjorie. That's what she wants. I should be the one to leave."

She shook her head. "What is this about? Why all of a sudden do you want to leave?"

I sat down on the bed. I had told her all that I could. "Like I said, my being here isn't good for my brothers."

"So they asked you to leave?"

"No, not exactly."

"Then why are you leaving?"

"I just have to."

Jade slowly brought her arm upward and cupped one of my cheeks, her thumb lightly massaging my upper lip. Oh, God—classic "I feel sorry for you" pose. I couldn't take it. I hated pity. I didn't want pity from anyone, and especially not from her.

I yanked her hand away. "Don't do that."

"Talon, please... I want to help."

"Help me with what?"

"Just...help."

"I don't need any fucking help."

She cupped my cheek again, and I couldn't bring myself to tear her arm away this time. Her touch soothed me, warmed me, gave me something—something I couldn't put into words.

This unquenchable hunger for her—was it because she had something I needed? But how would I have known that when I first laid eyes on her? Had her soul spoken to mine?

I was talking nonsense. My cock was hard, and I wanted to fuck her. That was all. I'd thought one time would ease my ache for her. All it did was make the ache worse. The second time the same. By that logic, if I fucked her again, I'd want her even more.

Go, Talon. Leave this room and don't look back.

But I couldn't. I placed my hand over hers, still on my cheek. I grasped it, brought into my mouth, and kissed her palm, her skin so soft and sweet beneath my lips. I gazed into her blue-gray eyes, so haunting, with a touch of sadness. Had I put that sadness there?

I brought sadness to everyone I touched. But then her lips, those beautiful full ruby-red lips, curved upward into a smile. She smiled at me, her steely eyes crinkling in the corners.

Her smile... My God, I'd sell my soul to the devil himself just to keep that smile on her face for all time.

Her lips began to move. "Kiss me, Talon. Please, kiss me."

I stood and pressed my lips to hers. She opened for me

immediately and slid her soft, sweet tongue into my mouth. I wanted to be gentle with her. I truly wanted to, but something about Jade Roberts brought out the animal in me. I wasn't used to being gentle. I wasn't used to thinking about my partner at all. I normally just took what she gave freely, unconcerned about whether she was happy with how I did it.

I slid my tongue into her mouth slowly, differently from how I usually dived straight in. My cock strained against my jeans. The urge to grind into her was great, but I held back, determined to take things slow this time.

But Jade had other ideas. She pushed me down onto the bed and straddled me, still kissing me, and unbuttoned my shirt. Soon only her flimsy cotton tank top separated us, and her hard little nipples poked into my bare chest. She kissed me with passion and fire, and my original plan to go slow was shot to hell. We kissed and we kissed, and then she rolled off of me, grabbed my hand, and slid it underneath her boxers.

"Touch me, Talon. Feel how wet I am for you."

I nearly exploded. She was soaking. I traced her slick folds with my fingers, circling her nub, exploring her wetness.

"Yes, just like that," she breathed. "I love it when you touch me. You make me so hot."

I plunged two fingers into her warm channel. She jolted, grinding against my hand. I shoved my fingers into her again and again, finding her G-spot, rubbing it, fueled by her groans of desire.

"Talon, yes. So good. It feels so fucking good."

If only those fingers were my cock, plunging into her, thrusting, taking her...

Slow, Talon. Slow.

But again, my plan went awry. She writhed against me,

her hard nipples poking from her tank top, her juices gushing over my hand. I had to have her. I withdrew my fingers, and she whimpered.

"Don't worry, blue eyes. I'm not going anywhere." I slid her boxers over her hips and discarded them. Then I spread her legs and dived between them. I slid my tongue up and down her wet slit, sucking all the cream out of that beautiful red pussy. God, she tasted so fucking good. Tangy, a little bit citrusy—I could live on her essence alone. I plunged my tongue into her opening, in and out, in and out. Then I swiped it over her slit and up to her clit, sucking while I forced the same two fingers back into her wet heat.

She arched her back. "God, I'm going to come."

"Yeah, baby, come. Come for me. Come all over my hand and my face. Let me see that sweet cream."

She clenched around my fingers, her pussy convulsing in orgasm. My cock was so hard I thought it might break through the denim of my jeans. Had to have her. Had to have my cock inside of her. But no. Not yet. She was going to come again. I pushed her thighs forward and swiped my tongue over her puckered asshole. She tensed a bit, and I waited. If she was going to protest, she needed to do it now.

When she relaxed, I continued my assault. I tongued her little hole until it relaxed against my lips. I lubed it up real good and then slid my tongue back up to her pussy as I breached her tight hole with a finger. She jerked.

"Relax, baby. You'll enjoy this. I promise."

I slowly inched farther, until her rim softened. Then I slid my finger in and out of her hole while I sucked her pussy lips.

I lapped up a fresh gush of cream and then flicked at her clit again, sucked at it, and soon she was awash in another climax.

"Oh my God, Talon. Oh my God."

When she came down, I withdrew my finger from her and stood for a moment to remove my jeans and boxers. God, my cock was so fucking hard. I fisted it, grasping the base to stave off my imminent climax. Her body was flushed pink from her orgasms, her pussy garnet red and puffy.

"Take off your tank top," I commanded.

She obeyed, and soon she lay before me, naked and ready, and oh, so beautiful.

"I'm going to fuck you now, blue eyes," I said. "I'm going to fuck you so long so deep, and you're going to come again and again around my cock."

I thrust inside of her heat. God, she held me so snugly. I could've blown then, but I truly wanted to go slowly, to make it good for her. I pulled out and thrust back in, and soon I was fucking her hard, hard, hard. She grabbed the cheeks of my ass, forcing herself to take me deeper.

And that made me harder. God, she was so hot.

"Take me, Jade. Take all of me."

"Give it to me, Talon," she said. "Give me all you have. I want it all."

"You got it, baby." I thrust harder, harder, harder, harder... I fucked her, taking her, but at the same time, a new sensation bubbled within me.

I wasn't just taking. I was giving. I was giving something to her that I had never given to anyone else.

I pulled out and sat up on the bed.

Her eyes shot wide open, their steely blue burning into me. "What's wrong? Why did you stop?"

I wasn't used to giving. I wasn't sure I wanted to give her

anything.

No. That was a lie.

I did want to give her something.

Something from deep inside me.

From my soul.

But I had nothing to give.

"Talon?"

My cock was still hard enough to cut through diamonds.

"Do you want me to suck you?" She rose and sat next to me.

I shook my head. Not that I didn't want that...

"What's going on? You're freaking me out here."

Still I had no answer for her.

"Talon, what is it that you want?"

I looked into her searing blue-gray gaze, and I could not lie to her. "You, Jade. I want *you*."

CHAPTER SEVENTEEN

Jade

I looked into his blazing black eyes. "You have me. I'm right here."

"But I don't want to want you so much."

"Why, Talon? I've already told you that I don't expect you to love me. So we have a lot of sexual chemistry. What's wrong with that? If you want me, take me."

"I don't want to take you."

"You've taken me several times now. What's the difference?"

He didn't answer. Not that I expected him to. His cock was still hard as a rock, and a small drop of liquid emerged from the tip. Without thinking, I reached toward him and smoothed the liquid over the head of his cock. He closed his eyes and shuddered.

I rose, dropped to my knees on the floor between his legs, and took his cock between my lips. I licked the saltiness from the head and then pushed my lips over his shaft. He was so large I couldn't get all the way to the base, but I got as far as I could until the back of his cock nudged my throat, and I withdrew. I licked the underside all the way down and then spread tiny kisses over his balls. I inhaled the musky scent, and then I moved away from his genitals to the sexy indentation of his hips. I kissed across his abdomen to his other side, his skin so warm against my lips. I spread tiny kisses over his thigh,

Returning to his cock, I nibbled the tip and looked up to him, meeting his gaze. "Tell me, Talon. Tell me what you want me to do."

"I want you to..."

"What?"

Instead of answering, he pulled me upward, flipped me over onto my hands and knees, and pushed his cock into me.

"I want to fuck you, blue eyes. I want to fuck you until there's no you left. Only me, you a part of me."

Exactly what I wanted. "Yeah, Talon, fuck me. Fuck me hard."

He obliged, pounding into me, his balls slapping against my cunt lips. A few seconds later, the blunt tip of his finger nudged my asshole. Yes, he was going to do it. He was going to finger my anus again. And I would not stop him. I hadn't stopped him the first time.

And it suddenly dawned on me that I would never stop him.

Never.

He could do what he wanted to me, to my body, and I would welcome it. I would welcome it all.

I arched when he breached the tightness, his finger sliding in and out in a different rhythm from his cock.

"That's it, blue eyes. I'm taking you. Taking your pussy and your ass. One day I'm going to fuck this ass. I'm going to fuck you so hard in the ass, and you're going to come for me."

His words made me gush. I exploded into a shattered climax. I cried out, my walls clenching around him.

"God, yes. That feels so good. Come for me, baby. Come

all over me."

The climax unfurled within me, taking me outside myself, making me tingle all over.

Rapture. Such rapture.

He fucked me harder, all the while drilling my ass.

"Yeah, fuck you. Want to fuck you, fuck you, fuck you." With each "fuck you," he plunged farther and farther into my pussy. "That's it, take me. Take me, Jade. Take my cock in your hot little pussy. Take it all. All of me."

And with one last thrust, he groaned out, "Yes, that's it, coming inside you. I'm marking you. Taking what is mine."

A few timeless moments passed with us joined, and then he finally withdrew from my pussy and my ass and collapsed on the bed, one arm over his forehead.

I wanted to say so much to him. I wanted to tell him that he didn't have to leave. I wanted to tell him that I had decided not to leave, that although I knew something tortured him, that something was poisoning him, I needed to stay here and help him. I wanted to tell him that he meant something to me. I wasn't sure what that was yet, but he meant something to me. Something important, something...essential.

But I couldn't say any of these things. Not yet, at least. I lay down next to him when a fist pounded on the door.

"Shit!" I grabbed my boxer shorts and tank top and threw them on. "Who is it?" I called out.

"It's Marj. Can I come in?"

I eyed the door. Had I locked it? I couldn't tell from where I was. I walked closer. Shit, it was unlocked. What had I been thinking? What would Talon think?

"Just a minute. I'm not decent."

"Oh, for God's sake, Jade, we were roommates for four

years." The doorknob turned.

Quickly I pushed in the locking mechanism just in time. "I'll be ready in a minute."

I went back to the bed. Talon was sitting up, grabbing his boxers and jeans.

"You need to hide in the bathroom," I whispered.

He let out a soft chuckle. "Are you insane? This is my house."

"Do you want your sister to know we were screwing?"

His eyes darkened for moment, and his lips turned down into a slight frown. Then he nodded. "You're right." He headed to the bathroom and quietly shut the door.

I unlocked the door and faced Marj. "What is it?"

She eyed me. "You're wearing your pajamas. You said you weren't decent."

"I...wasn't. I had started to go into the shower, and then you knocked on the door, so I had to put my jammies back on."

That seemed to appease her, although the skeptical eyebrow arch indicated she wasn't quite satisfied with my explanation. I pushed her out of the room. "Let's get some coffee. I need a caffeine boost."

She didn't argue with me, and for that I was eternally grateful. "Okay, there should be some coffee in the kitchen. Joe and Ryan were here earlier."

Sure enough, half a pot of brew sat on the burner, still warm. I poured a cup for me and for Marj, and we sat down at the kitchen table.

"So what did you want? Why were you knocking at my door?"

"I decided to see what you want to do today. It's Sunday, and in the small town of Snow Creek, that means everything is pretty much closed. It's Felicia's day off too, so I thought maybe we could have some fun."

"Oh?" I raised my eyebrows.

"Yeah. Let's make something. Let's cook today."

Although Marj loved to cook, I didn't exactly share the sentiment. I'd been cooking all my life because no one else was around to do it. "That's fun for you, not for me." I laughed.

She punched me in the arm. "If we don't cook, we either have to go into Grand Junction to eat, or we go hungry."

I rolled my eyes. "If you say so."

"Besides, we have the best beef in the good old US right here on Steel Acres. I'll pull out some steaks. How does that sound?"

One thing about Marj—she could put it away like a teenage boy and still keep that gorgeous figure of hers. Probably because she was so tall.

A smile crept up on me. "Let's make dinner for Talon."

Marj jumped up and hugged me around the neck. "Does that mean what I think it means?"

I froze. Did she know what was going on between Talon and me? Would she be okay with it?

"It means that...I'll help you cook dinner."

"Yay! So you're not leaving! I was hoping you'd decide to stay."

I heaved a sigh of relief. "Yeah. I guess so. For now. I should get my bar results next week. Maybe as soon as tomorrow." My nerves jumped. "God, I hope I passed."

Marj sat down. "You're brilliant, Jade. Of course you passed."

"I hope you're right. That test was pretty daunting. Two whole days. The essays weren't so bad. I mean, I know the material. But that multiple-choice test..."

"How could that be the harder of the two?"

"Because the essays were straightforward. The multiple-choice test had no 'right answer.' You had to choose the *best* answer. I could eliminate two pretty quickly, but then there were two that could go either way. By the time I started thinking about which one it could be, I realized I was wasting time. The test is timed, so I had to decide on an answer and move forward. I think I know four that I actually got right. The rest were a crapshoot."

Marj smiled and placed her hand on my forearm. "Jade, I'm really not worried. I know you passed."

"From your mouth to God's ears. I sure hope so. Although I have to tell you, I've really been enjoying working with Ryan at the winery."

"There's no reason why you can't continue to do that."

"With a license to practice law, I kind of feel like I should be practicing law. But at least I can continue working at the winery until I find a job."

Footfalls clomped behind me.

"Morning, Tal," Marj said.

I turned. Talon stood in his jeans and bare feet. He hadn't bothered to put his shirt back on. I hoped Marj hadn't seen him come from our side of the hallway. God, he looked good—his hair tousled and sexy, just hitting his shoulders, his long eyelashes fringing his dark-as-night eyes, his lips red and swollen from our kisses. Basically, he looked like he had just had hot monkey sex.

My skin tightened. Suddenly I felt very conspicuous. If he looked like he had just had amazing sex...what did I look like?

"Hey," was all he said. He walked toward the coffee maker

and poured himself a cup.

"Sit down with us for a few minutes," Marjorie said.

"Can't. Got work to do."

"Talon, it's Sunday. And you were just in the hospital yesterday. Take a load off, for God's sake."

Talon visibly tensed. "I'm fine. And the trees don't stop growing just because it's Sunday, Marjorie."

Marj rolled her eyes. "Fine, then. Go tend to your trees. But be back here by six p.m. sharp, because Jade and I are going to make a gourmet feast tonight."

"Oh, you are?" He turned to me.

"Hey, don't look at me. This is her idea. My contribution will be grilled cheese with tomato."

His cheeks reddened. Just a bit, but I noticed.

"We're having rib eyes, Tal. One hundred percent Steel-raised beef."

That got a dimple out of Talon. "Best there is."

"See if Joe and Ryan can come too. I'll get out five steaks."

"Sure, whatever." Talon took his coffee and walked out of the kitchen.

I sighed. "He sure is a man of few words." Except for when he was in the middle of hot monkey sex. But I kept that to myself.

"That's just his way. Although I am a little worried about yesterday."

I nodded. I was worried about him too, but I didn't want voice that concern to Marj just yet. I still didn't know how she would take the fact that I was sleeping with her brother, and not just any brother—the tortured one. Why didn't Marj see what I saw?

And then it came to me, like a concrete block hitting me

on the head. Talon must have been this way since Marj was born. She didn't know any other Talon.

But Ryan and Jonah knew. I had seen the awareness—the sadness—in their eyes when I had talked to them about Talon. They knew something—something they were keeping well hidden. Ryan had said it wasn't his story to tell.

Marj didn't know, or she would've told me. She and I didn't have secrets. Except now we did. I hadn't told her about Talon and me. A wave of guilt washed over me. I should tell her. But I couldn't. It wasn't just my story to tell. It was Talon's too, and I had to consider his feelings.

She chatted on and on about nothing in particular while I sipped my coffee—man, I needed to teach these people about brewing strong coffee—and listened with only one ear.

"So what do you think?" she asked.

I had no idea what she had asked me. "I'm sorry, what?"

"Jade, you have not been listening to a word I've said."

I sighed. "I'm sorry. My mind has just been other places, I guess. What did you need?"

"I said, 'what do you think about asparagus spears and twice-baked potatoes with our steaks tonight?'"

"Sure, that sounds great."

"I thought I'd grill the asparagus outside along with the steaks. Have you ever had grilled asparagus? It's to die for."

I smiled and shook my head. "Nope. At least not that I know of."

"Well, you're going to love it. What do you think we should make for dessert?"

Why was she asking me? My idea of dessert was opening a carton of Ben & Jerry's. Which sounded pretty darn good at the moment. "I don't know. Something chocolate?"

"Yes! Perfect. I'll make my famous French silk pie. I just hope we have all the ingredients in the pantry since the grocery stores aren't open today. I don't want to drive all the way to the city for graham cracker crumbs." Marj rose and walked across the vast kitchen to the walk-in pantry. "Sugar, check. Unsweetened chocolate, check. Crumbs, check." She came out of the pantry and walked to the fridge. "Butter, check. Eggs, check. No heavy cream. That's okay, I can substitute this half-and-half. It will be great. And we have plenty of asparagus and ten pounds of potatoes in the pantry." She opened the freezer and pulled out a couple packs of meat wrapped in white butcher's paper. "And rib eyes. Jade, tonight you will eat the best steak of your life."

I laughed. "I've had Steel beef before, remember? When I visited during college? And that's exactly what you said to me then."

She laughed. "Well, it's still true. I'm so excited to cook."

"You've been home for a while. How come you haven't cooked?"

"Well, I love Felicia's cooking so much. To tell you the truth, I don't really know. I should do more cooking."

"Have you reconsidered enrolling in culinary school?"

Marj tilted her head. "That's my dream. But I'm expected to stay here and help with the ranch. I mean, it *is* one quarter mine."

I nodded. I understood. Why should she walk away from this empire she lived on? I sure as heck wouldn't. Here I was, saddled with loans from college and law school, and currently living off Marjorie and her daddy's money.

I hoped I could find a job as an attorney. Until recently, I'd been planning to join the legal team at Colin's father's Denver satellite office. Those plans had blown up on my nonexistent wedding day.

But this wasn't about me. It was about Marjorie.

"If that's really your dream, why not talk to your brothers about it? Surely they'd understand."

"Yeah, I should. It's just easier staying here. I don't have to worry about anything."

Easy. Yeah, Marj did have it easy. I bit back a surge of envy. I certainly didn't begrudge her the good fortune, but man, my life would have been a lot easier if I'd had a little money. My dad did the best he could, and I never got a penny from my mother. Her much-younger second husband had seen to that.

I finished my coffee and stood. "I'm going to shower. What time do you need me in here to start our cooking extravaganza?"

"I'd say probably around five. No, make that four. The potatoes need to bake and then bake again. Plus we'll need to start the dessert so it can chill."

I nodded, put my coffee cup in the sink, and walked back to my room.

And on my bed sat Talon Steel.

CHAPTER EIGHTEEN

Talon

"Uh...hi," Jade said.

"My brothers don't want me to leave," I said.

She shook her head. "Hi to you too. What are you doing here?"

"Are you still leaving?"

She walked to her chest of drawers, opened the top one, and pulled out a pair of underwear. I tried not to imagine the plain white cotton panties clinging to her shapely ass. What was it about plain white panties on women? God, so hot.

"No, not yet, anyway."

"What changed your mind?" I dared to hope I had played a part in her decision.

"Nothing in particular. I mean, I took the Colorado bar, so I'll be living somewhere in the state anyway. And I promised Marj I would try to make it work here in Snow Creek."

Of course. For Marjorie. Not for me. Which was fine anyway, because I couldn't love her. I couldn't give her what she deserved. But her not being here... I'd be ripped in two.

I stared at her—at those blue-gray eyes that seemed to cut through my many tiers, at those red lips still swollen from her earlier kisses, at the lush golden-brown hair hanging in wavy layers around her creamy shoulders, at her perfectly shaped face, at her amazing and beautiful large breasts, at those brown-pink nipples poking through that damned white cotton tank. The woman could be wearing a lacy negligee from Victoria's Secret and she couldn't look any sexier than she did in a white tank and plaid boxers.

I wanted her again. My cock grew inside my jeans, and my balls tightened. How was this happening to me? I still hardly knew the woman. Was this simple physical chemistry? If it was only chemistry...why were my emotions involved?

Emotion... I had turned off myriad emotions long ago just so I could get through the craziness that was my life. Now feeling was creeping back into me, and as much as I wanted to stop it, I was powerless against it.

If Jade left, maybe I could get back to normal.

But if Jade left...she'd take a piece of me with her.

I had to get her out of my system once and for all. I could fuck her again. That would sate my physical hunger, but not for long, given the state of my cock at the moment. I had just had her an hour ago, and now I wanted her again. Truth of it was, I had wanted her as soon as we were done.

She fidgeted with the white panties she held, looking at the floor. "I need to shower, so if you'll excuse me..."

Shower. I could take her into the shower with me. But no. I would have her again on her bed.

"Look at me," I said.

She still looked down.

I rose and walked toward her. I lifted her chin and forced her to meet my gaze. "I said, 'look at me.'"

Her eyes burned darker, into an almost midnight gray-blue. I waited for her to speak, but she did not. My cock strained against the confines of my jeans. I ached to grab her, bend my legs, and grind my cock into her pelvis while we were still fully clothed.

Instead, I lowered my head and kissed her lips. She opened for me, and we kissed softly for a few seconds, but then the kiss became more fervent. God, to kiss her was heaven. Her soft sweet tongue, her firm full lips, the tiny nibbles from her teeth... Yes, it was heaven kissing her. And heaven was a place I hadn't known until Jade.

I brushed my hands over her shoulders, down her arms, and then up, cupping her firm full breasts. I thumbed her hard nipples through the flimsy cotton material. She groaned. I took them both between thumb and forefinger and pinched once, twice, three times...

She moaned into my mouth, the sound a tremor against the back of my throat. God, how I loved her nipples—so beautiful and so responsive. I pinched them again and again, her moans feeding my own desire. When I finally broke the kiss to take a breath, I leaned down and bit a nipple right through the fabric.

"Oh, God, Talon, yes. I love it when you pinch my nipples."

I continued sucking and nibbling her nipples through the cotton while I brushed the boxers over her hips and onto the floor. I touched her wet pussy with my fingers. Slick and ready for me...so hot.

"Yes, just like that," she said. "So good."

I let go of her nipple with a soft pop and turned her around so her beautiful ass was facing me. I squeezed the firm cheeks and then knelt and slid my tongue through the crease. She sighed. Her pussy was red and swollen, dripping with her sweet nectar. I buried my face in it, rubbing my cheeks, chin, and lips in her juices, sucking her clean. She tasted so good, like citrus and sex. I had to have her. Again.

I stood and removed my jeans quickly. My cock stood at attention, as hard as ever. I ached to be inside her. I sat down on the bed and motioned her toward me. "Come sit on my cock, baby. Take off your shirt first and sit on my cock. I'm going to play with your nipples while you fuck me."

She needed no further urging. When she sank her moist pussy onto me, I nearly shattered. So good, that suction, that sweet grip. Bracing her knees on either side of my hips, she rose slowly and plunged back down. A man of my word, I cupped both breasts, fingering one nipple and biting the other.

"Yes, Talon. Bite me. Bite that nipple. God, I'm going to come so hard."

"Yeah, blue eyes, come for me. I want that sweet little pussy to come all over my cock." I clamped my lips over her hard nipple again.

She rose and sank, rose and sank, and then imploded all over me. Her convulsions clenched me as she rode into her climax.

"Oh, Talon," she cried. "I'm coming, baby. Coming. So, so good."

I was ready to spew into her, but I wanted her to have another orgasm. Plus I wanted to taste that sweet little cunt.

I pulled her off of me and laid her down on the bed. I spread her legs and shoved my face between them, eating her. I sucked on her clit and stuffed two fingers inside her. Soon she was clenching around me again.

My God, I loved making her come. Her responses drove me insane. I had never been so concerned about a lover's pleasure before. I liked for them to come, but if they didn't, I didn't worry about it too much. But with Jade—every orgasm that shattered through her shattered through me as well.

Our pleasure was joined somehow.

One more climax with my fingers curled inside her, and I could take it no longer. I climbed atop her and thrust into her. Sweet, sweet home. She gripped me like no other, and as I pushed into her, bit into her neck as I fucked her, she moaned under my touch.

Two, three, four more thrusts, and I was coming all over again. Squirting into her, coming home.

I rolled over onto my back and closed my eyes, breathing hard.

A few minutes later, I opened my eyes. She was on her side, her head resting in her hand, her gorgeous hair falling over those creamy shoulders, staring at me. I waited for her to speak, but she didn't. I opened my mouth to speak, but nothing came out.

She looked at me expectantly.

"I'm glad you're not leaving," I whispered.

She smiled. "Not for the time being anyway, as I said."

I nodded and closed my eyes again.

"Talon?"

I recognized the tone of her voice. She wanted to "talk" about this. I didn't know what to say to her.

"Talon?" she said again.

Now or never. "What?"

"What exactly is this thing between us?"

I could more easily explain the meaning of life and the existence of God. "It's...sex."

She punched me in the arm, but at least it was a friendly punch...or so I thought.

"Clearly it's sex. But the first time you took me to your

bed, you said it would be the only time. That hasn't ended up being the case. So what is going on with us?"

"What do you want to be going on with us?" All the potential answers to that question scared the hell out of me, but it was easier to ask it than actually answer hers.

"Well...I haven't felt like I could tell Marj what's going on between us. Do you think it would be okay if I...told her?"

Not exactly what I had been expecting. Most women would want to talk about commitments, emotion, and all that other garbage. All Jade wanted to know was if she could tell her best friend. Something in me saddened a bit.

"Do you want to tell her?" Score two for me. Another question instead of answering hers.

"Honestly, I don't know. Normally I would. She and I don't have secrets. But something about this situation seems... very private to me. Why do you think that is?"

"Why do you think that is?"

"Oh, no, you don't. Don't think I haven't caught on. You're answering everything I ask with another question. I've been to law school. I know that tactic. I want an answer. What is this? And why do I feel like I can't talk about it?"

Her cheeks were red, her body still flushed from her orgasms. Private? I didn't know why it seemed private. I had no answer for her, and right now...I was longing for her again.

"I want your pussy again," I said.

"You can't be serious."

"I've never been more serious." I moved downward and spread her legs. "You're so beautiful down here. Especially after you've come. So red and swollen and juicy. I could eat you up."

"You've done that several times— Oh!"

I slithered my tongue over her wet folds. Delicious, perfect. I pushed her thighs forward, tongued her tight little asshole, and then sucked her entire labia into my mouth and pulled.

"God! God, that's good."

Between her legs, I met her blue-gray gaze. Her nipples were hard and puckered. "Touch your nipples for me, baby," I said. "Pinch those hard little nipples for me."

She brought her hands to her breasts and cupped them, fingering them lightly.

"That's hot, baby. Now pinch them. Pinch those hard little nipples while I suck your cunt."

She pinched them, and my cock hardened into granite. Damn, she was so hot. I lapped at her pussy, sucking, tugging, and then looked up again. "How does that feel, baby? How does it feel when you pinch your nipples like that?"

She moaned, writhing, grinding into my face. "Talon, I'm going to come again."

A thrill bubbled into me. "Yeah, baby, come for me. Come all over my face. Let me suck all that sweet cream out of your pussy."

She shattered, bathing me with her sweet essence. My cock throbbed, yearning for her hot sheath. While she was still coming, I inched forward and thrust into her. I fucked her. Fucked her harder. I got on my knees, lifted her hips, and plowed into her.

Thrust. Thrust. Thrust. Thrust. My balls tight. *Thrust. Thrust. Thrust.* Tiny convulsions started at the base. *Thrust. Thrust. Thrust.* My brain exploded, my skin tingled all over, my cock throbbed as I released into her juicy heat.

The most explosive climax I could remember...and still

I came and came and came...until finally I pulled out and collapsed in a heap next to her.

Calm peacefulness surrounded me as the afterglow whisked me to a different plane. I lay there, sated. Her presence next to me filled me with a tranquil headiness that was foreign to me. I floated downward, melting into the soft comforter.

God, dare I think it?

I felt...*good.*

But a few minutes later...

"What exactly is this thing between us?"

CHAPTER NINETEEN

Jade

He didn't answer me. Not that I expected he would. I got up to take my shower. I figured he'd let me this time. He'd had three or four orgasms already today. He wouldn't be after me for another.

I turned to look at him, his eyes still closed, his arm over his forehead as usual. One of his knees was bent and strewn over his other leg. Naked glory—he was indeed the epitome of masculine beauty.

I walked to the door to make sure it was locked, and I went to take a shower.

Twenty minutes later, when I walked out of the bathroom to dress, Talon was gone.

★ ★ ★ ★

"I can't believe this." Marj brought in the steaks from the grill and set the platter down harshly down on the patio dining table. "I told him six sharp."

Jonah and Ryan were relaxing in the hot tub with a beer. I was sipping a glass of Ryan's Rhône blend in a redwood Adirondack chair. My heart lurched. Worry for Talon consumed me. Had he fainted somewhere?

"Don't get your panties in a bunch, Sis," Ryan said jovially.

Always jovial, that one. Ryan always had a smile. I'd miss working with him when my bar results came in.

"Is it a crime to want to have dinner with my family?" Marj shook her head. "My *whole* family? I've been cooking for two hours!"

Jonah got out of the hot tub, his trunks dripping, and wrapped a towel around his waist. "It smells great. Don't feel bad, Marj. You know how Talon is." He sighed. "I just wish he were here. He was just in the ER yesterday, for God's sake."

So Jonah was worried too.

"He ruined my special dinner," Marj said, her dark eyes somber.

I gulped down the last of my wine. I hated to see my best friend upset. Yes, I was concerned, but I wouldn't let Marj down. I rose. "Come on." I put my arm around Marj's shoulder. "Joe and Ryan are here. I'm here. And everything smells great. Plus, I worked really hard sprinkling salt and pepper on that asparagus."

That got a slight smile out of Marj.

"Listen to Jade, Sis," Ryan said. "I could eat a horse. Let's pour some more of that Rhône and have some chow."

Dinner was delicious. At least I assumed it was. It all tasted like cardboard to me. Worry for Talon pounded in my gut. Alongside the worry churned anger. How could he do this to Marj? She had lightened up a bit after a couple glasses of wine, but she was clearly hurt that he had stood her up. I put on my happy face and talked with Marj and her brothers, but an underlying current of malaise was thick around us.

Where was he?

I helped Marj clear the table and then offered to serve the dessert. I went into the kitchen to fetch the French silk pie from the refrigerator, when the doorbell rang. Marj and the guys were outside and hadn't heard it. I walked out of the kitchen through the hall to the doorway. Who would be calling on a Sunday evening?

I opened the door. A cop stood on the front porch.

"Yes?" I said.

The cop cleared his throat. "I'm Officer Steve Dugan, ma'am. Is Mr. Steel at home?"

"Which one?"

"Talon Steel."

I shook my head. "No, he's out. But his brothers are here." I held out my hand. "I'm Jade Roberts, Marjorie's friend. Do you...want me to get Jonah and Ryan for you?"

Dugan nodded. "Yes, if you don't mind."

"Sure." I held the door open. "Come on in."

He stepped in and removed his hat. Polite.

"I'll just be a minute."

I walked quickly through the kitchen to the patio. They were laughing. At what, I had no idea. It was the first gale of laughter I'd heard tonight, and with the news I had, it would no doubt be the last.

I cleared my throat. "Excuse me, you guys, but there's an Officer Dugan here to see Talon. He wants to talk to the two of you."

Jonah arched his eyebrows. "Steve? What's going on?"

"I haven't a clue," I said, "but he's waiting in the foyer."

Jonah rose and walked past me, Ryan and Marj following. I strode quickly on their heels. I might not be family, but I needed to know what was going on. My nerves were a wreck.

"Steve"—Jonah held out his hand—"what's going on, buddy?"

"Hey, Joe." Dugan shook Jonah's hand and then Ryan's and Marjorie's. "I'm sorry to barge in like this."

"I guess you've already met Marj's friend Jade?" Ryan said.

Dugan smiled...sort of. "Nice to meet you." He shook my hand.

His hand was big and meaty. And clammy with perspiration. This cop was nervous. Or hesitant.

"Come on into the living room," Jonah said. "You want a drink?"

Dugan shook his head. "I'm here to see your brother."

"You putting together another poker game?" Ryan smiled. "Why don't you ever ask me to play?"

"Because you suck, Ry," Dugan said, "but that's not why I'm here." He cleared his throat. "I'm afraid this isn't a social call."

Apprehension clogged the air. Something was wrong. Very wrong.

"I need to take Talon in. I have a warrant for his arrest."

★ ★ ★ ★

I was helping Marion in the winery office the next morning, trying desperately to get Talon out of my mind.

He hadn't come home last night. I'd made several pilgrimages to the kitchen, hoping to find him staring at that damned glass of water, but to no avail. I hadn't slept, and from the looks of Ryan when I came in this morning, neither had he.

I nearly dropped the file I was working on when Marjorie burst in like a tornado, her cheeks flushed pink and her eyes rimmed with darkness, carrying a legal-size envelope. Clearly, she hadn't slept either.

"Jade"—she forced a smile—"your bar results came."

My stomach rose in my throat. The last thing I wanted to do was open that envelope in front of Marj and Marion.

"Morning, ladies." Ryan strode in, his signature smile missing from his face. "How's everything going this morning?"

And now in front of Ryan. Why couldn't he have stayed over at the warehouse with the barrels?

Goosebumps froze on my arms. "Marj..."

"Oh, what are you afraid of? You know you passed with flying colors. My brilliant BFF could do no less." She sighed. "Besides, we could all use some good news this morning."

I couldn't argue there. Marjorie, who usually slept like a baby, had clearly tossed and turned last night. Her eyes told the tale.

Ever since college, Marj had labored under the delusion that I was brilliant. The truth was I was no more brilliant than anyone else. I studied. I had to, to get scholarships. Marj, coming from the Steel Empire, hadn't needed to worry about money. I had worked hard in school my whole life, my father driving into my head that I needed to go to college and I needed to get scholarships to be able to do it. I'd always had scholarships, and I'd taken loans to cover the rest that my dad couldn't and then worked to cover my living expenses.

And here Marj was building me up in front of Marion and Ryan and waving my bar results in my face. What was I supposed to do? I had to open them. And if I didn't pass... Nothing much. I'd be mortified, that was all.

But as I had done for all tests in my entire testing career, I had studied for the bar exam. And when I studied for tests, I usually got As. So I had to go with the odds here. Why worry yet?

"I'm on pins and needles here, Jade." Marj thrust the envelope at me.

I reluctantly took it. Telling her I didn't want to open it in front of everyone would do no good. They already knew it was here anyway, and whatever the result was, they would know that eventually as well.

"Yes, please don't keep us in suspense." Marion smiled.

I took a deep breath and ripped open the envelope. Inside were two pieces of paper. My vision blurred as I tried to read the first piece. Name, address, *scan scan scan, scan scan scan...*

Status.

I drew in a deep breath.

Pass.

I widened my eyes to make sure I hadn't read it wrong.

Pass.

"I passed!" I squealed.

Marj launched herself at me, giving me a hug. She nearly stumbled, but Ryan steadied both of us.

"Easy there, squirt," he said. "Her first lawsuit will be against you."

Marj let me go, and I was shaking as I looked at the second sheet of paper.

"What's that?" Marj asked.

I scanned it quickly. "It's about the swearing in ceremony next month in Denver."

"That's great." Marj clapped her hands. "We'll all go to support you."

"That's not necessary. I may not even go myself. It's not like it's a requirement."

"Nonsense," Ryan said. "You should definitely be there.

We'll make sure we all get it on our calendars."

I took a deep breath. Thank God.

If only Talon were here...

Marjorie interrupted my worries. "You need to go look for an attorney job," she said.

"I'm kind of working here today, Marj."

"Actually, I was just coming in to tell you guys that there's not much to do around here today," Ryan said. "Marion can handle everything. Why don't you take the day off, go get your dress blues on, and go into town? There's only one firm in town, plus the city attorney's office. You can see them both today, strut your stuff. Maybe one of them will have an opening."

"See?" Marj said. "Everything is working out. Let's go back to the house, get you dressed, and I'll go with you. I'll treat you to lunch. Besides, it'll help get my mind off of..."

Talon.

She didn't have to say his name. We were all thinking it.

This was all hitting me so fast. I wasn't sure I could speak coherently, let alone try to get a job today. I opened my mouth to say as much, but Marion and Ryan ushered us out the door.

"Go on, you two," Marion said. "Ryan and I can hold down the fort here. You get yourself a job, missy."

★ ★ ★ ★

No sooner had we lunched at Enzio's Italian eatery—the eggplant parm, usually my favorite, had been flavorless due to my worry—than Marj was marching me toward the city attorney's office.

"The city attorney's name is Larry Wade. I don't know

him very well, but I believe he and my father did business together. Do you want me go in and introduce you?"

I shook my head. Marj had already done so much for me. Besides, I wanted to do this myself. "No, thanks. I'll go alone. I don't want it to get around town that I'm going around asking for favors because I know the Steels."

"I understand," Marj said. "Now run in there and show them what you've got."

I gathered my courage and walked through the door of the small city building. I was used to the massive city buildings and courthouses in Denver. This was a tiny brick building that apparently housed the mayor, the city attorney, and their staffs, which didn't appear to be very abundant.

A young lady sat behind a wall. I walked up to her. "Excuse me."

"Yes, may I help you?"

I cleared my throat. "I'd like to see the city attorney, please, if he's available?"

I let out a breath. I had done it again, inflecting my voice at the end of a statement and making it sound like a question, as if I were asking for a favor, as if I weren't worthy of seeing the city attorney.

I had to stop doing that.

"Do you have an appointment?"

I shook my head. "No."

"May I tell him what this is regarding?"

I drew in a breath and let it out slowly. "I'm an attorney. I'm looking for a job here in Snow Creek."

"Oh, then you came about the ad."

"The ad?"

"Yes, they're looking for an assistant city attorney. I'm

sure he'll want to see you. We haven't gotten many applicants. There aren't too many attorneys who choose to live in Snow Creek." She let out a quick laugh. "Let me tell him you're here."

My heart soared. They were actually looking for someone. Could my timing have been any better? Things like this never happened to me.

The receptionist turned back to me. "Larry is in the office and will see you. He's very excited that you're here."

I looked around. Surely there couldn't be that much work for a city attorney in Snow Creek. Why was he looking for an assistant? The money would probably not be much, but as long as I could get a small apartment and move off the ranch, it would be enough for me.

"Go ahead and have a seat." The receptionist gestured to the sofa and a few chairs in a sitting area. "He'll be down in a minute."

A few seconds later, a balding blond man of medium height, wearing khakis and a button-down shirt, walked toward me, his hand outstretched. "I'm Larry Wade. Are you the attorney?"

I stood and nodded. "I'm Jade Roberts." I took his hand. "It's great to meet you. I really appreciate you seeing me."

"Not at all. I'm thrilled you're here, to be honest. My workload is getting heavy, but as Carol likely told you, we don't get a lot of attorneys settling here in Snow Creek." He led me back to a small conference room and gestured for me to have a seat. He sat down across from me. "So what brings you to Snow Creek, Ms. Roberts?"

"Please, Jade. Actually, friends. Marjorie Steel is my best friend."

His eyebrows shot up. "The Steels?"

"Yes." Was that a problem?

"Good people, the Steels."

Okay, maybe not a problem. "Yes, they are."

"So how long have you been practicing law?"

Warmth spread over my cheeks. "I haven't, actually. I just got my bar results this morning." I tugged the paper out of the small briefcase I was carrying and slid it across the table to Mr. Wade.

"Well, congratulations, then." He smiled. "And welcome to the club." He took a look at my resume, scanning it. "So you clerked for Davis and Stubbs. Good, very good. You have any experience doing city work?"

I shook my head. "I'm afraid I don't, but I do know my way around a courtroom. I sat with Sherry Malone on several of her medical malpractice cases, did most of her legwork."

"As you can imagine, we don't have a lot of high-profile cases here in Snow Creek." He chuckled. "Anything big gets sent up to the County DA in Grand Junction. But we do have a lot of traffic tickets, curfew violations, drunk driving, assault and batteries, a little domestic violence sometimes. Nothing too exciting, but we make do."

"With all due respect, Mr. Wad—"

"Please, Larry."

I cleared my throat. "Larry. I guess I'm not sure why you need an assistant."

"I don't have an investigator on staff," Larry said. "At the city council meeting last month, I mentioned that I needed one, but the council suggested, and I agreed, that I hire an assistant city attorney instead, someone who could do investigation work but could also take over for me if necessary."

"I see." So I was to be a glorified law clerk. Great.

"Don't get me wrong. This will be a great starting job for you. You'll learn the inside out of municipal law and working for the city. And yes, you'll have to do some investigating, but most attorneys do that anyway."

I nodded, biting my lip. I wanted to ask how much the job paid, but I wasn't sure how to broach the subject.

"If you're interested, Jade, I'd love to have you start tomorrow."

"I'm definitely interested. And starting tomorrow probably wouldn't be any problem. But could I ask about benefits?"

Damn it, why had I asked like that? I had every right to know what kind of benefits and compensation I'd be receiving.

"Of course, of course. The city has an HMO for healthcare, paid in full for the employee. If you have a spouse or dependents, the excess will be taken out of your check."

"Well that's not a problem. I'm not married."

"Good, good. We also cover dental and vision. We're in the state system for retirement, so instead of paying Social Security, you'll pay into the state coffers."

I nodded. *Get to the money.*

"And the job starts at $65,000 a year."

Less than I wanted, but for a small town, probably pretty comparable.

"It may interest you to know that the median salary for city attorneys in the United States is about $90,000. But we're a small town, and you're a first-year attorney. I've been authorized to offer that same salary to any attorney with ten years or less experience, so you're getting a pretty good deal."

I couldn't really argue with his logic, and I wasn't really in a position to either.

"I don't know how serious you are about staying here in Snow Creek, but the only private law firm in town is not currently hiring as far as I know. There's also Newt Davis, a solo practitioner who hung his shingle on the other side of town a few months ago. But I hear he's having a hard time finding enough work just for himself."

Wow. He really wanted me to take this job. I wasn't exactly sure why, but I also didn't care all that much, at least not at this point.

"So are you offering me the job?"

He smiled. "I am."

I stood. "Then I'd be happy to accept. Thank you very much...Larry."

He stood, walked around the table to me, and held out his hand. "Then welcome aboard, Jade. I'm very happy to have you join us here. Let me give you a tour around our office. You can meet the rest of the staff, and then I'll give you your first case."

"That's great. Just let me go tell my friend that that I'll be tied up for a little while, and I'll be right back."

"Not a problem. Come on back in when you're ready."

I quickly told Marj that I got the job and that she could go ahead and go. Then I headed back to the office. Larry handed me a legal-size manila folder.

"Here's your first case, counselor," he said. "You can take it home tonight and then come back first thing in the morning to start work. We begin at nine around here."

"Sounds great to me." I placed the file in my small briefcase.

Larry showed me to a small office, but at least it had a window. It was sparsely decorated with a metal desk, computer table, desktop computer, and a couple filing cabinets and bookshelves.

"It's not much," he said, "but it works."

"Oh, it's fine. I'll be very comfortable here," I said.

He introduced me to Michelle, our secretary, and David, a file clerk. "We have a pretty small staff here. It's a small town, after all."

"I'm sure everything will work out just fine. It looks great to me."

"Excellent. We will see you bright and early tomorrow at nine o'clock."

"I look forward to it." As I began to walk toward the door, I pulled the file out of my briefcase to take a quick look.

And my heart plummeted to my stomach.

People versus Talon Steel.

CHAPTER TWENTY

Talon

The rag stuffed in his mouth made the boy gag. It tasted like mushrooms and dirt and vomit. His eyes were covered and his wrists bound with tight rope behind his back. Only his legs were free, but his exhaustion kept him from kicking his captors. He'd already kicked them and kicked them and kicked them some more...and still he'd ended up here.

"Get on in there, boy," a voice said.

Strong hands forced him down a long flight of stairs, and he nearly stumbled.

"Welcome home, you little bitch," another voice said. "You'll like it here. We'll make sure you're very comfortable." He laughed eerily.

Evil. Like a black snake slithering in the darkness, red eyes gleaming. That's what the voice sounded like. Pure evil.

The boy shivered. When he reached the bottom of the stairs, the men pushed him into a corner.

"You ready, boy?" the first voice said. "You ready?"

Still gagged, the boy couldn't answer. Ready for what?

He soon found out.

★ ★ ★ ★

"Please, Steve. I can't stand the handcuffs." I sweated in

the back of the police car, my hands bound behind me. I tried to draw in a deep breath, and then again. Couldn't get enough air.

"Sorry, Tal. Gotta do it by the book. You know that," Officer Steve Dugan said. "Why'd you beat that kid up, anyway?"

I didn't answer. I knew better than to talk. Besides, the guy was twenty-five years old, at least. He wasn't a kid.

A half hour later, we arrived at the Snow Creek Police Department and Courthouse, next to the City Administration Building. Steve got out of the car and opened the door for me.

"Come on, Tal."

I stayed seated, paralyzed. White noise echoed in my head.

"Commmme...onnnn...Tallll..." Steve's voice was deep and drawn out, like it was in a time warp.

A meaty hand grabbed my arm.

I jerked it away. "No!" I screamed. "I'm not going!"

"Christ, Talon, what's wrong with you?"

Snippets of images formed in my mind. Getting back from Grand Junction...alone in the house...doorbell...Steve... under arrest...handcuffs...

I hadn't resisted until now. Why hadn't I resisted? It was all a blur. A black evil blur. A blur with a phoenix tattoo...

I stood, got out of the car, and landed a roundhouse kick to Steve's chest. Steve went down, and I turned and ran. I ran and I ran and I ran...like I should have run all those years ago—

Until I straightened like a board. My body hit the concrete with a thud, my muscles spasming. Had to piss, had to shit. Couldn't fucking move.

"Help me! For the love of God, help me!"

No one came.

No one ever came.

Dying. I was obviously dying, and no one cared. Minute by minute by minute...

No one...

"All right, come on, Steel." An arm helped me to my feet. "What were you thinking, kicking a police officer?"

"It's okay, Sarge." Steve's voice. "He's just having a hard time. I'm not pressing charges. The Taser was punishment enough."

Taser. I had been tased. I looked down. My pants were dry, thank God. I hadn't made all over myself. Though my hands were still bound, I could move my fingers. I stepped forward. I could walk. My head hurt, like a hammer pounding my temple.

"You doing okay, Tal?" Steve asked. "Ten seconds from a Taser's a lot to take."

Ten seconds? More like an hour. "I don't belong here," was all I said.

"Yeah, you do, when you beat up a guy," a voice, not Steve's, said.

I turned. An older cop—must have been the sarge—had his pistol trained on me. He kept it aimed while Steve walked me into the building. I wasn't afraid of guns. The world contained much worse implements of torture.

White noise again as they filled out paperwork, took my fingerprints and my mug shot.

Again as they watched me undress and put on the orange prison clothes they gave me.

Again as they shoved me into a jail cell.

My hands now free, I huddled in the corner, the white

noise finally silencing. Dark and eerie voices replaced it, hurling me back through time.

★ ★ ★ ★

The boy huddled in the corner of the dark cellar, the pain cutting through him, his blood soaking the meager gray blanket his captors had given him. He had vomited what had been left in his stomach—oatmeal cookies and a slice of watermelon, his afternoon snack.

A sandwich sat next to him. They'd left it when they were done.

He couldn't eat. He'd never eat again.

At least he was no longer tied up. They'd locked him in. Alone.

"Get up. Get up and try to find a way out of here," the voice inside his head commanded.

But his body was weak. Torn up. Used. He couldn't move.

His little brother had gotten away. He'd run like the wind when the boy told him to. Thank God.

"Come on. Get up!" The inner voice again. "You don't deserve this. Get out of here. You can recover. You can go on. Fight, damn it, fight!"

The boy didn't move.

And the voice never spoke again.

CHAPTER TWENTY-ONE

J a d e

I quickly leafed through the folder. Colin had filed charges against Talon for assault and battery. Damn. This had never occurred to me, and it probably should have. One thing was for sure—I couldn't take this case. I had major conflicts of interest on both sides.

I opened my mouth to say as much, but Larry started talking.

"Talon Steel was just arrested today. As far as I know, he's next door in lockup at the police station. I'm sure one of his rich brothers will bail him out any minute now."

I gasped. At least he was safe. Where had he been? He must have been taken in after I left for work this morning. My skin prickled. I couldn't stand the thought of him in a dank little cell.

"Mr. Wade—"

"Larry, please."

I nodded. "Larry, you know I'm staying at the Steel ranch. And I feel I'm under obligation to tell you also that the alleged victim in this case, Colin Morse, is my ex-fiancé. So clearly, you can see how I have a conflict of interest here. I don't think I can work on this case."

"Nonsense. In a small town like this, there's always some

kind of conflict one way or another. We all know each other."

"But I—"

"This isn't anything different than what we see all the time around here. You will take the case. Mr. Morse is staying in a hotel in Grand Junction. His contact information is in the file. I don't know if Mr. Steel has retained counsel, but if you want to go next door to the police station and speak to him, now might be a good time."

I couldn't believe this. Perhaps Larry didn't feel what he was doing was unethical, but I sure did. Yes, I got that in a small town the potential for conflict was pretty great, but I had conflict on both sides of this case.

"Larry, I'm asking you as a professional. Please don't make me take this case."

"Jade, I've known the Steels since they were kids. I have just as much conflict as you do. But someone has to take this case."

"No, you don't have as much conflict as I do. I have conflict on both sides. I was engaged to the alleged victim, for goodness' sake. And I was a witness to the attack."

Larry's face turned red. Had I crossed a line? I did want this job, and I was thrilled that he was giving me the opportunity.

"If you're unable to take the work that I assign you, I will have to find another attorney for the position."

Yup, I'd crossed a line. I knew an ethical violation when I saw one, but I needed the job. I couldn't hang out at the ranch forever. And he did have a point about conflict being rampant in a small town. Plus, this way, I could make sure Talon wasn't too harshly punished. For some reason, turning over control of Talon's fate to Larry or anyone else didn't feel right to me.

I'd make sure Talon got an attorney, and any attorney worth his license would make sure I was removed from this case.

"No, you don't need to find another attorney. I appreciate the opportunity to work here. I will take the case."

"I think that's a wise decision. But I'll advise you, Jade, if you want to keep his job, do not question my ethics again."

I nodded. I had no doubts. From what I learned in legal ethics class, Larry was definitely violating ethics by putting me this case, and consequently, I was as well. But this *was* a small town. What he said made a lot of sense. If we were that stringent about conflicts, we'd have to bring in outside counsel to prosecute every case. That wouldn't be feasible. So I would work the case to the best of my ability. I didn't want Talon to go to jail. I could see that he paid restitution and got community service or something.

I walked out of the building, and Marj met me with some takeout.

"I grabbed us some food. I thought we could eat in the park. Such a beautiful day. Might help us take our minds off Talon."

Talon. Why did I have to be the one to tell her?

"Talon came back," I said.

She smiled. "Really? Where is he? What happened?" Then her happy face fell. "Oh, God."

I swallowed, nodding. "Marj, I can't have dinner with you right now. I have to go next door. I have a case to work on. Talon has been arrested. Colin filed charges against him for assault and battery. That's why the cops were looking for him last night."

Marj clamped her hand to her mouth. "What are we going to do? I'll go with you."

I shook my head. "I need to go alone. This is business."

"But he's my brother."

"That's exactly why I need to go. You're too emotionally involved." What a crock. I was just as emotionally involved, if not more so. "Besides, it's my job."

"But you're working for the city attorney. That means..."

I nodded. "Yes, that means I'm working against Talon. But don't worry. I'm going to take care of this so that he's in as little trouble as possible. I promise you."

"I need to walk over to the firm and get an attorney for him," Marj said.

I nodded again. "That's a good idea. Hurry. It's almost five. They might be closing soon. I'll let him know another attorney is on the way."

Marj ran off, still carrying our food, while I plodded over to the police station.

Fifteen minutes later, I was sitting in a witness room across the table from Talon. Even in orange, the man was a god. He made prison garb look like Armani.

He didn't speak, clearly on edge. Tense. It was written all over his face, from his pursed lips and clenched jaw to his wrinkled forehead.

I cleared my throat softly. "Talon, I want you to know that you can have an attorney present during this meeting."

"You mean you're not my attorney?"

I shook my head. How I wished I were. "No, I'm the assistant city attorney. Larry Wade just hired me and gave me this case."

Talon rolled his eyes. "Oh, for the love of God..." He glared at me, his eyes black and angry.

"You're not thinking anything I haven't already thought

myself. But this will be all right. I can make sure everything turns out okay. The first thing we need to do is get you an attorney."

"Jade, you have to get me out of here. I don't want an attorney."

"If you want to get out of here, you need one. Marj is heading over to the firm right now to find one for you."

"Those jokers? I wouldn't pay one of them to represent me."

"Talon—"

"I plead guilty, damn it. I fucking plead guilty. Send me off to prison."

My brain was rattled for a moment. Had I heard him right? "Talon, I'm going to consider this all off the record. You don't know what you're saying."

"You are a representative of the city of Snow Creek and consequently the state of Colorado. I am pleading guilty to you, an officer of the court. Take my plea, and send me up the river."

What was with him? Three seconds ago, he wanted me to get him out of there. "As I said," I continued through clenched teeth, "this is all off the record. This conversation is not taking place. Any guilty plea you want to enter with me is not going to get entered. I will not be taking any pleas from you, only from your attorney."

He leaned back in his chair and sighed. "Suit yourself."

"Now, I can help you. Colin is a reasonable man. I'm sure he will agree to drop the charges if you pay him restitution."

"I'm not paying that asshole off."

"Talon, you beat the crap out of him. He might have medical bills. You owe him that much."

Talon said nothing, just crossed his arms and glared at me.

"Be reasonable."

"Be reasonable? You want me to be reasonable? I had a cop come to the house this morning, took me away from my home in fucking handcuffs, like a common criminal. They locked me up, Jade. They locked me up in a cell. You have no idea..."

"Have no idea about what? What did you expect? When you beat the hell out of someone, that person might decide to file charges. You *are* a criminal, Talon. But this is fixable, if you'll just let me help you."

He closed his eyes. Dark circles rimmed them, his laugh wrinkles more apparent than usual. He obviously hadn't slept last night. Where had he been? I opened my mouth to ask, but he spoke.

"Maybe I don't want to fix it. Maybe I'm just too fucking tired to fix it."

"Look, even if you do plead guilty, you probably won't go to jail for a simple battery. Colin is fine. There are no lasting issues. You might get a fine, or restitution, maybe some community service and probation. You probably won't do any jail time."

"I happen to know that misdemeanor assault in Colorado carries a potential of three years jail time." He raised his eyebrows at me.

"I see you're familiar with the criminal code in Colorado."

"I do a lot of reading," he said. "I never sleep, remember?"

I sighed. What was I going to do with him? He seemed determined to destroy himself. Well, not on my watch.

A knock sounded on the door, and I turned.

A uniformed officer led a man in. "Mr. Steel, your attorney is here," the officer said.

I stood and held out my hand. "I'm Jade Roberts with the city attorney's office."

"Peter O'Keefe." The man took my hand. "Do you mind if I talk to my client alone?"

I shook my head. "Not at all."

Talon stood. "I mind. She stays."

"Talon, that's not a good idea. Mr. O'Keefe is here to help you." I turned to O'Keefe. "Maybe you can talk some sense into him."

"Mr. Steel, your sister explained the circumstances to me and also explained Ms. Roberts's involvement. I'm going to try to have her removed from the case due to conflict of interest."

"Just so you know," I said, "I tried to get out of this case myself. Larry wouldn't let me."

O'Keefe nodded. "Larry has a tendency to bend ethics whenever he can."

I didn't doubt it. "You can get me off this case if you want to, but I'm willing to strike a pretty good deal." I put my hand on the doorknob. "Let me know when you're ready to talk."

"Damn it!"

I turned and faced Talon after his outburst.

"Haven't I made myself clear? I said she stays."

O'Keefe let out a heavy sigh. "Fine. But if I tell you to shut up, you better damn well shut up. Maybe we can get this settled today."

"It's already settled. I plead guilty. I want to go to jail."

I shook my head. "Talon, please. There's no reason for you to go to jail. Colin is not even that injured."

"I'm afraid I don't quite understand what you're saying,

Mr. Steel," O'Keefe said. "The city attorney here is clearly willing to work with us. Why are you so against it?"

"I committed a crime. Criminals belong in jail."

"Technically this is a misdemeanor, not crime," I said.

"Ms. Roberts is correct. You haven't been accused of a crime. You haven't even been charged with anything. You've only been arrested. Your sister is arranging for bail right now. You should be out of here within a couple of hours."

"Nope, I think I'm staying."

I threw my hands in the air. "I'll leave you two to battle this out." I turned to O'Keefe. "Afraid I don't have a business card yet. I just started work today." I hastily scribbled my cell phone number on a Post-it. "You can reach me here."

"Thank you. I'll be in touch," he said.

"I told you, she stays!"

I left anyway.

CHAPTER TWENTY-TWO

Talon

Peter O'Keefe was an idiot. What had Marj been thinking, sending him? He sat across from me, drenching me with saliva every time he spoke. He asked me a bunch of questions about that asshole Colin, and I answered them truthfully.

"So I'm pretty sure we can get this down to reckless endangerment, maybe get some community service. Shouldn't be a big deal."

"Jade says she thought she could get the guy to drop the charges."

"We can't count on that. But it would be great if she could."

"Whatever. I don't care if I stay here. I really don't." Fucking lie that was. I couldn't bear the thought of being locked up. My nerves were a jumble of jelly. But I would take care of it and I would do it if it meant no one else would be destroyed because of me. I belonged somewhere where I couldn't hurt anyone. Even if the walls caved in on me. I could do it. I'd lived through it before.

"Mr. Steel, you're talking nonsense. Once you get out of here, you'll see that." O'Keefe took a card out of his wallet and slid it across the table to me. "I'm going to ignore your guilty plea because you aren't in a position to make a plea at this time. The charges haven't even officially been filed."

"I don't care."

"Well, start caring. I'll be in touch."

O'Keefe stood, but before he could open the door, it opened from the other side and a uniformed officer entered.

"Steel," he said, "your bail's been posted. You're free to go."

Great. Free to go. Free as the birds in the sky. Free to enjoy life.

What a fucking crock. I would never be free.

I followed the officer to a locker room.

He handed me a paper bag. "Here are your personals. Go ahead and get changed. I'll meet you up front, and we'll process you on out of here."

I took the bag without saying a word. What was there to say? Thank you? He didn't stay to watch me dress this time. I threw the bag down on the bench and sat, the white concrete walls beating in time with my heart.

The walls advanced again...

Won't go there. Can't go there.

But the monstrous walls lurched forward. The floor tilted, and I slid off the bench, my skin clammy, my heart thundering. I stared at the stark ceiling, the fluorescent lights blinding me. My bowels churned, and bile inched up my throat.

Needed to breathe. Couldn't...fucking...breathe...

Help! The words stuck in my throat. I climbed back to the bench, back to safety. *Breathe, Talon. Breathe. If you lose consciousness again, they'll never leave you alone.*

★ ★ ★ ★

The boy's voice had grown hoarse from screaming. His fingernails were filed down and his fingertips scabbed over from clawing at the concrete walls.

After a while, he no longer screamed, and eventually his voice repaired itself and his fingers healed. He sat, his arms around his legs, his chin resting in the indent formed by his two knees.

He had gotten used to his circumstances. A bucket sat in the corner of the room where he took care of his needs. His captors only changed it when they came for him. The days grew together. Had they been there yesterday? Or had it been longer? Sometimes he got three meals a day. Sometimes he got nothing. His stomach had long ago stopped growling for food. Sometimes they brought him water. More often they taunted him with the full icy glass.

The nights were the worst. The concrete floor was often chilly, even though it was summer. Was it still summer? The days had rolled together. How long had he been here? At first, he'd kept track of each time they came to him, but he stopped doing that. He didn't want to think about those times.

The door to the small room opened, and one of them came down the stairs, wearing a mask, of course. They always wore masks.

He didn't speak to the boy, just set out a tray of food. The boy didn't dare move until the man had ascended and closed and locked the door. Then he scrambled to the tray and gobbled up every bit of tasteless food. Maybe it was poisoned.

★ ★ ★ ★

I stood abruptly when the officer walked back in. The walls flew back to their normal places.

"Ready, Mr. Steel?"

I nodded. I was okay. Everything was okay. Needed to get home. Needed to see Jade. She'd make it all right.

Marjorie and Jade sat in the waiting area. Marj ran up to me and flew into my arms.

"Talon. I was so worried. Are you okay?"

I couldn't tell her I'd just had a panic attack. "I'm fine."

Jade said nothing, but she stood, her blue-gray eyes piercing into me like two spears.

"Let's get you home," Marj said.

Home. Where was home, anyway? I hadn't felt like I'd been home for twenty-five years. We walked out together. Marj's car was parked nearby on the street. Jade still hadn't said anything.

"Are you hungry?" Marj asked. "We can stop and get something. Jade and I already ate."

I shook my head. No, I wasn't hungry. I was rarely hungry. I ate for sustenance. Fuck. I'd missed Marj's steak dinner last night. I'd have to apologize. God... I hated hurting my sister. Hated hurting my brothers.

"I'm so sorry all this happened, Talon." Marj's eyes misted up.

I could stand anything but her tears. So many tears had been shed over me during my life. I was damned sick of it.

After that, Marj stopped talking, and we were all silent during the half-hour ride out to the ranch. I sat in the front seat next to Marj, and Jade sat in the back. I couldn't see her, but her presence surrounded me, enveloped me, permeated me. She was inside me, and I was being pulled in different directions. One part of me wanted her more than anything, but the other part pushed her away. I couldn't bear the thought of hurting her, and if she stayed near me, she would get hurt. I was a mess—a mess she, or anyone else, shouldn't have to deal with.

We pulled into the ranch, and Jade went into her room without another word. I watched her walk down the hallway. Only she could make a navy-blue conservative suit look hotter than hell. I wanted to rip that tweed off of her and fuck her good right there.

But that would have to wait. Marj was coddling me, fawning all over me. Guilt raced through me. I'd missed her dinner, but she didn't mention it. Instead, she made me a pot of tea and told me to go to my room and rest. Rest was the last thing I needed. Yes, I was perpetually tired, but right now, my body was agitated. I needed to keep moving, needed to work off some steam. Needed to release...

And I knew just where I could find one. How to get past Marj was the problem.

After I had waited a while, I sneaked out of my bedroom and down the hallway toward Jade's room. I knocked lightly on the door.

"Come in."

She had changed out of her stuffy suit, and she sat on her bed in a pair of denim cutoffs and a hot-pink tank top. My cock reacted at the sight. On the bed was a manila folder, and several documents were splayed out.

She looked up at me. "Hey, I was just looking over your case file."

"So you're really going to prosecute me, huh?"

She shook her head. "Not if I can help it. But I need you to cooperate."

"You think you can get pretty boy to drop the charges?"

"I will try. Even if he doesn't, you have a great chance to get a good plea bargain. But honestly, we're putting the cart before the horse. Formal charges haven't even come in yet."

"Well, you're the city attorney. You file the charges, right?"

She shook her head. "Larry does that, I'm afraid. But I will certainly recommend to him that we go lenient on this."

"Don't hold your breath," I said. "The good folks of Snow Creek like to stick it to the Steels."

She arched her eyebrows. "Why would you say that?"

I wasn't sure why I had said that, to be truthful. As far as I knew, no one had anything against us in town. "I don't know. Because we're the rich ranchers. We own half the damn town."

She nodded. "I see." She paused a moment. "So where were you last night, anyway? Marj worked her butt off cooking that great dinner for all of us. She was really hurt when you didn't show up."

I gulped. What could I say? Turned out I didn't need to say anything, because Jade kept talking.

"And then that cop comes around looking for you, saying he has an arrest warrant. Do you have any idea what you put all of us through? I was worried sick. But never mind me. What about Marj and your brothers? None of us got any sleep last night."

I let out a guffaw. "Join the fucking club."

"No way. Don't turn this around. I get that you have trouble sleeping, and I'm sorry. But that doesn't negate what you did last night. And you have sleeping pills now. Why aren't you taking them?"

I didn't know what to say. She kept talking.

"You owe your sister an apology. And for God's sake, where were you last night? People here care about you, you know. You can't just take off like that when your sister is expecting you for dinner, and then have some cop come along—"

"Hey, I didn't know Steve was coming around. It's not my fault that jerk ex of yours had me arrested."

"Not your fault? Do you listen to the words that come out of your mouth, Talon?" She shook her head.

I looked down. I don't know why I'd said it wasn't my fault. But he'd been kissing her, touching her... "I told you I'd plead guilty."

"And back to that again." Jade sighed. "You really are determined to fuck up your life, aren't you?"

I didn't have to fuck up my life. It was already fucked up beyond recognition. "Fine. What should I do? Will he drop the charges?"

She looked back down at the files on her bed, shaking her head again. "All right, we'll talk about your case, since whenever something personal comes up, you clam up." She cleared her throat. "Honestly, I don't think you have a lot to worry about. I tried calling Colin and left a voice mail. When he calls back, I'll get this taken care of. After all, he owes me a lot more than this."

"Why does he owe you anything?" The thought of him owing her made my teeth rattle.

"Hello? He left me at the altar and humiliated me beyond repair. He did come back here to apologize and try to make things right, though. I'll just tell him that he can make things right by dropping the charges."

"You don't have to use your favors on me."

Jade gathered the papers together and stuck them back in the file, slid the file into a slim briefcase, and set it by the side of her bed. Then she looked up at me, her eyes slightly misty. "Why are you resisting my help? I'm here and willing to help. I care about you."

Pinpricks covered my body. "No, I don't want you to care about me."

She scooted to the edge of her bed and stood, facing me. "I don't understand you, Talon. We've had some amazing times together, and don't tell me you haven't felt the connection. I know you have."

I said nothing. I couldn't deny it. I felt the connection, and it scared the hell out of me. As much as I wanted to disconnect from it, I couldn't stay away from her.

"Look, you made it perfectly clear where you stood when this first started. You're not going to fall in love with me. Fine, I can deal with that. But for God's sake, I can help you here. Please, let me." Her red lips trembled.

All thought fled from my head. I grabbed her, pulled her to me, and kissed her.

As usual, she responded right away, opening, sliding her silky tongue against mine. She tasted of strawberries and sweetness, and I was hungry, hungry for the flavor that was her.

She wrapped her arms around my neck and pressed her breasts into me. When I needed to take a breath, I broke the kiss. "My God, what have you done to me?" I said into her neck.

She didn't reply. She just pressed tiny kisses to the top of my chest that was exposed. Her touch, I hungered for it.

Something about her... Being with her...

I almost felt whole.

I pushed her slightly away. "Take off your clothes," I commanded.

I turned and walked back to her door, locking it. When I returned, she stood before me, naked and inviting. So beautiful. I trailed a finger down her cheek to her chin, down her neck, over the plump swell of her breasts, and flicked a nipple. She moaned and jerked.

"Now undress me," I said.

She pushed me down until I was sitting on the bed, and then she knelt before me, pulling off my boots and socks. She slid up, unbuckled my belt, and unzipped my jeans.

My cock was straining. I wanted her so much. I ached to have her beneath me, obeying me.

She stood and pulled me into a standing position. She brushed my boxers and jeans over my legs, and I stepped out of them. Then she worked at my shirt, unbuttoning it and pushing it off my shoulders until I was as naked as she was.

"Lie down on the bed," I said, "facedown."

She gazed at me with those steely blue eyes and then did as I bid. I could take her now, have her any way I wanted her. She would let me. She gave me that power. She trusted me. Unworthy as I was, she trusted me.

I grabbed my jeans off the floor and pulled the blue bandanna out of my pocket. Quickly I bound her hands together behind her back.

She tensed but said nothing.

"Okay?" I asked.

She moved her head in what I thought was a nod, but because her head was on the bed, I wasn't quite sure.

"You have to answer me. Verbally."

"Okay," she said.

I trailed my finger over the globes of her beautiful ass and then between the crease. She shuddered.

"Close your eyes," I said.

She complied.

"I'm going to do what I want to do to you, blue eyes," I said. "If you want me to stop, you tell me to stop. Okay?"

Again, she attempted a nod.

"Verbally," I said.

"Okay," she said, her voice shaking a bit.

Was she truly ready for this? I didn't know, but she would stop me if she needed to.

Starting at her toes, I grazed my fingers all the way up her smooth legs to her ass, up her back to her shoulders. No millimeter of skin went untouched by me. When I trailed back down and touched her between her legs, she was dripping wet. Oh, God. No woman had ever responded to me quite like Jade did.

"You're wet, baby. You're so wet for me."

She attempted her nod again.

"I'm going to slide my cock into you, baby," I said. "Keep your legs together like that, and I'm going to slide right into that sweet cunt. It's going to be so tight, and it's going to feel so good."

I gave her a gentle slap on the ass. She jerked but didn't say anything. I had told her to tell me to stop if she needed me to, so I continued. I slapped her ass again, a little harder this time. It turned a luscious shade of pink. Then I leaned down and spread kisses over her pink cheeks to soothe the sting.

"You like that, baby? You like it when I slap your little

ass?"

"Y-Yes," she stammered.

I would go easy this time. As much as I wanted to smack her cute little butt until it was bright red, I couldn't. She would need to understand me better before we could go there. And she would never understand me fully. I couldn't let that happen.

I climbed on top of her and rubbed my cock between her ass cheeks. I dipped the head into her slit and then slid it between her ass cheeks again, lubricating with her wetness.

"Keep your legs together, baby," I said again. "I'm going to slide into that tight heat just like this." I knelt, my knees on either side of her thighs. I notched my cock at the entrance to her pussy, and slowly, achingly slowly, I slid into that wet paradise.

She let out the softest, sweetest sigh as I entered her.

That sound was better than the sweetest music I'd ever heard, better than the soft patter of rain on the roof, better than a baby's laugh. And with that sigh, something opened inside me. A tiny bit of my heart that had been hard as stone for so long broke free.

A tear slid out of the corner of my eye. I didn't know why. I had no idea where it came from. But something inside me broke, if only for that single moment. I pulled out slowly and slid back in, letting her warm suction surround me, take me, make everything okay.

Was this the person I had been looking for? Was this the person who could take all the bad away? Did such a person even exist? She lay still, not resisting, letting me take what I needed from her.

And even though she knew nothing about my past, what I

had been through, something inside me, something on a deep carnal level, knew that she understood.

I slid back into her one more time and let my orgasm take me. More tears fell down my cheeks as I moaned and released.

I poured everything inside me into that release, into her. She lay beneath me, moaning into the comforter, her hips bucking, her hands tied behind her back. Taking me, trusting me, and giving me so much in return.

If only I were worthy.

CHAPTER TWENTY-THREE

Jade

He convulsed into me, and although I hadn't had an orgasm, something about this joining of our bodies was more special and sweet than any before.

When his cock stopped pulsing, he withdrew. He released my hands, and I turned to face him. His dark eyes were sunken and wet, and moist trails lined his face where tears had fallen.

I cupped his cheek, thumbing the remainder of a tear away. I longed to ask him what was wrong, why he was crying, but I knew he would not respond. So I said nothing, and after cupping his cheeks for a few more seconds, I crawled into his arms.

He held on to me, and I burrowed my face into his chest. I inhaled the salty cinnamon masculine aroma. I loved his scent. I loved how I smelled like him for hours after we'd been together. I sometimes hesitated to shower so I could keep the scent on me longer.

He didn't say anything, didn't offer any explanation as to why he had been crying. I didn't ask for one. I just held him, and I let him hold me.

And we came a little bit closer that night.

★ ★ ★ ★

"If you just drop the charges, I can get him to pay restitution. I'm almost sure of it."

"Why should I? The jerk beat the shit out of me. If you're the new city attorney, aren't you supposed to be on my side?"

I pushed my chair back and sighed into the cell phone. "I'm on the side of the city, Colin. Taking this to trial would be a waste of the city's resources. You told me yourself that you're okay. That you didn't have any lasting effects from the incident."

"He damn near broke my nose."

"But he didn't." I was surprised he hadn't. Colin's nose had been bleeding pretty badly.

"He could've broken my ribs the way he was kicking me."

"And again, he didn't."

"Only because I knew how to protect myself by getting in the right position."

"We can all be thankful that you knew how to protect yourself." I let out another sigh. "Don't you need to get back to Denver? You really want to hang around here to testify?"

"I can fly out here anytime to testify. Has your office filed charges yet?"

"Yes, my boss did this morning. But, Colin, this is a misdemeanor assault. He didn't use a weapon, and you didn't sustain any lasting injuries."

"I'm not dropping the charges." Colin clicked the phone off.

Now what? I'd have to talk to Talon's attorney and come up with a plea bargain. Would Larry object? I smiled to myself. He couldn't possibly. He had given me this case. If he objected,

I could easily go to the judge and tell him that Larry had given me in this case in spite of all the conflicts. It was my case. I would handle it as I saw fit.

I perused the Colorado criminal statutes. Reckless endangerment carried a maximum sentence of six months in prison and a maximum fine of five hundred dollars. I could probably get Talon to plead down to that and get him a fine instead of prison time. God knew he had the money.

I laughed out loud. I was the prosecution, for God's sake. The defense should be pleading down the case. Where was O'Keefe? He should be taking care of this.

I pulled his business card out of my briefcase and punched in his number.

"Peter O'Keefe please."

"May I ask who is calling?"

"Jade Roberts from the city attorney's office."

A few minutes later, "Peter O'Keefe here."

"Mr. O'Keefe, hi, this is Jade Roberts at the city attorney's office. I'm calling about Talon Steel."

"Yes, what can I help you with?"

"I've been going over the file, and I don't think there's any reason to take this to trial. The people are willing to plead down to reckless endangerment and a five hundred dollar fine plus restitution to the alleged victim."

"That's a generous offer, Ms. Roberts. I think I can probably sell that to my client."

"Great. Let me know." *And please do sell it*, I added myself.

Now, to convince Talon. I checked my watch. It was almost five. Larry had left an hour ago to take his grandkids for dinner and ice cream. I'd put in a full day, so I gathered my things. I said a quick good-bye to Michelle and left.

When I walked out of the building, there stood Talon.

My breath caught. I would never grow tired of looking at him. He wore a black cotton shirt, short-sleeved, his forearms tanned and sinewy. His denim jeans hugged his hips and thighs. He was rugged through and through, all the way down to his black cowboy boots. A black felt Stetson sat on his head, and I thought I might swoon. He looked every bit the cowboy today, and I wanted to launch myself into his arms.

"What are you doing here?" I asked.

"I came to plead guilty."

I let out a sigh. "Haven't we been through this?"

"I changed my mind. I want to plead guilty to a lesser offense. I...don't want to be locked up."

"Well then, you're in luck. I just talked to your attorney on the phone. I'm offering a plea of guilty to reckless endangerment and a five hundred dollar fine, plus any restitution Colin demands."

"Your boss will go for that?"

"My boss has no choice. He gave this case to me even when I told him I shouldn't take it."

"Why shouldn't you have taken it?"

"I have a major conflict of interest. The alleged victim is my ex-fiancé, and the defendant—that's you—well, you're my best friend's brother, and you and I are..."

His lips trembled a bit. Only a bit, but I noticed. He looked down and mumbled something I didn't understand.

"What? I can't hear you."

He looked up, his dark eyes burning into me. "Thank you," he said softly.

Those two words permeated my soul and lifted me high. Instinctively, I knew saying them had been difficult for him.

"You don't have to thank me, Talon. I'm doing my job."

"Blue eyes, your job is to prosecute me, not get me off."

"Actually, you're wrong. Colin is not my client. The city is. My job is to do what's in the best interest of the city of Snow Creek. And quite frankly, it's my professional opinion the interests of the city are best served if we don't spend the taxpayers' money to prosecute this case."

"What if you're wrong? What if I should be prosecuted? What if I beat the shit out of someone else?"

"You won't."

"How do you know that?"

"Because, Talon, I won't let you."

To my surprise, he nodded. "What do I do now?"

"Your attorney will call you and give you the details. There will be a hearing sometime soon, and we will present the plea to the judge."

"All right." He dug his hands into his pockets and looked down again. "For what it's worth, Jade, I'm...sorry."

I smiled. More difficult words from him. "Sorry for what? For beating Colin?"

He let out a chuckle. "Only for taking it as far as I did. The jerk deserved a good ass whooping for what he did to you."

"I can't say I disagree with you there. And Talon, I'm sorry too. I'm sorry that Colin put you in a position to do what you did. He should never have come here. I didn't want him to. It's over between us. I hope you understand that."

He didn't respond. Not that I thought he would.

"Well," I said, "I guess I'll get back to the ranch."

"I thought maybe..."

"What?"

"You might like to have dinner or something?"

"Are you asking me out?"

"Well...you're here, and I'm here, and it's almost dinner time..."

I couldn't help a laugh. He was something else. "Talon, I would love to have dinner with you. Where do you want to go?"

"Follow me." And then he smiled.

My heart nearly burst right there. The man had a beautiful smile. I just wished I could see it more often.

We walked a couple of blocks to the greenbelt area. A path of bricks led about a quarter mile into the park under a big shaded oak tree. A red-and-white checkered cloth had been set out along with a picnic basket and a bottle of wine. My breath caught, and I silently thanked God that I had worn pants instead of a skirt to work this morning.

"Did you do all this?" I asked.

"Well, no. Felicia made the food. I just brought it here and set it out."

Tears emerged from my eyes. Talon Steel was a man of many facets, and I liked almost every single one of them.

To keep him from further embarrassment, I walked forward. "What's for dinner?"

"Good ol' country food. Felicia's famous fried chicken, potato salad, and fresh fruit salad."

I laughed. "No Steel beef?"

"Steaks don't make for an easy picnic, unless we grill them here, but grills aren't allowed in the city park."

Talon opened the basket and pulled out a corkscrew. He deftly opened the bottle of red wine and poured two glasses, handing one to me. He looked at me for a moment, and I almost thought he was going to propose a toast of some sort, but he didn't. He simply took a sip, so I followed suit.

Then he opened the basket and pulled out a couple of plates.

"Here, let me help you." I pulled out the container of fried chicken and opened it. "I like thighs. What do you like?"

"Thighs? Really? You mean you're not a chicken breast girl? The leaner cut?"

"Do I look like I try to be supermodel thin? I may be Brooke Bailey's daughter, but my figure comes from my father's side. Besides, once it's battered and fried, the leaner cuts really don't matter."

He laughed. A happy laugh. "I actually do like the breast, but not because I'm worried about my weight."

I scanned his beautifully sculpted body. Nope, he sure didn't need to worry about his weight. I placed a breast on his plate and a thigh on mine. He scooped some potato salad and fruit on my plate. I smiled and thanked him. We began eating, and we didn't talk much, but oddly, the silence didn't seem awkward. I laughed when he dropped a piece of potato salad on his shirt. I wiped it up with my napkin. For a few fleeting moments, we were almost like a couple, and I wanted to enjoy it. Appreciate it.

My feelings for Talon had grown deep. I wasn't ready to say I loved him, and I knew he didn't love me, but some of the emotion I was feeling went beyond anything I'd ever felt with Colin, someone I'd supposedly been in love with. Something infected Talon, and I wished I knew what it was so I could help him. Since I couldn't, I wanted to just enjoy this simple meal with him. Maybe he was enjoying it too, and maybe we'd have another one sometime.

"Do you want another piece of chicken?" I asked when I

saw he had finished his breast.

He nodded. "Yeah, let me try the other thigh, unless you want it."

I shook my head. "Nope, it's yours. If I want more, I can have a drumstick. I'm pretty easy to please." I cursed myself the moment after the words left my lips. I didn't need him to take that the wrong way.

But he went right on eating, sipping his wine, spearing a strawberry or a chunk of pineapple with his fork. He seemed... comfortable, and I wasn't sure I'd ever seen him comfortable.

I finished my thigh and decided I didn't need a drumstick after all. I was getting full. "Felicia is a great cook. I've really enjoyed my meals since I've been here."

"She's the best."

"Did you know Marj would like to go to culinary school?"

He shook his head. "Really? She is a good little cook, that's for sure."

"I'm surprised she doesn't cook more often."

"She's not used to working hard. She's so much younger than the rest of us, and she was the baby and very spoiled. So she just lets Felicia do most of it."

I nodded. I loved Marjorie dearly, but she *was* a bit spoiled. Four years of living with her as a roommate in college had taught me that. "Maybe I can get her to cook more often. I'll tell her how much I enjoy her cooking. In fact, why don't you, Jonah, and Ryan tell her, too? It might mean more coming from her brothers."

"Jade..."

I looked up. His eyes had darkened. I had the feeling we were done talking about Marj's cooking.

"Yeah?"

"I don't want to..."

"What?"

"I don't want to hurt you."

I cupped his cheek. "Do I look hurt to you?"

"You're good at that, aren't you?"

"Good at what?"

He let out a tiny laugh. "At asking a question instead of making a comment. You'll make a good attorney."

"I hope so. And Talon, you haven't hurt me."

"I don't understand what it is about you. Right now, I'm hard as a rock just sitting near you. Something in you calls to me, and I'm powerless to resist it."

Even in the warm sun summer evening, my cheeks heated further. I was wet for him too. "If you've noticed, I haven't been resisting you either."

"I guess that's what I mean. Maybe you should be resisting it."

"Why? If we're both enjoying ourselves, why not do it?"

"Because, like I said, I don't want to hurt you."

"Do I look hurt?"

He huffed. "Would you stop doing that please?"

"You won't hurt me. I won't let you. If I think I'm going to get hurt, I'll end this..." This what? I had no idea how to finish that statement. "This..." I said again. "What the hell is this thing between us, anyway?"

CHAPTER TWENTY-FOUR

Talon

My craving.

This thing between us was my craving. How could I tell her that she had become as necessary to me as food and water? That she was my sustenance? That I'd gladly crawl through the depths of hell just to have her for a few seconds each day? That when I wasn't with her, half of me was missing? My skin rippled. This had gone beyond craving. She was becoming my obsession.

I didn't understand it myself. How could I explain it to her?

So I took the easy way out.

"I don't know," I said.

"I don't know either." She sighed. "You said you didn't want a relationship, and you said you would never love me. I'm not asking for your love, Talon. I just got out of a seven-year relationship, and I care too much about you to make you a rebound guy. So why not just let it be what it is? Why not just enjoy each other while it lasts?"

I nodded. What she said made a lot of sense. But what if it didn't last? What if she left someday? She had almost left a couple days ago. To not be able to see her smile, her steely gaze, to hear her sweet voice... I closed my eyes. I couldn't bear it.

I had told her I couldn't love her. I had never loved anyone, other than Marj, since before I was ten years old. I loved my brothers, and I had loved my mother and father. I loved them all enough not to torture them, which is why I had told Jonah and Ryan I would leave.

If Jade stayed, I would only cause her pain, like I caused my siblings pain. An invisible knife sliced through my gut. She was an angel, and she deserved happiness, not a torturous existence because of me.

I would have to leave her eventually. I knew this truth in my heart. But for now, perhaps it was okay to do as she said—to enjoy it while it lasted. I took a sip of my wine and let the smooth acidity slide down my throat and warm me. Ryan's Rhône blend, my personal favorite, though my drink of choice was a nice smooth whiskey, neat.

She chewed on her beautiful full lower lip, her hair as sexy as could be even though it was wrapped up into a bun on top of her head. She wore black stretch pants and a white V-neck pullover shirt. Her cleavage was evident.

What if I could never love her? Someone else could, and she would leave me.

Suddenly my skin tightened, and my breathing quickened. No. She couldn't leave me. I gulped down the rest of my wine and grabbed her arm.

"What?" she said, her eyebrows arched.

"I want you. Now."

"We're in a public place."

"I don't care." And I didn't. I was ready to rip our clothes off and take her up against the oak tree, forcefully, marking her, making her mine and only mine.

I moved the plate from her lap and stood, pulling her with

me. I clamped my lips down on hers and kissed her ferociously. My cock strained against my jeans, and I ground into her.

She ripped her mouth away. "Talon, stop,"

But I couldn't stop. I was going to have her and have her now.

I cupped her breast and squeezed it, finding her nipple through the flimsy fabric of her bra and pinching it.

She gasped. "Talon, please!"

I didn't care who saw us. I didn't care who was witness to my taking. I was going to have her. My body cried out for hers.

"Get hold of yourself," she insisted.

I pinched her nipple again, and again she gasped.

And she pulled away from me. "What the hell do you think you're doing?" she said through clenched teeth. "You need to stop this. Now. What we do in the privacy of the bedroom is one thing, but you absolutely cannot do this to me in public in broad daylight. I don't care what has gone on between us before. I won't stand for this."

Her skin was bright pink with her anger. Her nostrils flared, and her silvery eyes bored into mine, her lips red and puffy from our raging kisses. I only wanted her more.

I grabbed her to me again and took her lips, gliding my tongue into her mouth.

Instead of squeezing her nipple, I slid my hand down and cupped her mound through her stretch pants.

She pushed me away again. "Goddamnit. Didn't you hear me?" She raised her hand and slapped me across the cheek.

I didn't even feel the sting. She fidgeted with her pants and shirt. I reached for her again, but she stumbled backward, nearly losing her footing.

"I'm going home," she said. "Don't bother coming

anywhere near me tonight." She picked up her briefcase and stomped off.

My whole body was on fire. Her ass swayed slightly as she walked. I itched to run after her, but…damn! I was nursing a raging hard-on. I'd barely be able to walk, let alone run. I could drive into Grand Junction and call any of about a dozen women who would be happy to have me warming their bed. But that wouldn't work. I had tried it before. My body cried out for Jade and only Jade.

I needed a fucking drink.

When I had cooled down a bit, I walked away, leaving the picnic basket and cloth sitting on the lawn. After a couple of blocks, I entered Murphy's bar.

"Hey, Steel," Sean Murphy, the owner said. "Long time no see. What can I get you?"

I took a seat at the bar. "Peach Street, neat."

"You boys do have taste," Sean said. He poured my drink and set it in front of me. Then he went about his business.

I liked Sean. He wasn't the kind of bartender who tried to get a guy talking. He poured a drink and then made himself scarce.

I wanted to be alone. I took a sip of the smooth whiskey, letting it float over my tongue for a moment before I swallowed, its spicy warmth coating my throat. What the hell? I finished the rest like a shot and set my glass back on the bar. "Another, Sean."

"You got it." Sean took my glass and filled it again. "How's everything at the ranch?"

"The same."

"Jonah was in here the other night. We chatted a little bit."

I nodded. Sean set down my glass with a smile and then turned to another patron.

I downed the second and ordered another. Luckily, I hadn't drunk much wine with dinner. My mind churned. What was I going to do about Jade? This incessant need was eating me alive, destroying me, consuming me. She was like a drug I couldn't live without. Was it time to go cold turkey? If she were truly like a drug, would I suffer withdrawal symptoms?

I let out a chuckle. Of course I would. I suffered withdrawal every time I was away from her. I would have her, and then within seconds of completing, I would crave her again. What could I do? Maybe I should leave. I shouldn't have let Joe and Ryan talk me into staying.

I couldn't have a life with Jade. I didn't even want a life with Jade. Did I? This desire, this all-consuming passion... was it indicative of something else? Did I want more than just sex? Was I feeling something I had never felt before?

I finished the third drink and plunked the glass back on the counter. No. I wasn't feeling anything like that. I couldn't allow myself to feel anything like that. It would only lead to more heartbreak. Jade deserved better than to be saddled with my baggage.

She deserved the best.

I stood, a little buzzed but not drunk. Good thing, because I had to drive home. I would go home, I would find Jade, and I would apologize.

And then I would tell her that whatever this thing between us was, it was over.

I just hoped the withdrawal wouldn't be too painful.

CHAPTER TWENTY-FIVE

Jade

I was in the shower when he came barreling in without even knocking. I screeched, grabbing the shower door and nearly falling. He caught me, his hands steady, though the aroma of alcohol hung on his breath. He handed me a towel.

"Dry off. We need to talk." He left the bathroom, shutting the door behind him.

Damn right we needed to talk. He owed me a big apology. And if he thought I was going to fall right into bed with him...

Fuck. Who the hell was I trying to kid? Of course I would fall right into bed with him. I had been wet since we sat down at that sweet little picnic. I dried off quickly, squeezed the moisture out of my hair, slipped into a short satin robe, and left the bathroom.

He was sitting on my bed, looking sexy as hell. His hair was a mess, but then it was always a little tousled. His dark eyes were burning, singeing me. They could melt right through my robe.

"What do you want, Talon?"

He stood, his eyes full of passion. "We...need to stop this."

I raised my eyebrows. Not exactly what I had expected, and a jolt of sadness coursed through me. Even though part of me—a big part of me—agreed with him, I didn't want to stop this.

"We do? Why?"

"The why doesn't really matter," he said. "Just trust me. We need to stop this."

"The why matters to *me*, Talon." I walked toward him and stopped when our bodies were no more than two inches apart. The air was thick with lust. Passion swirled around us almost as if it were visible. My heart beat quickly, and my skin tightened. "If you truly wanted to stop this, you wouldn't have walked in on me in the shower. You would have waited until I was fully clothed."

He moved backward, away from me, hitting the bed and sitting down. "Just trust me. It needs to end."

"I don't accept that." Slowly I untied my robe and let it fall over my shoulders onto the floor. I stood naked in front of him, like an offering. I licked my lips and cupped my breasts, holding them out. I pinched one nipple and then the other, and a jolt of desire arrowed straight into my pussy. "Are you ready to accept that?"

He pulled me down into his lap. "Please. Don't make this any harder than it is."

I wrapped my arms around his neck and nudged one breast up to his lips. "Kiss my nipple, Talon."

He closed his eyes, but he did not turn his head away.

I began undulating my hips, driving my pussy against his denim-clad erection. "I'm wet for you, Talon. I've been wet for you since you met me at the office. I turned you away because we were in a public place. I had to keep my head. But I wanted you. I wanted you then, and I want you now."

He opened his eyes. "This doesn't have anything to do with that."

"Then tell me what it's about."

He closed his eyes again, and I raised my hips again, nudging his lips with my nipple.

"Jade..."

"Don't resist me, Talon. I know you want me. I want you too."

He closed his lips around my nipple and sucked. Sweet surrender.

And it came to me, as if I'd known it all along. I would always surrender to this man. We might not have a future together, but as long as we were anywhere near each other, I would surrender to him, no matter what. He did something to me, something I didn't understand. Perhaps I'd never understand it. Craving was the word he had used. Maybe that was all it was—a craving that might never be satisfied.

He sucked harder on my nipple, and my skin tingled. My pussy ached for his cock.

"That feels so good, Talon. No one sucks my nipples like you do."

He bit down, and I let out a squeal. I almost came right then and there. My pussy was swelling. I could feel it against the denim of his jeans.

I would ask for what I wanted.

"Pretend we're still in the park, Talon. Pretend people are watching, and take me. Take me right here."

He groaned and stood, lifting me and then laying me down on the bed. He quickly undressed and pulled me up to him. He lifted me, and, still standing, sank me down on his cock.

A sigh escaped my lips as he filled me. Sweet joining. Every time was better than the last. Each time I was sure that he couldn't fill me more completely than he had last time, and each time he did.

His eyes were closed, but I wrapped my arms around his neck.

"Open your eyes. Look at me. Look at me."

He opened his eyes, and his gaze blazed into mine. He lifted me by the cheeks of my ass and set me down again and again, filling me with his cock each time. Our gazes stayed glued together, and I swore his eyes were seeing straight into my soul. I never let our eye contact waver, and when the tingling began in my clit, the tickling inside my cunt, and I knew I was on the edge, I touched his cheek.

"I'm going to come, Talon. Come with me, baby. I want us to come together."

He groaned and began moving me up and down off his cock faster and faster, harder and harder, until, just when I exploded, he groaned and sank me down so deep on his cock I felt like he was touching my heart. So good, such bliss.

My pussy pulsed and pulsed and pulsed, shattering my nerves, making my skin burn. When my climax finally started to slow, I threaded my fingers through his thick locks and brought my lips to his.

He gently laid me on the bed and then lay down beside me. He kissed me again, a sweet kiss. A kiss of joy, a kiss of satiation. Our lips slid against each other, our tongues swirled together.

We kissed and we kissed. Lying naked on my bed. For a long time.

★ ★ ★ ★

I didn't remember stopping kissing, but we must've fallen asleep. When I woke up in the morning to my phone alarm, Talon was gone. I was still lying naked on top of the covers. I smiled, letting the memories of our passion overtake me. As much as the sex had been satisfying, what I had loved most about last night was lying together afterward and kissing. We had kissed for so long. He had been so sweet, and so gentle, so... un-Talon-like. His kisses had been laced with the spice of his whiskey and his own sweet musky flavor. I let out a happy sigh and stretched my arms over my head.

But enough daydreaming. I had to get to work.

★ ★ ★ ★

When I got home from work, Talon was nowhere to be found, but Marj was in the kitchen.

"Hey," she said. "I'm making manicotti."

"Oh, yeah? Where's Felicia?"

"I gave her the afternoon off. I felt like cooking tonight."

I inhaled. "It smells delish. Can I help?"

"Sure. Why don't you put together a salad?"

I headed to the fridge and pulled out a head of romaine, a tomato, some radishes, and some baby spinach. "Where is Talon?"

"I haven't the foggiest. I haven't seen him since this morning."

She was ahead of me. I hadn't seen him this morning. He'd left my bed sometime during the night.

"By the way, Ryan and Joe are coming for dinner."

Good. Maybe Marj and I could talk to them about Talon.

"Okay. When?"

"They should be here any minute."

"But Talon's not coming?"

Marj shrugged. "As I said, I haven't the foggiest. His car is gone, and I've no idea where he went. I've given up on him. After all, he stood us up last time, remember? My guess is he's gone for the day and evening. He does that sometimes, goes into Grand Junction on business and has dinner there."

"Did he ever apologize to you about the other night?" He hadn't told me where he'd been. Maybe he'd told Marj.

She nodded. "Yeah. Sort of. Talon has issues with apologies. But he felt bad. I could tell."

"Where did he go?"

"Same thing. To Grand Junction. He didn't say why."

I let it go. The guys arrived shortly thereafter, and Marj poured us all a glass of Ryan's Italian blend. The robust aroma of the zesty tomato sauce wafted out from the oven as we sat at the kitchen table to drink wine and munch on skewers of honeydew melon and prosciutto drizzled with olive oil.

We engaged in small talk, until finally the perfect moment arrived for me to bring up Talon.

"I haven't had a chance to thank you, Jade," Jonah said, "for getting that good deal for Talon with the city."

"You don't have to thank me. I was glad to do it. You guys have all done so much for me, letting me stay here, and you, Ryan, letting me work at the winery the first few weeks I was here."

"We miss you over there," Ryan said. "Anytime you want to come back, there's an open invitation."

"She has a license to practice law now, Ry," Jonah said. "I doubt she wants to make wine for living."

"Actually, that doesn't sound too bad. Honestly, I'm not sure law was ever my true calling. I knew I wanted to do something where I could draw good pay. My dad and I pretty much lived paycheck to paycheck, and I didn't want to do that for the rest of my life. Plus, I'm not really happy with my boss right now. It was a clear breach of ethics for me to even work on Talon's case, but I'm glad I could help. I'm not sure what Larry would've done with it."

Jonah scoffed. "Larry Wade is a moron. Of course he didn't see any ethical problem with you working on Talon's case. He wouldn't know ethics if they hit him in the head. Honestly, I'm glad you're working on it, breach of ethics or not. I don't trust Larry as far as I can throw him."

I nodded. I didn't really trust the guy either, and I'd only known him for a couple of days. "Talon originally wanted to plead guilty and get jail time. Did you guys know that?" I said.

Jonah raised his eyebrows. "That doesn't sound like Talon."

Ryan shook his head. "It sure doesn't. Talon hates being locked up."

"Well, I'm sure no one likes being locked up," I said. "Is he claustrophobic or something?"

"Well, not exactly..." Jonah looked down at his glass of wine.

Marj piped up. "Then what *exactly* do you mean?"

"Nothing," Ryan said. "He means nothing. It's like Jade said. No one likes being locked up."

"I don't buy it," Marj said.

I didn't either, but as a visitor, I wasn't really at liberty to say so. I was glad Marj had.

"What exactly is there to buy, Marjorie?" Jonah asked.

Marj let out a chuckle. "Using my full name? I've hit a nerve somewhere." She turned to me. "Why don't you guys tell us exactly what's going on here? Jade's been asking me for weeks what the story is with Talon, and I've been telling her the same thing you guys have always told me. It's just his way. He's always been that way. But it occurs to me that you guys have known him a lot longer than I have. He's my brother, and I love him as much as I love the two of you. What is going on?"

Ryan and Jonah exchanged a fleeting glance. Very fleeting, actually, but I noticed it. I was on high alert when it came to Talon. I would've noticed anything.

"Let it go, Marj," Jonah said softly.

"I can't let it go any longer," Marj said. "He's my brother too, damn it. What are you hiding?"

"We're not hiding anything," Ryan said. "Talon probably has post-traumatic stress disorder from his time in the military. We've talked to him about getting help for it, but he's not open to that. There's nothing more we can do."

"He went to see a doctor, though, that Dr. Carmichael who was at the ER. So maybe he *is* open to it."

"And you saw how that went," Jonah said.

Marj didn't respond. I had lots more questions, but I let them go. It was one thing for Marj to demand answers, quite another for me to. When the timer rang on the oven, Marj got up and pulled the manicotti out. She set it on the table and brought over my salad. She passed the salad bowl around, and we each took some.

"This is great dressing, Marj. New recipe?" Ryan asked.

Marj shook her head. "Jade made the salad."

"It's just a simple French vinaigrette," I said and took a bite.

Back to small talk for the remainder of the dinner.

And I was still filled with questions about Talon.

★ ★ ★ ★

I was lying on my bed reading when a knock sounded on my door. My heart skipped a beat. Perhaps Talon had come back. "Come in," I said.

Marj walked through my door. Though I was little let down not to see Talon, I was glad to see her. Jonah and Ryan had volunteered to clean the kitchen after dinner, so Marj and I had gone our separate ways, but we still had that college roommate bond. We could each tell that we wanted to talk, but we couldn't with the brothers there.

"Did they leave?" I asked.

She nodded. "And I got a text from Talon. He's staying in the city tonight."

My heart lurched a bit. Why was he staying in the city? Why had he the other night? Did he have a woman there? Probably many women. The thought broke my heart a little.

On the other hand, if Jonah and Ryan had left and Talon was gone for the night, Marj and I could talk.

"So what do you think?"

"They're lying," Marj said. "I've been wondering about Talon for a long time, and he may very well have post-traumatic stress disorder. I was a teenager when he left for Iraq, but even still, I remember him being pretty much the same way before he left. So I'm not sure it can all be blamed on his service."

"I guess there's not much we can do about it," I said.

Marj gave me a devious grin. "Want to bet? I think we need to do some investigating. We can start with my father's old files. I've always thought about going through them, but then figured it was none of my business. But you know what? I own a quarter of this ranch. And Talon is my brother. I love him. So it *is* my business." She grabbed my arm and yanked me off the bed. "Come on."

Marj led me not to the office, where I thought we would be going, but down the stairway to the basement. The basement was finished into a gorgeous rec room and three extra bedrooms, but she took me to none of those places. In the back was some crawl space. She slid the door open and crawled inside, beckoning for me to follow. I did, hurting my knees in the gravelly dirt. It smelled musty and moldy.

"Marj, do I really need to be in here? Can't you just find what we need and pull it out?"

"It's just that I'm not quite sure what we need, Jade. There are a bunch of boxes in here marked private. They're taped up pretty good."

"What are they?"

"Old stuff of my father's. I was always told it was junk, but I'm not so sure anymore."

My eyes adjusted to the dark. Lots of brown cardboard boxes, well over twenty, sat in the space, taped up just as Marj had said.

"Let's get them all over here close to the doorway," she said. "Then we can pull them out one by one and go through them."

I nodded. "Okay."

The two of us yanked all the boxes near the entrance. By the time we were done, my knees were crusted with dirt and hurt like hell. I crawled out of the crawl space, and Marj followed, lugging the first box. She pulled it down into the extra bedroom and then repositioned the door to the crawl space.

"We're going to need something to cut through this tape," I said.

Marj smiled. "Not a problem." She pulled a Leatherman out of her pocket. "I always come prepared."

She quickly cut through the tape and opened the first box. "Just as I suspected. Bunch of old files and records." She sighed. "Well, let's go through them." She handed me a pile.

I opened the first file and went through it. "This looks like mostly old quitclaim deeds. I mean, these go way back, over a century ago." I leafed through the delicate papers. "There are even some old chattel mortgages in here. You don't see those anymore."

"What's a chattel mortgage?" she asked.

"A mortgage on a thing, rather than on a piece of property. These are old ones, from England."

"The Steels are originally from England," she said.

"You don't see them in the US," I said. "What we have here are secured transactions."

"You mean like collateral?"

I nodded. "A chattel mortgage is basically the same thing. For example, it looks like this one is on a threshing machine." I handed it to her.

She shook her head and gestured for me to put the document back. "I probably wouldn't understand it anyway."

"What exactly are we looking for?"

"To be honest, I have no idea. But I bet we'll know when we find it."

I let out a giggle. This was kind of fun, like a game, looking for clues. I finished going through my stack of documents and reached for another. "What do you have in your stack?" I asked.

"Some old census documents, it looks like, from when the Steels first came over here from England several generations ago. A couple of birth certificates for relatives I've never heard of." She kept going. "Are these more of those chattel mortgages you were talking about?" She handed me some papers.

"Yep," I said. "We've got to be getting to the bottom of this box soon."

Marj let out a sigh. "Is it worth going through these boxes? This is all ancient history."

"Yeah, you could be right." But something in me wanted to continue. "Maybe we should look at one more box."

"Okay." Marj put the lid on the first box. "I'll re-tape this later." She opened the door to the crawl space, pulled out the second box, and opened it.

She handed me a stack of files and took a stack for herself. I opened my first file, and lo and behold. "I think this is your dad's birth certificate," I said, handing her a document.

"Yeah. Bradford Raymond Steel. I wonder why his birth certificate has been boxed up with all this other historical stuff?"

"I think what that means is that this *is* all historical stuff," I said. "We may have to go through all these boxes after all."

"You're probably right."

I kept shuffling through the folder. "Hey, I have your parents' marriage certificate. Bradford Raymond Steel to Daphne Kay Wade."

"Wade?" Marj bit her lip. "Are you sure?"

I handed it to her. "Pretty sure."

She perused the document. "I'm not sure what this

means, but I was always told that my mother's maiden name was Warren. In fact, Ryan's middle name is Warren, after my mom's maiden name."

I didn't see how this could have any relation to Talon, but it was definitely suspicious. "We should probably ask Jonah about it."

Marj nodded. "Absolutely. If they lied to me about this, they could easily be lying about other things."

"Hey, look," I said, leafing through the rest of the papers. "Here's Jonah's birth certificate. And Talon's and Ryan's. And look, here's yours, Marj." I glanced at the document. "How come you never told me your first name is Angela?"

"What?" She grabbed the document from me.

"Be careful. These are old documents."

I looked through the others. Jonah Bradford Steel. Ryan Warren Steel. Talon John Steel, all born to Bradford Raymond Steel and Daphne Kay Steel, née Wade.

Talon John. Such a strong rugged name for a strong rugged man.

"This is totally bizarre, Jade. My name is not Angela. They always told me my name was Marjorie Steel, no middle name."

"Who always told you that?"

"My dad, when he was alive. And I never asked my brothers, but I assume they would tell me the same thing."

That was odd. "Maybe they just decided to call you Marjorie."

"Well, sure, I could understand that, but why wouldn't they tell me that I went by my middle name? My signature should be A. Marjorie Steel. Not just Marjorie Steel. And come to think of it, all three of my brothers have middle names. Why would they decide not to give me one? It doesn't make sense." She stood. "Come on."

"What?" Talon's birth certificate fascinated me, and I wasn't quite ready to stop looking at.

"We're going to go see Joe. I want some answers. And I want them now."

I glanced at my wristwatch. "It's after nine o'clock."

"I don't care. I just found out my name is Angela. I suppose it's not that big of a deal, but why didn't anyone tell me?"

"Okay. You go ahead, and I'll keep looking through these documents."

"No, I want you to go with me. Please? He'll be less likely to get all big brother on me if you're there."

I let out a laugh. "Okay, good point." I closed my folder, placed it back in the box, and stood, brushing off my knees again. "You're driving."

CHAPTER TWENTY-SIX

Talon

The boy didn't wear pants. They had been taken away from him the first day. He wore only his T-shirt. Even though it was summer, he was cold most of the time in the dank concrete basement. He spent most days and nights wrapped in the dirty blanket they'd given him.

Hot breath on the back of his neck—that's what the boy hated the most. The rank stench of stale cigars and liquor. They'd always been drinking when they came. Sometimes they drank during.

The pain, the humiliation—as much as he hated them, he had learned to detach himself. One day he would be so used up he would die on the hard floor. No one would notice or care.

But the hot breath...the demonic stench...that wind from hell wafting over him.

He never detached from that.

★ ★ ★ ★

Hot breath...stench of alcohol, stale cigar smoke...

A blunt object poked me in the back. "Your wallet, asshole," the voice said.

I elbowed the assailant in the ribs, knocking him to the ground. I kicked his weapon down the alley and then booted him in the side a few times. "Who the fuck do you think you are? You think you can just take what you want? Life doesn't work that way, you dumb fuck."

I kicked the bum's face and walked away.

This wasn't the first time I had been mugged. I often walked through the seedy area on the outskirts of the city at night, just waiting for some dumb-ass to try to jump me. Two times before tonight I had been jumped, and two times before tonight I had disarmed the mugger and beat the shit out of him. No one had ever called the cops on me. I didn't care if they did. I was careful never to do any lasting damage. Plus, self-defense and all.

I wanted to go back to that one, though. I used my will not to go running back and pummel him to his death.

The sickly heat of his breath on my neck. The acrid stench.

I wanted to see him dead.

But I wasn't crazy. I knew killing was wrong, despite my time in the Marines and despite everything else I'd been through. I still had morals, and I knew how to exist in society. I knew right from wrong. I wasn't a sociopath. I knew this as well as I knew anything. I'd done my share of research.

I didn't beat people up indiscriminately. But hey, try to mug me, take what is mine, and I'll make you pay. Not too many would argue with that thought process.

The face of Jade's ex emerged in my mind. He was the exception. He hadn't tried to take anything from me.

Or had he?

I had become an animal when I saw him kissing her. All rational thought had fled, and I had lunged forward to protect... what was mine.

I had no right to think of her as mine. I had nothing to

offer her.

She was the only thing I had ever truly wanted.

And I had no right to her.

I walked into a seedy little dive that served rotgut whiskey and catered to two-bit whores. I wasn't proud of it, but I had spent more than my share of time in the little alcove. There had been a time, after I turned twenty-one, when this place was my second home. I drank and fucked myself into oblivion, trying—and failing—to ease the pain that consumed me. I hadn't been here in years, but still it stood, a haven for the melancholy, the outcasts—the people like me.

I sat down at the bar next to an old geezer in a blue-and-yellow plaid flannel shirt and a hunting cap.

A bartender who looked like he'd seen damn near a century strolled up to me. "What'll it be?"

I cleared my throat. "Whiskey, straight."

He poured me a drink from a bottle I'd never seen or heard of.

I downed a shot, burning my throat. Yep, rotgut. But I was in a rotgut kind of mood. I pushed my glass to the edge of the bar and signaled the bartender for another.

The old geezer next to me turned toward me. "Troubles, son?"

I shook my head in the low chuckle. "You don't know the half of it."

"You need an ear? I got nowhere else to go." He held out his hand. "Name's Mike."

I shook his hand. "Talon."

"Talon, like a bird's claw?"

I nodded. "That's the one."

"Mighty unusual name."

Not the first time someone had commented about my name. "My mother liked it. My dad wanted to name me John. That's my middle name." I took a sip of my drink. I'd take this one a bit more slowly.

"That's some real crap you're drinking," Mike said.

"So?"

"So, you look like the kind of guy who can afford the good stuff."

"Why do you say that?"

Mike looked down. "Those ostrich cowboy boots, for one."

I let out a huff. "Maybe I like the crap."

"If you say so. Me, I love to taste that good stuff once in a while."

I took another sip. Mike looked tired. Old and tired. "What you do, Mike?"

"Worked construction all my life. I'm retired now. My wife passed away a year ago, so it's just me and my dog. What about you?"

"I'm a rancher."

"That can be a hard life," he said.

I laughed. Yeah, for most, ranching was hard. For the Steels? Not so much. We were lucky. Great-Grandpa Steel had started out with nothing, and between him and Grandpa, they built an empire, adding the peach and apple orchard to the already thriving beef ranch. Dad had built the winery, and he and Ryan had created another empire.

Not that we didn't work hard. We did, Jonah and Ryan especially. They were known to put in twelve-hour days. But money was never a worry.

No, my ranch wasn't the source of my problem.

"We do okay," I said.

"Then what's eatin' at you, boy?"

I glared daggers at him. "Don't call me boy."

"Sorry. Meant no disrespect. But something's bothering you. I can tell."

I sighed. "I just got mugged."

"Don't surprise me none, walking around this area dressed like that." Mike coughed.

"Last time I checked it was a free country, Mike. I should have the right to walk where the hell I want without someone trying to take something that's mine."

"I can't argue with you, son. But you gotta use your smarts, too. You don't look stupid to me, but it seems stupid for someone like you to be walking around here after dark and not expect to get mugged."

"I took care of it."

"You don't look any worse for the wear."

"I don't, but the dumb-ass mugger sure does."

Mike raised his eyebrows and took a long draft of his beer. Then he let out a laugh. "So you didn't give in, I take it?"

"Hell, no."

"And you kicked his ass?"

"Into next week." I took another sip of the rotgut.

Mike chuckled. "Can't say he didn't have it coming." He finished his beer. "So tell me, what's eating you? And don't tell me you're upset over the mugging. If you didn't want to be mugged, you wouldn't have come down here."

"You don't know what the fuck you're talking about."

Mike let out a little chortle. "I'm thinking I'm hitting a little too close to home for you, son."

"So you're a shrink now?"

"Not by a long shot. Just an old guy who's been around the block a few times. I've been told I'm good at reading people. And I think I just read you better than you wanted me to."

"You don't know a damned thing about me."

"Now that's not true. I know you're a rancher. You said so yourself. I know you were walking outside in the dark in this area with those boots on, and that made you prime meat for the muggers. I also know that you knew damned well you were likely to get mugged, and you did. You didn't let the mugger have anything, and you walked away unscathed."

I downed my drink and motioned for another. "You don't know shit, old man."

Mike gestured the bartender for another beer. "You get to be my age, and you know a lot. I know right now that you're hiding something. Now, I don't know what it is, but you're going to have to deal with it sooner or later if you want to live a happy life."

"I'm perfectly happy." What a crock.

"Son, perfectly happy people don't walk around asking to get mugged."

I downed my third rotgut whiskey and threw some bills on the counter. "I'm out of here." I stood and turned around, ready to walk.

"Running away is never the answer, son."

I didn't know why I turned back. I had heard those words before, from my brothers, from myriad other people. But something in Mike's voice spoke to me.

I sat back down and looked into his watery blue gaze. These were eyes that had seen a lifetime, eyes that seemed to hold...something. Was it empathy? "You really think you know me, old man?"

Mike coughed again and smiled. "I don't know the color of the socks I put on this morning, but I know you need to face your life. Just like everybody else in the world."

I shook my head. "Everybody else in the world doesn't have my life."

"Maybe not. But they have their own hardships. Never doubt that."

I didn't doubt that, not really. Did I? Maybe this old man had something to say after all. "All right. I've got a few minutes. Give me your wisdom, Mike."

"Hell, I'm no sage. And even though I know you're hiding something, I don't pretend to know what it is. But you've got to let it go. There is no great secret to life. It's pretty simple. You've read Thoreau, haven't you?"

I nodded. I had read Thoreau, but I was pretty surprised that Mike had.

"It's like he says. Suck out the marrow of life."

"Thoreau was living in the wilderness. Refusing to do his duty. Pay his taxes. Pretty much being a spoiled brat, if you asked me," I said.

Mike laughed aloud. "I can't really disagree with you there. But the man had a lot of worthwhile things to say. You need to concentrate on the good things, no matter how small. Find the good in everything, and suck it out."

The man was hardly eloquent. But Mike's words resonated with me. Could I?

"Tell me something good about your life," he said.

I remained silent.

"Don't tell me you've been in this funk so long that you can't see what's good in your life. Clearly, you have no financial worries, judging by those boots you're wearing. That's got to be a good thing."

I took a sip of drink and nodded. "Yeah, that's a good thing."

"For God's sake, son, don't be so blasé about it. I scrimped my whole life, and now I'm existing on what little I get from Social Security. Financial worries are a big part of most people's lives. Be thankful you don't have them."

I raked my fingers through my hair. Suddenly I felt like a very small person. "You're right."

"Now what else?"

"I have two brothers and a sister. They're all really great."

"Good, good. Family is everything. And what else?"

Jade. She was actually the first thing that had popped into my mind when he asked about something good in my life. For some reason, I couldn't bring her name to my lips. She wasn't mine, as much as I wanted her to be, because with the same amount of desire, I didn't want her to be. I didn't want to bring her into my tortured existence. I didn't want to ruin her. She deserved so much better.

"You got yourself a girl?"

I looked away.

"Or a guy? I don't judge."

My nerves prickled. "There's a girl. But she's not mine."

"She doesn't feel the same way about you?"

I didn't know. She was clearly not repulsed by me. "She seems to like me okay."

"Then what are you waiting for? Tell her how you feel."

"I don't really know how I feel." It was the God's honest truth.

"I don't buy that."

"I'm no good for her. She deserves better."

"You need to stop that self-defeating attitude, son, if you're going to be happy in life."

Happy? I had given up the notion of happiness twenty-five years ago. "I'm not being self-defeating. This is just a fact. She deserves better."

Hell, she deserved the best. Unfortunately, that wasn't me.

"What could be better for a woman than a man who loves her? You do love her, don't you?"

Did I? I didn't know what that kind of love was. I had no frame of reference. I was used to taking what women offered. I had never given them anything in return.

And then it hit me like a house falling on my head. That was the problem with Jade. I didn't want to just take from her. I wanted to give everything back to her as well, and I didn't think I was capable of it. I hungered for her, longed for her. Was that love?

"I don't know," I said honestly.

"Don't you think you owe it to yourself to figure out what your feelings are for this woman?"

I stayed silent.

"Don't you think about her at all?"

Again, I stayed silent.

"Look, son, take a look at your life. Maybe it hasn't been a joyful one, and I'm sure sorry about that. But there have to be moments of contentedness. Sift through the crap. Find those moments. When have you felt the most content?"

I smiled. I actually smiled at this old man who was the wisest person I'd met in a long time.

"I've been the most content when I've been with her." I stood.

"Now where are you off to?"

"I'm going home. But before I do, give me your address, Mike."

"Whatever for?"

"You've helped me a lot. I'd like to send you something in gratitude."

He scribbled something on a napkin and laughed. "Well. I won't turn that down. It's been great talking to you, Talon. I honestly do wish you happiness in the rest of your life."

The road would be rough and icy, but maybe I could trudge along and find happiness.

One thing I knew. By tomorrow evening, Mike would have a case of the good stuff delivered to his door.

CHAPTER TWENTY-SEVEN

Jade

"Where the hell did you find this?" Jonah held the birth certificate, his eyes blazing.

"Jade and I did some investigating."

"What the fuck?"

I warmed all over. This was clearly a family moment. I felt totally out of place. If a hole had swallowed me up, I would have been glad.

"Yeah."

"Damn it, Marj, this isn't funny. Tell me where you found this."

"In the crawl space in the basement. Those old boxes of Dad's that you always told me were nothing of importance."

"They're not."

"Apparently they are. I don't even know what my legal name is."

He handed the birth certificate back to her. "I don't know anything about this."

Jonah's words hung in the air.

Marj whipped her hands to her hips. "I don't buy it, Joe. You know something. Clearly, my real name is Angela Marjorie Steel. I want to know why no one told me."

"I don't know. Maybe Mom and Dad had your name

changed."

"Why would they do that?"

Jonah shrugged. "Beats the hell out of me."

"You're lying," Marj said, her dark eyes laced with anger. "Why didn't Dad tell me what my real name was? Why didn't *you* tell me?"

"It's a nonissue, Marjorie. Leave it."

"What exactly is the big deal here? It's my name. It's not some criminal record or anything horrible. I just want to know why no one told me what my name is. Is that so wrong?"

"Marj..."

"And while you're at it, you can tell me why you always told me that Mom's maiden name was Warren, but her marriage certificate to Dad says it's Wade."

Jonah widened his eyes. Only slightly, but I noticed. Had Marj noticed as well?

"Leave these things be," Jonah said, his tone serious. "And don't go snooping around anymore in that stuff."

"I will snoop around as much as I want. This property is one quarter mine, in case you've forgotten."

"No one has forgotten that. But I'm warning you. Don't go snooping. It's none of your business anyway, and you might not like what you find."

★ ★ ★ ★

I lay in bed, unable to sleep. The clock ticked by. Midnight. One a.m. One thirty. I could get up, get a cup of tea from the kitchen, but Talon wasn't home. He wouldn't be sitting at the table with his glass of water.

Finally, as I was drifting off to sleep, my door creaked

open. I sat up quickly.

"Don't be afraid. It's just me, blue eyes."

My eyes adjusted to the dark, and I looked up. Talon stood a few feet away from my bed, looking mussed and fatigued.

"Where have you been?" I asked.

"Grand Junction."

"Why did you come back? Marjorie said you usually spend the night when you go to the city."

"I wanted to see you."

My heart jumped. "It's the middle of the night, Talon."

He raked his fingers through his gorgeous head of hair. "I know. I just...couldn't wait."

"I have work in the morning."

"I know. I just..."

He looked so sad and forlorn that my heart went out to him. I patted my bed. "All right. Come on and sit down."

He sat down and took my hand. He had never done that before. He stayed silent for several moments.

"So what is it?" I nudged him.

Again, he stayed silent. I squeezed his hand.

"I can't do this," he said.

As much as I needed to know what was on his mind, I knew better than to push Talon. We hadn't known each other that long, but he would not respond well to pushing.

"All right," I said. "Why don't you lie down? You can stay here with me or go to your own room. Either way, you look like you could use some sleep."

I lay back down, scooting over to make room for him in case he wanted to stay. I hoped he would stay. I couldn't think of anything sweeter than sleeping in his arms.

"Could we have dinner tomorrow night?" he asked.

"Sure. You want to meet me after work?"

He shook his head. "Marj told me this morning that she'd be gone tomorrow evening."

I nodded. "Yeah, she signed up for some kind of cooking class in Grand Junction. I'm so glad she's finally pursuing her passion."

"I want to have dinner here. Will you have dinner here with me?"

I couldn't help but chuckle. "Are you cooking?"

He smiled. "I wouldn't subject you to that. I'll have Felicia make something nice."

I smiled. "That sounds great. Now if you're not going to lie here with me, go to bed. You need to rest."

He got up and left without saying another word.

★ ★ ★ ★

I spent the next day at work on the computer, investigating. It wasn't practicing law, but I was beginning to like the investigation portion of this job. I was learning a lot, and with the Internet and social media, I could track down almost anything.

Larry left at five and told me to go ahead and take off as well, so I did. I wanted to go home and shower and change before my dinner with Talon.

An hour later, I was combing out my wet hair and putting on a slinky sundress when a knock sounded on my door.

Talon was the only one home. "Yeah?" I said.

He opened the door. "Dinner is ready." Roger panted happily at his feet.

"Okay. Can you wait a few minutes? I just need to dry my

hair."

"Your hair looks great."

I laughed. "It's wet, Talon. I just got out of the shower."

"Are you kidding? It's sexy as hell."

Men certainly had interesting taste sometimes. "Okay. If you say so." I smiled. "Let's go to the kitchen."

"We're not eating in the kitchen."

"In the formal dining room? Just the two of us?"

He shook his head. "We're dining in my bedroom."

My skin pricked. Obviously, he had more than dinner on his mind, and that was fine with me. He didn't take my hand as he had last night. I simply followed him across the house to his suite.

"Oh!" A small table had been set up, complete with fine china and candlelight. "This is lovely. Did Felicia set this up for you?"

He shook his head. "No. I did it myself."

"Wow." I was stunned. "It's really beautiful, Talon."

He pulled out a chair. "Have a seat."

I sat, and he poured me a glass of red wine.

"This is Ryan's top-of-the-line Cabernet Sauvignon. This particular bottle has been aged ten years. I hope you like it."

"Are you having any?"

"I will with dinner. I prefer a good strong whiskey as an aperitif. This is Peach Street, made in a bourbon style right here on the western slope." He lifted his old-fashioned glass.

I took a sip of the wine. "Delicious. Berries on the nose, with some subtle black pepper and cinnamon."

"Ryan taught you well."

"I enjoyed working with him a lot. In fact, I miss it. Though I'm enjoying my new job as an attorney."

"I'm glad you're happy there."

Small talk. I was dying to know what he had wanted to tell me last night. "So what did you want to talk to me about?" I asked.

"Let's have our dinner first."

Fine. I could wait. "What's on the menu?"

He lifted the silver dome from my plate. "Tenderloin with green peppercorn sauce, broccoli rabe, rosemary polenta, and a sunflower seed baguette."

I inhaled. "It smells great." I took another sip of wine. "Felicia must've really outdone herself."

"I asked her to make something special, and this is what she came up with."

"Special indeed. Although any of her delicious meals would have sufficed. She's a wonderful cook."

Now I was making small talk. But we had to talk about something while we ate.

Talon picked up a steak knife and cut a piece of meat. "How was your day?"

"Good. A lot of investigating on the computer. Next week I'll probably have to do some footwork for a new case. I'm sure glad today is Friday. I can use a day off."

More small talk. How could we have so little to say to each other? Was sex all there was between us?

No. There was more. So much more. Love.

For the first time, I admitted it to myself. I had fallen in love with Talon. It scared the hell out of me, but it was the truth. Sometimes we were so close I felt like we were one person. And other times, like now, he was miles away, across from me at the table. His walls were up, and the only time he let me through them was when we were intimate.

I looked down at my plate. My filet was cooked to perfection—rare, just how I liked it. The red juice meandered into my polenta. I mashed the polenta with my fork.

Marj's birth certificate popped into my mind. Jonah had told us to leave it be, but maybe Talon knew something.

"Talon?"

"Yeah?" He took a bite of steak, chewed, and swallowed.

"Marj and I found her birth certificate the other day."

"So?"

"Well, it's kind of confusing. It says her name is Angela Marjorie Steel. But she says you guys always told her that her first name was Marjorie and she had no middle name."

He was quiet a moment. Then, "Why do you care?"

"I would think that's obvious. She cares because it's her name. I care because I care about her. We asked Jonah about it, but he wouldn't tell us anything. He told us not to go snooping or we'd find things we didn't want to know."

He looked down at his plate. "If I were you, I'd take Joe's advice."

"Do you know anything about it?"

"I'll just echo Joe's sentiments. Leave it alone."

"That's not fair. Marj only wants to know who she is."

"She knows who she is. She's Marjorie Steel. She's my sister. She owns a quarter of the goddamned richest ranch in Colorado. What the hell more does she need to know?"

"Well, her name for one."

He raised his gaze and glared at me. "Don't push this, Jade."

"So you're going to clam up, just like your brother. Great. Something is going on around here, Talon, and if you don't want me to know about it, that's one thing. But Marj is your sister."

"Marj is better off. She has a great life. She doesn't want it screwed up."

"But, Talon—"

His fist came down on the table, jarring my plate of food. He stood. "Damn it, Jade. Don't push it," he said through clenched teeth. He came toward me, grabbed my arm, and jerked me into a standing position.

"But—"

His mouth came down on mine violently.

I responded to him as I always did. Our bodies were drawn together, our lips perfect matches for each other's. I opened to him, and his tongue dived into my mouth. We kissed with passion, with fervor, our mouths open and clamped together.

When he finally broke the kiss and we both gasped in much-needed breaths, he trailed his lips to my ear.

"You're the only thing I've ever wanted in my life," he whispered.

"What?" I gasped. My heart was beating a mile a minute, stampeding against my chest. My breath was coming in rapid puffs. I couldn't breathe. What had he said?

"You, blue eyes. You are the only thing I've ever wanted."

His lips came down on mine again. We kissed and we kissed, and he edged me toward his bed.

Within seconds, we were lying together, still fully clothed, making out on his bed like a couple of sex-starved teenagers. Our mouths were melded together. Boiling honey flowed through my veins.

He cupped one breast and found my nipples through my sundress as he continued to violently love my mouth.

My body quivered. I was ready for him. My pussy pulsed,

and I knew I was wet.

"You," he said, panting. "You. All the other women. Never one of them. Just took what they gave freely. But you...you..."

"Talon..."

"You, Jade. I want you."

"Then take me. Take me tonight. Make me yours."

He grimaced. "Can't. Can't. Can't make you mine. You don't want to be mine."

"I want to be yours," I said.

"You don't. You can't. I can't have you."

"Talon, I'm right here. You *have* me."

He looked at me for a moment, his eyes on fire, but something clawed at him. He was scared.

"Whatever it is, Talon, we can face it together. Let me help you."

"Need you. Need to be inside you. Need you to take the demons away." His body trembled.

He needed me to take the lead this time. I sensed it, knew it in my very soul. I moved away from his body, sat up, pulled my sundress over my head, and tossed it on the floor. I hadn't worn a bra, and my nipples were already stiff and hard. I flipped my sandals off and removed my thong. Then I slowly began to unbutton his burgundy cotton shirt. With each button, I exposed more of his beautiful bronze skin, and my pussy throbbed harder.

I eased the shirt over his shoulders, helped him pull his arms out, and discarded the garment. I unbuckled his belt, and though I wanted to strip him naked quickly, climb on top of him, and fuck his brains out, I went slowly. I needed to calm him down. Slowly, each tooth of the zipper released, and I moved down to the foot of his bed and pulled off his boots and socks. Then I pulled his jeans over his legs and finally removed his boxers. He was erect, as big and proud as I'd ever seen him, a pearl of pre-come beading on his slit. His black nest of pubic hair drew me, and I bent down and inhaled his musky maleness.

"You're so beautiful, Talon. Every part of you. I've never seen a more beautiful man. Never."

I kissed the tip of his dick, and then I kissed his abdomen, trailing my tongue up the hard muscled bronze to his copper nipples. I flicked my tongue over one of them, and he jerked.

I kissed up to his shoulders up his neck to his earlobe. I sucked it into my mouth and gave it a tug.

"Let me take care of you," I whispered into his ear. "Please. I want this."

He squeezed his eyes shut, and the beginning of a tear emerged in the corner of one.

"Don't fight this, baby. I've got you. I'll take care of you." I kissed around the outer shell of his ear, pushed my tongue inside a few times.

He shivered and sighed. I moved away from his head for a moment and threaded my fingers into his gorgeous mop of hair. I combed my fingers through it, massaging his scalp, digging my fingernails in just a little.

He sighed again. "That feels nice."

"You just relax, baby. I'm in charge tonight."

I continued my assault. Once I had given him a good scalp massage, I moved my fingers to his cheeks and massaged his cheekbones, his temples, and then his jawline.

"You're so tense. Relax. Let it go." I massaged the tops of his shoulders and his pecs. "Turn over, baby. I want to give you a back rub."

"Jade, as much as I would love a back rub, I'm hard as a rock right now. I need you on my cock."

I chuckled. "I thought I was in charge here."

"Just sit on me, baby. Fuck me. Then you can help me relax. And pretty soon I'll be hard for you again."

I couldn't say no to that. My pussy was dripping. I wanted that big cock inside me so bad I thought I might die if I couldn't have it.

"Please, blue eyes. Come ride me."

I moved toward his hardness and slowly, inch by succulent inch, I lowered myself onto his cock. *So complete, and so full. Never like this with anyone else.*

"Yeah, baby," he said. "So perfect. So right."

I let out a soft sigh as I took in the last glorious inch of him.

"God, I love that. That sound you make when I first go inside you. So sexy. God, Jade, fuck me good. Fuck me hard. I need you."

I lifted myself and plunged back down on his cock.

"Yeah, baby. Faster though. I want you to fuck me. Send me to the fucking moon."

I thrust faster, my hips pistoning. So fast, so good, and within moments I was edging toward climax.

"Touch your clit, baby. Make yourself come. Let me watch you pleasure yourself. That's so hot."

I trailed my hand over my breasts and down my tummy onto my very bare vulva to my clit. It was sopping wet with my juices. I trailed my finger around it, and that was all it took.

I exploded. Stars whirled above me. My whole body shattered around me, and kaleidoscopes and rainbows appeared in my mind's eye. I continued riding Talon as hard as I could.

"Yeah, baby, yeah. You're so beautiful. Come for me. Come for me, baby." And then he pushed into me hard with one last thrust. "God. Feels so good. Nobody but you. Want you. Only thing I've ever wanted."

When we both finally calmed down and our breathing had returned to normal, I let his cock slide out of me and I crawled into his arms. "Rest for a few minutes," I said. "But then I owe you a back rub."

CHAPTER TWENTY-EIGHT

Talon

Reluctantly, I moved facedown when she asked me to. This was a submissive position for me, and I was not comfortable. My nerves were jumping, but then again, my nerves were always jumping. It was part of being Talon Steel.

"Let me take care of you, baby," she said, her voice sexy, comforting.

I tried to relax, tried to find peace. But I wasn't sure how to do that.

"Baby, relax. It's not so hard." She started at the back of my neck, rubbing with her thumb.

It felt good. It felt right.

"So tense. How do you exist this way?"

I had no answer for her. This *was* my existence. I was always in a constant state of alertness. Always tense. I could never explain to her why.

"Just relax. I'm going to work all this tension out of you, Talon. All of it. If it takes me all damn night."

I closed my eyes, trying to find serenity. Her soft lips whispered against my skin. She kissed me between my shoulder blades.

And then her talented fingers went to work. She kneaded my shoulders and my upper arms, and she pushed through my shoulder blades. The lactic acid crinkled through my muscles.

"So tense," she said again.

"Story of my life," I said softly.

"This doesn't have to be your story, baby. Let me help you create a new ending."

If only it were that simple. No new ending existed for me. It wasn't possible. Still, as her fingers maneuvered my muscles, I started to feel better. Cared for.

She worked out lots of kinks in my shoulders and then maneuvered down to my middle and lower back. She worked those for a while, her warm hands bringing me comfort, solace. Down farther, she kneaded my glutes.

"So tight," she said again as she worked my hamstrings, the backs of my knees, to my calves. And then to my feet.

"Have you ever had a foot massage before, Talon?" she asked.

I shook my head against the bed. "Don't believe I have."

"Then you're in for a treat."

She started with my left foot, massaging my heel and then my instep. Then the ball of my foot, to each toe. Her touch was perfect. Just firm enough to feel good but not to hurt.

She worked on that foot for about ten minutes before she went to the next one.

I wanted so much to relax. I wanted so much to let everything go and lose myself in her.

Could she be my salvation?

That would be too good to be true. But God, when I was with her, when her tight little body encased mine, when she looked at me with those steely blue eyes...

The bricks around me started to crumble down.

And that scared the hell out of me.

She began kneading my calf again. "You're tensing up again, baby. Relax."

I tried. I tried to sink into the comforter, sink into a sea of Jade and perfection and joy and rapture.

She worked her way up to my thighs again, massaging my hamstrings, and then up to my ass again, massaging my glutes.

"You have a gorgeous butt, Talon. I've never seen any man who looks as good in jeans as you do."

I smiled against the comforter.

Her hands, so good, so right, so perfec—

★ ★ ★ ★

The boy screamed.

A thick finger breached his behind. He was being torn in half. Ripped apart. Thousands of needles forced themselves into him. Nothing could ever hurt so much. He screamed in agony.

"Stop that! You're hurting me! Mama! Daddy! Help me! Please!"

This wasn't normal. People didn't do these things. Not to kids... Not to...

His blood curdled as a high-pitched screech ripped from his throat. More pain. Shards of jagged glass tore into him, stretching him, breaking him.

"That's it, boy. Take it all."

The boy would never recover. He would die right now. This was the end of his short life. The end...

★ ★ ★ ★

"Talon!"

I was on my knees, my hands clamped over my ears. The

noise. So much noise. *Make it stop, make it stop, make it stop!* A blood-chilling screech. Malignant and wretched.

"Talon!"

Through the noise, a sweet voice called my name. *Talon.* Far away, someone called...

God, please, the noise. Make it stop make it stop make it stop.

"Talon!"

The noise stopped. I looked at Jade. She was beautiful. So beautiful. But fear, terror, laced her steely eyes.

"My God, what's wrong?"

And I knew. The deafening noise had been coming from me, my voice. What had happened? I looked at her. So beautiful, so innocent. She had been taking such good care of me, massaging my thighs, my lower back, my ass, and then dipping...

She had touched me there—on my anus.

I squeezed my eyes shut. *Cannot go there. Will not go there.*

"Talon, let me help you. Tell me what's wrong."

I stood. My cock hung flaccid. I had been so looking forward to making love with her again. Yes, making love. Not just fucking.

But this would never work. I put on my jeans and boxers. Then I picked up her dress and handed it to her. "Leave," I said.

She arched her eyebrows, and her beautiful lips formed an O. "Leave? I don't understand."

"You know what the word means." I looked away.

She walked to me, still naked, holding her dress. She cupped my cheek and forced me to gaze into her eyes. "I'm not leaving. I'm not going anywhere. I'm here for you. Please, let me help you."

How I wanted to believe her. How I wanted to grab her in my arms, hold her against me until the last monster disappeared into the fog of the night. Could I try? Could I risk everything and keep her with me?

I shook my head. "You need to leave. Now."

"I don't understand. Please. I don't want to leave. I want to stay and help you."

I gritted my teeth. "No. Leave."

She bit her lip, and two tears, one from each eye, rivered down her cheeks.

I had never loathed myself more.

She put her sundress over her head and covered her shapely body. She sniffed and said, "All right, Talon. I will leave. But tomorrow, we're going to talk about this. You can't push me away. I won't let you."

I didn't want to push her away. All I wanted was her. She was all I had ever wanted. I had never wanted anything until I met her. But I had to push her away. I had to protect her from the horror that was my life.

I grabbed her arm. "You're not understanding me."

"Talon, I have never understood you. But right now, you clearly need me to leave, so I want to leave. But we will talk tomorrow."

Except that we wouldn't talk tomorrow. We wouldn't talk tomorrow or any other day.

"When I say leave, I'm not talking about leaving for now. I want you out of this house."

Sadness shone in her beautiful eyes. "You can't mean that."

"I've never meant anything more in my life."

"When I tried to leave before, you wanted me to stay."

Hell, I wanted her to stay now. But what happened tonight had been like a freight train running me over, crushing me into dust, and forcing reality into me. I couldn't give her anything. She needed to get away from me and have a life. She was wonderful, the most wonderful woman I had ever met, and she deserved to find someone who was capable of giving her what she deserved.

An anvil of jealousy hit me in the gut. God, another man touching her... Fucking her...

Loving her.

I squeezed my eyes shut again, trying to erase the images from my mind. *Have to let go. Have to let her go.*

"Things change, Jade."

"We just made love. I'm so sorry. I don't know what I did. I was massaging you, and then—"

"Enough!" I raked my fingers through my hair. "Leave my room. Leave this house."

"I-I can't leave tonight."

"First thing in the goddamned morning, then. I don't want to see your face here again."

"But...what will I tell Marj?"

Thank God my sister was in the city tonight. "I'll deal with Marj. You just get your ass out of this house in the morning."

Her beautiful lips trembled, and her hair fell around her shoulders in unruly waves.

She turned and walked out of my room.

Out of my life.

Taking my only chance of happiness with her.

★ ★ ★ ★

Hot breath singed the back of the boy's neck. He had learned to separate his mind from his body. It was the only way to survive. But still, the breath. Always the breath, no matter how far away he was into his mind.

He had stopped fighting back. He had stopped begging them to leave him alone. It was useless. They seemed to like it when he resisted.

He was used to the pain. Tonight was bad though. The one with the tattoo went first, and he was the biggest.

The boy winced and cried out when Tattoo breached him. He hated himself for screaming. Each time he promised himself he wouldn't scream, and then he did. Next time, he said to himself. Next time I won't scream.

Tattoo grunted as he forced his way into the boy's body. As much as the boy hated being penetrated, it was better than having it stuffed inside his mouth. He threw up either way, but at least with penetration he could hold off until they left. Then he would heave and empty his stomach.

"Yeah, give it to him good," Low Voice said.

The three men always wore black ski masks, so the boy had no idea what they looked like. Just as well. He didn't want to see their faces. This way, not knowing what they looked like, he could think of them as inhuman. Pure evil.

"You like that, don't you, boy?" Tattoo said, pumping into him. "You like being fucked in the ass."

The boy said nothing. The first couple of times he had screamed, "No. I don't! Stop this! I hate this!" And he'd paid for it with a beating as well as a fucking.

"Come on, boy. Tell me you like it."

Still, he remained silent except for a few wails and sniffs.

Until a cool metal blade touched his neck.

"You say you like it," Low Voice said. "Say you like his big hard cock in your ass, or I'll slit your pretty little throat."

★ ★ ★ ★

I like it.

I'd said the words. Like a goddamned little pussy, I'd said the words to stay alive. Alive in the hell that had become my life.

Why? Why had I bothered to stay alive?

Cold desperation paralyzed me.

The boy. He was me.

He *is* me.

God help me.

CHAPTER TWENTY-NINE

Jade

I cried into my pillow until finally, my nose clogged, my face swollen, I fell asleep.

I woke the next morning, rose, and walked into my bathroom. A look in the mirror was a terrible reminder. My eyes were swollen from sobbing, my nose red. My hair was matted with tangles. I grabbed my brush and put it through my hair, wincing when I hit a knot. I brushed it through, reveling in the pain of tearing the tangle out of my hair.

It hurt, but no tears came. I was all cried out. I turned the shower on, and the whoosh of water was somehow comforting. Once the bathroom was good and steamy, I stepped in, letting the hot water scald my skin. I stood there for a few minutes, not washing my hair, not washing my face, just relishing the hot water on my body.

After a few more moments, I shook my head, sniffed, and squirted some shampoo into my palm.

Time to move forward.

When I finished washing, I stepped out of the shower and dried off, taking a dry cloth and wiping a circle in the steam on the mirror. I still looked like hell, but my face would recover from the crying jag. My face, my body—they would show no sign of my time with Talon Steel.

Not so for my heart.

I toweled off, dried my hair, and went back into the bedroom. I grabbed some underpants out of my top drawer.

My top drawer.

It was no longer my top drawer. I was no longer welcome here.

I thought about Marj. She would tell me to stay, no matter what Talon had said.

Which was exactly why I wasn't going to wake her. She had gotten in late last night from her cooking class. I'd heard her after midnight. Today was Saturday, and she would be sleeping in. I could pack up fairly quickly, call a cab, and go to Grand Junction. It would be a hefty fair, but I didn't care.

I'd have to call Larry and quit my job. I actually liked the job, but I definitely had issues with Larry's ethics, so I'd find a better job in Grand Junction. I'd find work with lawyers I respected. I would have liked to give Larry two weeks' notice, but that wouldn't be possible, and I couldn't very well commute from Grand Junction without a car. The cab fare alone from here was going to take all of my spare cash.

I bit back more tears as I pulled all my underwear and socks out of my top drawer and walked over to my bed to set them down.

I gasped.

On my pillow sat one perfect red rose.

★ ★ ★ ★

I had scarcely gotten settled in my hotel room when my cell phone rang. It was a number I didn't recognize.

"Hello?"

Silence for a moment. Then, "Jade?"

The voice was familiar, so like my own. Even though I hadn't heard it in years, I knew exactly who was on the other end of the line.

"Hello, Mother."

"Jade, darling, how are you?"

Seriously? How did she think I was? And if she really cared, she would've asked a long time before now. But I was not in the mood to get into anything with her. After what I had been through with Talon at the ranch, I didn't want any more drama. "I'm fine, Mother. How are you?"

"How nice of you to ask. Things are going well for me. I'm dating a wonderful new gentleman, and I'm going to write my memoirs. Can you believe it? Me, a writer."

Yep, always about her. Classic Brooke Bailey. I say "fine," and she gives me her life story.

"That sounds nice," I said.

"I'm in town, darling. Nico—that's my new beau—and I would love to take you to dinner."

"You're in Grand Junction?"

"Yes, isn't that just a hoot?"

A hoot, indeed. "What are you doing here?"

"Nico is originally from Colorado, and he has family here. So we came for a short visit. You'll have to tell me how to get to your ranch, though, and we'll pick you up."

"That's not necessary, actually. I'm in Grand Junction now. I moved off the ranch."

"You did? My goodness. Well, tell me where you are, and we'll pick you up."

And that was that. No questions about why I had left the ranch. No questions about what I was doing in Grand Junction.

No questions about me at all. Did she know I'd passed the bar exam? Hell, did she even know I'd gone to law school?

"There's no reason for you to pick me up. I have a car and I can come to you." A lie, of course, but I didn't want her to see me in the seedy hotel I had rented by the week until I could find an apartment. Not that she would care, but I had a little pride.

"That would be fabulous, darling. We're at the Carlton Downtown Grand Junction. They have a marvelous restaurant here. I thought we could have some dinner and then an evening swim in the hotel pool. It's such a gorgeous night. So don't forget to bring your suit."

I hadn't even said I'd go yet. But hey, a girl had to eat. Since I was no longer getting free food at the Steel ranch, I'd much rather eat at a five-star restaurant than have a fast-food burger, which had been my plan. "All right, I'll meet you at your hotel. What time?"

"How about six o'clock? That will give us time for some cocktails before dinner. I'm just dying to hear all about what you're up to."

She didn't fool me for a minute. If she had any interest in what I'd been up to, she would've asked before now. I wasn't sure what Brooke had up her sleeve, but it wasn't any grand desire to see her long-lost daughter.

"Sure, Mother. That sounds great. I'll see you at the Carlton at six."

"Perfect, darling." She made a kiss noise into the phone.

And I nearly threw up.

"Ta-ta. I'm so excited for you to meet Nico. Until then."

I ended the call and flopped down in my bed. Just what I didn't need. Whoever this Nico was, he would be footing the bill this evening. My mother's second husband had drained her coffers dry with some investment scam. In fact, I wouldn't be surprised if she tried to get money out of me. Not that I would give her any even if I had it.

But dinner with Queen Brooke would at least keep my mind off Talon. It was inevitable. Brooke would talk about herself all evening, I wouldn't get a word in edgewise, and I wouldn't have time to think about Talon.

★ ★ ★ ★

Turned out, I was wrong. As Brooke droned on and on at dinner about this new opportunity and that new opportunity, I tuned her out quite easily, and Talon crept into my mind. I tried to erase him. Truly I did. But I could no longer hide from the truth.

I loved him.

I was in love with Talon Steel. All six-feet-three inches of screwed-up man. I didn't delude myself into thinking he could ever love me back. He had too much baggage. I only wished I knew what it was so I could help him. But did he even want my help? He'd made it pretty clear he didn't.

Jonah's voice still haunted me. *Don't go snooping. It's none of your business anyway, and you might not like what you find.*

There was a riddle in those words, and also a warning. I could go digging myself, but where would I start? And here was the irony—had I stayed at my job with Larry at the city attorney's office, I would've been an investigator. I would've had all his investigative tools at my disposal. I could've learned a lot in that job, whether or not I respected my boss.

But I'd had to leave. I couldn't take any more of Talon and

his drama. It had nearly destroyed me.

How could I have fallen in love with him?

"Don't you think so, Jade?"

I jerked my head up, forced out of my thoughts. My mother had spoken to me, but I had no idea what she'd said.

"I'm sorry, what?"

"I was just saying that if Nico plays his cards right, within a few years he could be a candidate for president."

I looked over at my mother's new love interest. Nico Kostas was a good-looking man. A dark Mediterranean type, he had black hair, olive skin, dark-brown eyes, rugged features, and a stocky, muscular build. He was graying at his temples and had laugh lines around his eyes. I guessed him to be in his early fifties.

He had been perfectly polite to me all evening, and he treated my mother like a queen. But something was off about him. I couldn't quite put my finger on it, but something about him rattled my nerves a little, made my skin crawl.

"I don't pretend to know much about politics," I said. "But I wish you the best of luck if those are your aspirations."

Nico smiled. "Oh, I think every politician dreams at one time or another of getting to the White House. But right now, I'll settle for just being one of the two senators from Iowa."

I nodded. Maybe that was the weird vibe that I was getting from him. Merely that he was a politician. So many of them were crooked. No...something else wasn't right, and even though there was no love lost between my mother and me, I didn't really want him near her.

I let out a sigh. None of this made sense. I took a sip of my merlot, which Nico had ordered. It was boring and a little sour. I had learned so much from Ryan at the winery. I could've chosen a better wine.

My mother picked at her striped bass, leaving most of it on her plate and scraping all the creamy sauce to the side. Still a supermodel, still afraid to eat.

I, of course, had cleaned my plate of my chicken piccata.

No doubt about it, my mother was a gorgeous woman. She was taller than I easily by three inches and probably weighed about twenty pounds less. Of course, she had no boobs. Mine had come from my father's side.

She hung on Nico's every word, never letting an opportunity to touch him pass by.

The waiter came and cleared the table, asked if we wanted dessert.

"Oh, heavens, no," Brooke said. "I absolutely couldn't swallow another bite."

She hadn't swallowed too many bites yet anyway.

"Just coffee for me," I said.

"Excellent idea, Jade," Nico said. "Make that three coffees, please. And I'll have a Courvoisier also."

"What a wonderful idea, Nico," Brooke bubbled. "Make that two on the cognac. Jade?"

I shook my head.

When the waiter had left, Nico said, "This will give our stomachs a chance to settle before we go on our evening swim."

Yes, the evening swim. I'd skip that.

But when the time came, Brooke would hear nothing of it.

"Of course, darling, you must come along. Nico looks amazing in his Speedo."

Oh, God. Just what I didn't need—to get a good look at my mother's boyfriend's package.

But what the hell? The fleabag I was staying at didn't

have a pool, and even if it did, I wouldn't set foot in it for fear of contracting some kind of disease.

I accompanied them to their suite on the top floor. My mother ushered me to a lush bathroom.

"You can change in here, darling."

I hurriedly changed and took a look at my reflection in the mirror. Not too bad, after that huge meal I had just eaten. I might not be waif thin, but no one could call me fat. I smiled to myself. Talon had certainly liked what he'd seen.

I walked out of the bathroom and tried to ignore Nico's lascivious gaze. The man made me squeamish.

But then a flash of color caught my eye. A tattoo on his forearm.

"Oh, you have a tattoo," I said. Tattoos fascinated me. I hadn't gotten one myself yet because I hadn't found the perfect image.

"Oh, yes, isn't it beautiful?" my mother said.

I walked closer to get a better look. It was indeed beautiful—a bird enveloped in colors of fuchsia, purple, orange, and teal. Its wings were flames, and it rose from ashes.

It was a phoenix.

Talon and Jade's story continues in

Obsession

Keep reading for an excerpt!

CHAPTER ONE

Talon

"You what?"

My sister, Marjorie, whipped her hands to her hips, her eyes wide and angry.

I let out a sigh. "You heard me the first time. I asked Jade to leave."

Marjorie shook her head, her lips trembling. "I don't get you, Talon. Jade is the sweetest person in the world. She's the best friend a girl could have, and she's been there for me every time I've needed her. It gave me great joy to help her when she needed help, to let her come live here and start her life over after her she got humiliated at her wedding. Why in God's name would you ask her to leave?"

How could I answer? Jade had only been gone since this morning, and already an emptiness had surfaced. Even in this sprawling ranch house, the loss of Jade's body, her soul, was measurable—a thickness that was damn near visible. It percolated through me like a cold fog.

"Damn it, Talon, you owe me an explanation."

Marj spoke the truth. I just didn't know how to put my explanation into words without telling my sister things I didn't want her to have to deal with. My brothers having to deal with them was bad enough.

"So you're really just going to stand there with your mouth hanging open like an idiot, huh?" Marj bit her bottom lip. "Fine. I'll call Jade." She stomped off.

My skin tightened around me. Jade would probably tell my sister that I'd been screaming like a maniac before I booted her out of our house, but at least she wouldn't be able to tell Marj the truth. Jade didn't know the truth. She didn't know I'd had a flashback while she was massaging me.

I reached down and gave my mutt, Roger, a pet on the head. He licked my fingers.

Even canine loyalty wasn't going to cheer me up today. Life was about to get hard. Not that I wasn't used to that, but this time, emotion was involved—emotion that was new to me. I sucked in a deep breath. I'd go to the guest house and talk to Ryan. My younger brother's door was always open. After all, I was a hero in his eyes.

What bullshit.

But Ryan would listen. He always listened, and I had to tell someone what had gone on between Jade and me.

I had to tell someone that I had fallen in love.

MESSAGE FROM HELEN HARDT

Dear Reader,

Thank you for reading Craving. If you want to find out about my current backlist and future releases, please like my Facebook page: https://www.facebook.com/HelenHardt and join my mailing list: http://helenhardt.com/signup/. I often do giveaways. If you're a fan and would like to join my street team to help spread the word about my books, you can do so here: https://www.facebook.com/groups/hardtandsoul/. I regularly do awesome giveaways for my street team members.

If you enjoyed the story, please take the time to leave a review on a site like Amazon or Goodreads. I welcome all feedback.

I wish you all the best!
Helen

ALSO BY HELEN HARDT

The Sex and the Season Series:
Lily and the Duke
Rose in Bloom
Lady Alexandra's Lover
Sophie's Voice
The Perils of Patricia (coming soon)

The Temptation Saga:
Tempting Dusty
Teasing Annie
Taking Catie
Taming Angelina
Treasuring Amber
Trusting Sydney
Tantalizing Maria (Coming October 25th, 2016)

Daughters of the Prairie:
The Outlaw's Angel
Lessons of the Heart
Song of the Raven

The Steel Brothers Saga:
Craving
Obsession
Possession
Melt (Coming December 20th, 2016)

DISCUSSION QUESTIONS

1. The theme of a story is its central idea or ideas. To put it simply, it's what the story *means*. How would you characterize the theme of *Craving?*

2. Compare and contrast Jade and Marjorie. How are they alike and how are they different?

3. What do we know so far about Talon's past? How does this explain some of his actions?

4. Discuss Jonah's and Ryan's feelings about Talon's ordeal. Why do they feel the guilt that they do?

5. Discuss Jade's relationship with her mother. How has it affected the woman Jade has become?

6. We know little, yet, about Talon's experiences in the military. What do you think might have happened there? How might this have affected the man he is now?

7. Why is Talon so reluctant to help himself? What does this say about his character?

8. Discuss the author's use of flashbacks in the story. Though the book is written in first person, she shifts to

third person for the flashbacks. How does this add to the story, and what is its significance?

9. What do you think the brothers might be hiding? What might be the significance of Marjorie's birth certificate? Of her mother's maiden name?

10. Discuss Jade's role in the sexual relationship. Is she a submissive? Why or why not?

11. Discuss Talon's role in the sexual relationship. Why is he so drawn to Jade? Why is he unable to love her?

12. What do you think the future holds for Jade and Talon in *Obsession?* What about Jonah and Ryan? Marjorie?

ACKNOWLEDGEMENTS

Starting a new series is always exciting. These characters are very special to me, and I hope you all love them as much as I do. I've written the tortured hero before, but Talon is in a class of his own. Keep reading. I promise he will get the happy ending he deserves!

As always, thank you to my brilliant editor, Michele Hamner Moore, and my eagle-eyed proofreader, Jenny Rarden. Thank you to all the great people at Waterhouse Press—Meredith, David, Kurt, Shayla, Jon, and Yvonne. The cover art for this series is beyond perfect, thanks to Meredith and Yvonne.

Thank you to the members of my street team, Hardt and Soul. HS members got the first look at Craving, and I appreciate all your support, reviews, and general good vibes. I have the best street team in the universe!

Thanks to my always supportive family and friends, and to all of the fans who eagerly waited for this new series. I hope you love it!

ABOUT THE AUTHOR

New York Times and *USA Today* Bestselling author Helen Hardt's passion for the written word began with the books her mother read to her at bedtime. She wrote her first story at age six and hasn't stopped since. In addition to being an award winning author of contemporary and historical romance and erotica, she's a mother, a black belt in Taekwondo, a grammar geek, an appreciator of fine red wine, and a lover of Ben and Jerry's ice cream. She writes from her home in Colorado, where she lives with her family. Helen loves to hear from readers.

Visit her here:
www.facebook.com/HelenHardt

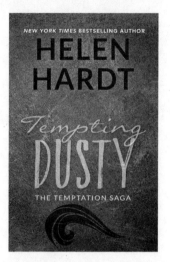

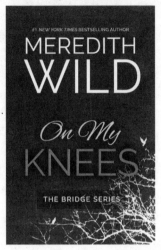